D0263831

RUNNING

CHILDREN'S BOOKS BY BARBARA SPENCER

Scruffy

A Dangerous Game of Football

BARBARA SPENCER

RUNNING

Matador
5 Weir Road
Kibworth Beauchamp
Leicester LE8 0LQ, UK
Tel: (+44) 116 279 2299
Email: books@troubador.co.uk
Web: www.troubador.co.uk/matador

ISBN 978 1848763 241

Cover Design: Aimee Hibberd

British Library Cataloguing in Publication Data.
A catalogue record for this book is available from the British Library.

Typeset in 12pt Sabon MT by Troubador Publishing Ltd, Leicester, UK

Printed in Great Britain by the MPG Books Group, Bodmin and King's Lynn

Matador is an imprint of Troubador Publishing Ltd

For Melissa
who stayed up all night reading

PROLOGUE

Simultaneously mobiles rang in every corner of the world, the trapped and dying reaching out for a lifeline, as if a miracle of modern technology could rescue them. Last words of love and desperation soared into the air, with radio masts quivering under a deluge of calls. Within seconds the besieged towers were screaming *no network coverage* to the millions who, witnessing the disaster live on television, heedlessly keyed in the numbers of anyone that might be caught up in the quake, even now wiping out the Californian coastline.

A skyscraper, which five minutes before had been central to a vast hotel complex, nosedived into the ground. The resulting tremor catapulted the camera sideways so that, to the people staring at the screen, it was as if they were standing on their heads. Blackness followed then silence, the calm voice of the anchor man trying to reassure viewers they would be *back at the scene momentarily.*

In London, the cab driver, chatting amiably with his passenger and ignorant of the unfolding drama, had one eye on traffic, which appeared to be fast backing up, and one eye on his mirror, nodding in agreement to the various subjects offered up for discussion.

'It's a long time since I was in England,' the man said, the faintest trace of an American accent marking his voice.

That was when the cab driver began to wonder if his fare could be a film star. Even features, excellent teeth, not an ounce of extra flesh, with a thatch of light brown hair tipped blond by the sun, and steel blue eyes of a shade that only ever belonged to Americans.

The mobile in the American's jacket pocket rang. 'Excuse me,' he said. 'Sweetheart, where are you calling from? Everything okay?'

Since mobiles were designed only to be heard by the person into whose ear they were pressed, the cab driver couldn't hear the terrified syllables speeding across the saturated airwaves. He could only watch with astonishment as his passenger's face turned into a mask of dangerous impotence.

'They told us we had to work for them to stay alive,' the whispered words flew across the Atlantic. 'But they tricked us. Can you hear it? The earthquake!'

'What are you talking about? *Who tricked you?*'

'The Styrus Project – they want it. We said no.'

'Who, goddamn it! *Who?*'

There was a blur of static then the line cleared. '… there's no way out.'

'Yes, there is,' the man snapped. 'There's always a way out – find it.'

'I'm trying, that's what you can hear – me – running. But it's hopeless. Charlie's dead, so's James. It's impossible. We're trapped.'

'Try, g*oddamn it!* If someone's after you, they won't let you be killed, you're too valuable. And if they can get in, you can get out. Stay alive, *do you hear!*' The pleasant quality of the man's voice had vanished his tone vicious, as if it could force a reaction thousands of miles away.

The mobile crackled, the words becoming staccato. 'There's no way. Can't make it… Sky … keep him safe. The building … it's toppling … *Sky* … safety.'

'You're not checking out on me. *Crawl* if you have to, *but don't you dare check out*,' the passenger yelled into the static.

The cab driver watched in a state of near panic. Whatever had happened? His passenger's face was now chalk-white under its tan, his expression animal-like in its ferocity, his eyes glittering as he swiftly keyed in a number, speaking briefly.

'Get me back to Grosvenor House – fast,' he snapped, his eyes fixed on the small screen in his mobile, where newsreaders crowded to report events.

The cabby stuck his arm straight out of the window and, heedless of the vehicle bearing down on them, swung the cab round, saluting the driver's blast on the horn with two fingers. Grosvenor House came into view and he swung the cab along the apron in front of the hotel and stopped.

'*Wait!*' his passenger took the hotel steps in a single bound. 'Get me on the next flight to New York,' he snapped to the Bell Captain, scarcely hesitating in his path to the front desk.

Ten minutes later he reappeared, clutching a small valise. The cabby, who had considered jettisoning his lucrative fare and fleeing the scene, convinced he was carrying a knife-wielding maniac, obligingly pulled back into the traffic. There'd been no lack of volunteers in the cab rank eager to update him on the disaster taking place in California. He viewed his passenger with careful sympathy; someone belonging to the American was caught up in the earthquake, that much was evident. He fished around for something to say but found nothing. He didn't know the bloke and *sorry* was an empty, meaningless word, trotted out when you bumped into someone. Instead, he cursed the traffic and urged his cab forward, one eye on the crowd of onlookers that had spilled on to the roadway outside Debenhams. Ignorant to the danger, they had their gaze fixed on the television sets in the shop's window display, where live footage of the disaster was being transmitted.

'*Son of a bitch!*' his passenger cursed. 'The vacuous pleasures of the petty-minded, who derive their kicks from someone else's misfortune.'

'That's not fair, guv,' the cab driver rebuked. 'The English don't celebrate tragedy. Those people watching, they'll be putting their hands in their pockets tomorrow to help.'

'I know,' his passenger said, his tone bleak. 'Excuse me.'

'Look, guv. I can't help much but I can drop you by a tube station. You'll reach the airport quicker that way. It's not fair to take your money.'

He pulled in to the side of the road, opposite the entrance to the underground at Oxford Circus. 'Good luck, sir. Who was it?' he said, the traditional inner core of reserve, so great a part of being English, battling with his cabby's nose for entertaining titbits to pass on to his next fare.

'My wife!' The man pressed a twenty-pound note into the cabby's hand. He glanced up briefly, meeting the concern in the driver's eyes. 'Only my wife.'

At dawn the following morning, a rental car made its way down narrow, dust-filled tracks that wound across the slopes of the Sierras. The driver knuckled his eyes. He felt bone weary, but thanked God he had at least made it. If the call had not got through – if the taxi driver had been lazy or greedy and withheld information about travelling by subway – if he had missed his connection in New York, he would now be stranded. The rental car's stereo, his only companion, had kept him abreast of the news. And less than six hours after he reached New York, the President had declared a State of Emergency closing every airport on the continent. By then he was landing in Las Vegas. Now nothing moved in the skies, unless by order of the Federal Government.

Beyond that nothing had happened, the lessons learned from the tragedy of New Orleans too far distant to be remembered. In any case it had been a double whammy. Participants at meetings, hastily convened to set up a rescue operation with help for survivors, had awakened to find their decisions literally wiped out, as a deadly wave submerged the battered coastline in the dead of night, sealing the fate of those who had somehow survived the earthquake.

To the American driving through the night, the horrific details of the tsunami constantly tore holes in his belief that his wife had somehow survived. Nevertheless, each time he stopped for coffee he punched in numbers on his speed dial, praying someone, somewhere, would have news, only to be met with silence.

The couple waiting for him out on their porch had no news either. They only knew what the television had relayed and prayed their son had something more hopeful. In their sixties with white hair, they continued vigorous and upright; the husband still carrying the firm muscle of a sportsman, his clear grey eyes watching the distant track as the car appeared through a cloud of dust.

The disaster hadn't reached them, high in the hills above Sacramento; but the slopes, a mile below them, were thronged with battered survivors, many still in night wear. Anxious residents had opened their doors and ransacked closets for clothes and shoes, handing out water and blankets, all the time desperately searching the skies for some sign the government cared.

The man pulled the Chevy to a halt and got out, his face grey with fatigue.

'Any news?'

A unified shake of the head spoke volumes as to the length of time the couple had been married. The older man put a gentle arm round the younger man's shoulders, escorting him onto the porch, his expression carefully noncommittal. 'We were hoping you had something, son. But it was not to be. Seems like it was totalled all the way to San Francisco. Sacramento escaped the water, but it's raining refugees. Lord knows when help's coming; seems like our government's got itself frozen. Come in, lad, you need food and sleep.'

'Any strangers?' the man said, looking round.

'No son, you're safe. You only got here with help. How can anyone else?'

From the sky, the man thought, but he didn't offer up the words, they had enough to worry about, no point adding more. He rubbed his eyes. 'You're right, I need sleep, but straight after we must all leave ...'

His father nodded. 'We're already packed up. We'll go up to my cabin. No one can find that. Wish you'd come, too.' He held up his hands, backing away. 'Yeah, I know we've discussed it. You have to get out of the States. But that's not going to be as easy as you think,' he added. 'There's lock down on the roads, nothing's moving and the only things flying belong to the Federal Government and there's a chronic shortage there, too. I expect the quake put paid to State Government. But I guess you'll find a way.'

The man nodded, smiling briefly at his mother, who had put a heaped plate of bacon and eggs in front of him and was busily pouring out a cup of coffee, strong enough to hold a spoon upright. 'It won't keep you awake,' she said, her voice stern. 'I doubt anything will.'

The food appeared to revive him, his blanched cheeks resuming their normal tanned appearance, although the deep black smudges under his eyes remained. He got up and went into the back room, where there were two beds, stripping off his shirt. A smile lifted the lines of fatigue on his face, as he stared down at the bed where a small child lay sleeping.

The four men that deplaned from the Lear jet a little after two o'clock in the afternoon were young, in their late twenties. The jet, which had landed them at the airport fifty miles east of Sacramento, was of military design sporting the crest of the Federal Government, the men's combat gear only serving to confirm their status.

A few mechanics sat idly. With all planes grounded they were unemployed. Although a few had stayed on, feeling the need for human companionship in the face of what was happening on their doorstep, the majority had left in a rush to check their family weren't among the victims. The handful now remaining, concentrated alternatively on their mobiles and the larger TV screen in their rest room, endlessly chewing over events. They eagerly inspected the four men, hoping they were the vanguard of a rescue mission. But what could four men do when news readers were crunching numbers like a million dead? Still, at least their appearance spelled movement.

The door to the office opened abruptly, slamming shut behind a bespectacled clerk waving a slip of paper. He trotted out over the tarmac towards the party, bending slightly as the slipstream of the Lear hit him.

'Is there a Lieutenant *Dervoy?*'

The officer, his shoulder sporting the stripes of a lieutenant swung round. 'Davois,' he snapped.

'Message for you, sir. Came through ten minutes ago.'

The lieutenant took the slip of paper, scanning its message.

'Your ride's waiting, sir,' the clerk said stating the obvious, an army chopper which had clearly been sent to collect the four men, already parked near one of the sheds, its engines idle.

The officer crossed to the helicopter, speaking briefly to the pilot. A couple of mechanics, who had been checking its rotor blades, heard the heavily accented voice but didn't bother with it, so used to Mexicans and their broken English. He returned to the little group.

'The address just came through. Our pilot says 'e knows the place we want. It's about an 'alf hour ride.'

To the watching mechanics the lieutenant and two of the three men came across exactly as they were meant to look – regulation; their carriage upright as if a twenty-five-mile run was no more than a gentle stroll, although the frame of the lieutenant would pile on fat in middle life, a half-inch of spare flesh already showing above his belt. The fourth man, his words lost in a roar of noise as the chopper's engines burst into life, appeared an unlikely sort of soldier. Bone thin and rangy, he gave the impression rather of long days spent in the saddle, with walking a painful necessity rather than a pleasure. Shouldering his kit bag, he moved out slowly towards the chopper, followed by the other three.

The engines cut back making it possible to be heard.

The soldier, his reflective lenses leaving his face a blank

canvas, lacking expression, tossed his bag up onto the cabin floor. 'Hope it's not a wild goose chase.'

'Where else would 'e go?' said the lieutenant. 'Pity about 'is wife.'

'They found her body yet?'

'The wave put paid to that. But we 'ave to find the 'usband. I'm not expecting any bother. You two …' he called to the two men, already strapping themselves in for the ride. 'If 'e's not there, you two 'ave got the job of asking 'is parents where 'e is.'

The two men grinned, saying nothing.

Preparations for leaving were almost complete when they heard the chopper.

The man stared at the moving silhouette. 'How long?'

'Twenty minutes – tops,' said his father. 'You sure about this?'

A Harley-Davidson stood ready to go, the open doors of the outhouse sheltering it from view. The man adjusted his goggles. 'Can't afford to take the chance, Dad, you know that.'

'I've filled the panniers full of food and clothes, but I don't like it,' his mother said tearfully. 'It's running away. I'm sure they won't hurt us.'

'For God's sake, woman,' snapped her husband. 'If they're responsible for a million people dying, they're hardly going to lose sleep over two more.'

Her son put his arm round her, giving her a hug. 'Dad's right, Mum. I'll phone when it's safe but you know I won't be back – not yet anyway.'

She slipped back into the house immediately reappearing with a heavy rucksack, only the top of the child's head showing. She strapped it firmly to the man's back. 'That's the best I can do,' she said. 'Promise me?'

Her son smiled briefly and touched her cheek. 'I'll buy something more comfortable.'

'Go slow,' the older man warned.

'Five minutes and you're gone. *Clear?*'

'We're gone, now. I'm not stupid, boy. Mother, go and get your bag. Leave the door open.'

'But …'

'If they find it locked they'll kick it in.'

'Don't come back, Dad.'

'Teach your grandmother to suck eggs. I wasn't a marine for nothing.'

A brief smile flicked across the younger man's face.

'It's not a good day, son,' his father said, 'but I've survived worse and we'll survive this, I can promise you that.'

The couple, linking arms, watched sadly as the Harley-Davidson disappeared with a cloud of noise and dust, its rider returning the way he had come.

Taking a final look at the dust-blown track down which their son and grandchild had vanished, they climbed into the heavily laden rental car, its rear bumper now decorated with branches, trailing the ground behind it. The ex-marine turned the ignition and leisurely, as if he had all the time in the world, moved out along the track, the densely-packed leaves sweeping the roadway clear of all tyre tracks.

ONE

Fifteen years later ...

'*So who can tell me, what dramatic events of the last twenty years have changed the world into what we know today?*'

Scott, putting the finishing touches to the drawing of a motor bike he'd been doodling on his rough pad, looked up. So did the rest of the class, aware this sudden change of subject by the Newt represented a last-ditch attempt to gain their attention. Droning through the rainfall of the Sahara had been deadly dull and a waste of time; no one ever the slightest bit interested in Africa, since it was unlikely any of them would ever get there. Perhaps, at long last, he had come to his senses and had chased his brain for something actually exciting.

The interactive screen, on the front wall of the classroom, changed shape, a map of the world now filling the space. Hands flew into the air as the year -11 students finally woke up.

'So, Mary, give me one of these events.'

Mary's brown eyes brightened enthusiastically. 'The blowing up of the Iran Nuclear Facility.'

Mr Newman, whose nickname referred to his size rather than his ability to turn into a frog, nodded. 'And the other?'

Scott didn't move. Long habit stopped him joining the barrage of hands waving at the Newt. He glanced across at his friend Jameson, eagerly bouncing up and down in his seat, his dark hair and glasses joining in the fun.

'Me, sir, *Me!*'

'*Jameson – Jameson* – please give someone else the chance to talk for a change. Scott – you rarely say a word in class. Do you know the answer?'

Scott shook his head. He knew the answer all right. It was the earthquake that killed his mother.

'Pity! Okay – Hilary then.'

'The earthquake in the United States.' The girl sitting next to Scott said, 'with its resulting tsunami.'

It was a surprise to hear Hilary speaking up. Since she'd joined the school the previous month, when her parents relocated from London into the calm atmosphere of the Cornish countryside, she'd hardly said a word. And that was such a shame. Scott glanced surreptitiously at her; since she was easily the best looker in class, with a neat figure, a blonde ponytail and a smile a mile wide. Regrettably, she'd also made it abundantly clear to every boy who tried to make a move on her, that she wasn't interested.

Mr Newman picked up the plastic pointer touching it to the screen and a faint green shadow appeared in the background of the world map. As it mingled with the blue of the ocean it turned turquoise, padding out the landmass of three of the five continents: America, Africa and Asia.

A gasping 'Wow!' came from the class.

'This was the ribbon of land known as California.' Mr Newman highlighted the turquoise bulge on the south-west corner of the North American continent. 'It lay along the St Andreas fault, a notoriously unstable area. There had been a devastating earthquake one hundred years prior to this event, but nothing on this scale.'

'Sir?'

'Yes, Jameson?'

'Was the earthquake connected to the blast in Iran?'

'What an extraordinary question.' Mr Newman beamed his delight at the interest his class was showing. 'There's only a few minutes till the end of the lesson, we can spend it discussing the two events, if you like. Do you think they're connected, Jameson?'

'Well, sir, they could be. I mean, except for the great meteor which did the dinosaurs in, there's been nothing on this scale for millions of years. It's too much of a coincidence for two such events to happen within a few days.'

'But, sir?'

'Yes, Wesley?'

'They couldn't have been linked, sir. The United States were behind the Iran blast, everyone knows that. The earthquake had to be a coincidence. Not even those lunatics in the United States would go round blowing up their own country or would they?'

'Okay, anyone?'

Hands waved madly in the air.

'Travers.'

'But the US denied it, didn't they, sir?'

'They did, Travers. Unfortunately the world didn't believe them. We were on the brink of a world war, this time between the Middle East and the US, when Al Zaitigh claimed responsibility. According to their broadcast, they blew up the nuclear facility because the Iranian people were moving away from the laws of God.'

'Yes, sir, but that's the point, sir,' protested Jameson. 'The explosion in Iran effectively closed down the world. Nobody was looking anywhere else. I mean, Wesley's right in a way. The United States wouldn't have blown themselves up, so somebody else must have done it.'

Scott could see where Jameson was heading – and it made perfect sense. The moment the world knew of the explosion in Iran, the developed countries – the United States in particular – had mobilised their forces to send massive aid and, as a result, became vulnerable to attack.

'Say it had been planned,' Jameson plunged enthusiastically into his argument. 'When the blast happened it was like the entire world lost its head and went running round in circles. If you were a terrorist organisation, wanting to damage the US – that was the perfect time. An undersea nuclear explosion could easily have triggered the earthquake.'

'It would have had to be a very powerful blast,' their teacher pointed out.

Hilary raised her hand.

'Go on, Hilary,' Mr Newman nodded in her direction.

'But if there *had been* an organisation with that sort of nuclear capability, surely someone would have known about it. I mean, Iran's nuclear programme was well documented.'

'Good point, Hilary. Nice to see you joining in. Keep it up. Anyone else?'

'What about China, sir? They had the knowledge.'

'They did, that's right, Mary. Well, we appear to have strayed over the boundaries into the realm of historical fact, but it doesn't matter. Personally, I never saw China as a threat. They were busily becoming powerful enough to rival the US by trading – they didn't need to destroy the world. Yes, Jameson?'

'That's the whole point, sir. They didn't destroy the world, did they? We're all still here. But whoever did it, they couldn't have foreseen the tsunami and the rise in sea levels could they?'

'Valid argument.'

Scott listened. Even if his father hadn't advised him to play his cards close to his chest, he wouldn't have joined in. You learned more by listening.

'Sir?' A tall, athletic-looking girl, her swimming captain's badge in a prominent place on her sweater, waved her hand in the air. 'What exactly did happen?'

'I'll go into it in more depth next lesson, Jenny. Briefly, the earthquake went off the Richter scale, and the western coast of California ...' The plastic pointer rapidly covered the screen, highlighting the turquoise-coloured ribbon of land, 'disappeared into the Pacific ... from here ... to here.' The pointer swung up and down the coast. 'Between the Iran blast and the earthquake, millions of people were killed. Then, while the US was still reeling from this, the tsunami struck. It killed several million more people worldwide and sea levels were left elevated, so enormous flooding took place ... here ... here ... here ... and here.'

The pointer flicked quickly over the west coast of the United States, the Caribbean and countries bordering the Atlantic as far north as Norway, before moving across to the Pacific islands and the eastern seaboard of Russia.

The class fell silent, staring at the rapidly moving pointer, the areas affected lit up like a Christmas tree.

Mary leant across and tugged at Travers's sleeve. 'Was it really like this?' she whispered, a horrified expression on her face.

'And some,' he replied.

'I had no idea. If there's a documentary on telly, Mum usually says: *we don't want to see this* and Dad changes the channel. But it's crazy,' she hissed.

'What were you saying, Mary?' Mr Newton turned back from the board. 'Share it with the class, please.'

Mary flushed pink. 'I was saying to Travers, that no one in their right mind would kill all those people on purpose. I mean …' she paused and burst out, 'Anybody who did that has to be a serious head-case.'

'Exactly so,' their teacher agreed with her. 'Unfortunately, there was a consensus of opinion – by the nations of the world – that America had become power crazy. Despite the confession by Al Zaitigh, the world believed then, and continues to believe now, that the US was behind the Iran blast and quite possibly the Californian earthquake, too. It was known that America had a secret research facility in the area and, although the Americans strongly denied it, it was concluded they had triggered the underground explosion in error. That is why the United Nations moved to Switzerland. America, accused of mass murder, was immediately ostracised by the rest of the world and all ties severed. Fifteen years later they still continue to protest their innocence, but it will take a hundred years or more – long after the last survivor of the event has died – for them to be readmitted into the global community.'

The jangling of the bell interrupted the appalled silence in which the class had listened. Normal conversation broke out again as the twenty or so students packed away their books and put on their specs. Mr Newman gazed round his class, delighted that for once his students were leaving one of his lessons on a high.

'Remember,' he called after the hurriedly departing throng, 'exams are in a few weeks and the occasional peek into the Internet might prove useful.'

Five pairs of feet fitted neatly in a row against the wall. Four of the five pairs belonged to Jameson, Mary, Travers and Scott; the fifth to Hilary. She had been walking down the corridor behind the group, quietly minding her own business, when she'd been hijacked. She just had time to hear a muttered, *this way*, before Mary dragged her off down the corridor at high speed.

It was Hilary that broke the silence.

'Can someone tell me why we're sitting eating our lunch in the janitor's cupboard?'

The four friends grinned at her.

'Jameson's in hiding,' explained Mary turning round, her glossy, short brown hair swinging across her face with the movement.

Jameson grinned wickedly. 'From the Weasel.'

'It still makes no sense, unless I know who the Weasel is.'

'You don't know?' A chorus of reproaches broke the air.

Hilary flushed. 'I'm new, remember.'

'So is Wesley the Weasel,' groaned Jameson. 'But, except for using words like janitor, you're perfectly acceptable because you've never once tried to push your way in. Quite the opposite. But Wesley … he's a right pain with all his questions – never stops. He's got this obsession about what subjects I'm planning to study at university. He was spotted by Travers bearing down on us, hence the rapid escape – sorry.'

'That's okay, but what's wrong with janitor?'

'It's American.'

'Oh God! I'm *so* sorry. There was an American girl at my old school,' said Hilary, adding quickly, 'I must have picked it up from her.'

'American girl! How come?' Jameson said, eagerly picking up on the word like a puppy worrying a ball.

'Most probably a refugee. There's a whole community in London.' Hilary shrugged. 'No one talks about them, but they're there.'

'Okay, you're excused.'

'Okay is American – was, I mean,' she added.

Travers groaned and buried his head in his hands. 'I know the government is always on about getting rid of all the Americanisms in our speech, but that's impossible. It's like they invented speech.'

'Do you really think someone set off the earthquake in California, Jay, or were you saying it just for the hell of it?'

Scott quickly changed the subject, the conversation about refugees too close to home for his liking. He was American, even if his birth certificate did say he was born in London. That was one of the secrets – and a big one. *If you're American you don't talk about it,* that's what his dad said when he went to primary school. 'Never tell anyone anything about your family, not even to your best friend.' And if you don't talk about that, it becomes easier and safer never to talk much about anything – even to friends.

'No, I was searching the net. There was this article. I wanted to find out more.'

'So what was she like, Hilary – the girl at your school?'

'Like a girl, Travers, *did you expect something different?*'

Travers, who openly boasted he was as thick as two short planks but get him on the rugby pitch and he had brains enough for fifteen men, was perfectly typecast. Dark and athletically built, he had a broad face almost as wide as it was high. His heavy eyebrows overhung deeply-set brown eyes, with a short muscular neck dissolving into powerful shoulders and chest.

'You know what I mean,' he growled. 'How did she get here?'

Hilary pulled a face. 'No idea. It's got to be one of those embarrassing questions you never ask.'

'I read this article, on the Internet, that thousands of Americans were stranded worldwide. Some of the stories are really interesting, too. For a while there was even an underground organisation, using Canada and Mexico to get them back into the States,' Jameson leaned forward to look along the line of his friends, 'so any still left here are probably legal.'

Scott wished he could say, 'I'm legal.' Except he didn't know if they were. Again he tried to change the subject. 'Dad was saying he'd read a report about kids vanishing – did you see that, Jay?'

'What sort of kids?' Jameson asked, taking the bait.

Scott relaxed. 'Clever ones.'

Travers burst into laughter. 'Thank God for that, Scott. That rules out Mary and me.'

Scott grinned. 'Me too! Holy crap, that's it!'

Hilary jumped and stared at Scott across the line of feet. 'That's another American expression,' she rebuked him.

Scott stopped dead, his cheeks tinged pink, wondering if she could be one of those girls that hated swearing, although to be honest, *Holy crap* could hardly be considered swearing.

'It's just an expression,' Jameson broke in. 'It doesn't mean anything. Actually, when you know Scott better, you'll be grateful for every single word he does let fall, whether it means anything or not. *You've* just been in receipt of three whole sentences – count yourself lucky.' He smiled ruefully. 'Besides it's impossible to eradicate every single word – like Travers said – speech would be pretty dull without them.'

'Thanks for that!' Scott overlaid his laugh with a scowl. 'That wasn't it. I've just worked out why the Weasel is stalking you, Jay, he's after your brain. Better take care. No going out after dark.'

Scott said it seriously but it came out like a joke and four pairs of feet drummed the wall in appreciation.

'Your dad never said that, Scott, you're conning us,' Mary said, when she'd stopped laughing. 'If it was true we'd have heard it on the news.'

'That's what I told him,' said Scott. But he had.

'Oh, forget all that,' Travers said now, taking charge of the conversation. 'We've got a week off. To celebrate; how about you all come over to my house on Saturday – you too, Hilary? Dad's taking out the boat and we're going up-river. Mary's coming.'

'That is a surprise,' Scott said with a grin.

'Love to but can't.' Jameson groaned and pulled a face. 'Family wedding. Got to go to that, worse luck. Can't you do it Sunday, Travers?'

'Not my party – shame though. Hilary?'

'That would be nice. I'll come but only if Scott's coming.'

'Oooooer!' Jameson fluttered his eyelashes.

'It's nothing like that,' she retorted. 'If you aren't there and Scott isn't either, I shall be playing gooseberry to Travers and Mary – and that will be ghastly. And I'd love to go out on the river.'

'The ball's in your court, Scott. By the way, Dad said you simply had to bring your dad. Says he's got something important he wants to talk to him about. I asked Mum. She said it probably meant he'd get some decent conversation if your dad was there.'

Scott kept his face neutral but inside he was cheering. Wild horses wouldn't keep him away. 'Okay, I'll be there. But you know my dad ...'

'Actually, to be truthful, Scott, we don't.'

And neither, thought Scott, do I.

TWO

Scott dropped his bag on the kitchen floor and, grabbing a Coke from the fridge, kicked the door shut again with his foot.

The two-bedroom cottage he shared with his father was quite small, with its front door opening straight onto the kitchen; while the door connecting the kitchen to the rest of the house had been removed altogether and now propped up a wall in the garage. Originally an old bake-house, this had been rebuilt and, besides racks of shelving for sailing and climbing equipment, housed a washing machine, a Four by Four and a 1000cc motorbike.

Munching a biscuit he flicked the intercom. 'Dad, I'm home – want anything?'

'Tea – and some conversation.'

Scott grinned and grabbing the kettle set about filling it. They had developed a habit of drinking tea together when Scott got home from school. The Coke was a stopgap. It was quite warm outside and he was thirsty after his ride. And while they drank tea they talked, Scott's father eager to hear every detail of the day's events.

The kitchen was bare, only essential items – like the kettle, juicer and microwave, all of them in constant use – allowed to corrupt the uncompromisingly tidy appearance of its laminate surfaces. The rest of the house continued the minimalist theme; no pictures and nothing on the walls, only Scott's bedroom breaking the mould and filled with toys and games, suitable for a boy growing up from six to sixteen.

The kettle clicked. Scott made a pot of tea and, dragging the kitchen door closed with his foot, crossed the yard and entered the building in which his dad worked. The door swung shut behind him. Balancing the tray on a low table, the only item of furniture in an otherwise bare lobby; he removed his specs, placing them in their holder next to his dad's, before pulling open the door to the inner room.

His dad looked up.

'Thank God for the cavalry,' he said.

For the thousandth time Scott asked, 'So what are you working on?'

Ever since he'd reached an age to find his father a subject of interest, Scott had wondered exactly what his dad did. Jameson's dad owned a chain of restaurants. Travers's dad worked in television. But his dad? He never spoke about work. No one came to the house, although to be fair Scott was at school five days a week, and the only letters they received were bills and junk mail. Did he work? If so, who paid his wages? Someone had to. There always appeared to be enough money in the bank to buy things, so …

And, for the thousandth time, his question went unanswered.

'So what's happening in the real world? Anyone new in town?'

Since town referred to the small village, two miles away, Scott had long since decided the question was rhetorical and didn't require an answer. Nevertheless, he always gave it due consideration.

'No, nothing new. A tractor broke down in the main street causing a traffic jam …' he pulled a face. 'You know – three cars! Jean at the pub is advertising for a chef. Oh yes, the new girl, Hilary? She actually broke her silence and spoke up in class. She's nice.'

'What were you talking about?'

'Well, the Newt is wanting us to study the effects of the Iran fiasco and the tsunami on …' Scott hesitated, 'world climate – I guess.'

His father sipped his tea, his eyebrows prompting Scott to continue.

'Well, Jameson has this theory that the two events were related and that far from being the aggressor, America was the victim.'

Bill Anderson put down his cup. 'What makes him think that?'

Scott leaned up against the work bench. Idly, he glanced down noticing a loose sheet of paper scrawled all over with letters and numbers. Part of his dad's work? 'Because nothing like it has ever been experienced in thousands of years of world history, so it was too much of a coincidence.'

'An interesting theory. Has he anything to back it up?' Bill Anderson leaned over and, picking up the sheet of paper, fed it through the shredder.

'I don't know. Jay's pretty clever and he made some good points. Dad? I know you never talk about the tsunami ... because of Mum, I mean. But if we're going to study it in school, I'd like to know what happened. Okay ... and even before you ask, I'd never, never say anything to anyone ... I don't even know how Mum died.'

'There were millions of people lost, Scott, for whom there's never been an answer. So what do you know?'

It appeared to Scott that, even after fifteen years, his father remained in shock, incapable of talking about the death of his wife. He would talk about everything under the sun, bar that. Had he regretted that freak trip to London to meet up with a colleague, a trip coinciding with the earthquake and tsunami? Not long ago, when he was sick to death of chasing puzzles round and round in his head, Scott had summoned up the courage to ask the question: 'Did you wish you'd died, too, Dad?'

'Hell, no,' he replied. 'Never once. There was you, remember. Look what I'd have missed, my daily living reminder of my wife.'

'Well, I know it was the St. Andreas fault – a shifting of the earth's plates,' Scott said now. 'But I was thinking, there are other regions just as unstable. Jameson's right, nothing like this *has* ever happened before. Villages, towns, even whole cities get churned up and spat out again, but this was – like a whole country.'

'It also contained the nerve-centre of Silicon Valley, an area boasting more professors per square inch than any other real estate in the world. It just so happened, a world computer symposium was taking place – with a gathering of brainpower powerful enough to rival the planets in the night sky. It had taken years to organise. US-led, even the venue was kept secret till the last minute, in case of terrorist activity.'

'So what was it about?' Scott asked.

'Viruses.'

'You mean things like disease?'

Bill laughed. 'Nope! Computer viruses. The decade before had been plagued with the problem. The moment virus software was created someone discovered a virus that could breach it. The computer world had become a nightmare. It was hoped that a worldwide accord ... *agreement*,' Scott nodded, 'could be formulated, with a global virus ... police ... if you like. Everyone wanted to attend. The hotels along the strip were overflowing with boffins of one sort or another, eagerly swopping software secrets. Most of those who survived the quake perished in the tsunami. Over ninety percent of the finest brains lost in five minutes,' he finished, his voice clipped, snapping the phrase off as abruptly as the lives he'd been referring to.

'Including Mum,' Scott gave a sad smile. 'So what about the ones that were left?'

'They now live under constant protection or, if they are American – in a city specially built for them somewhere in the States that doesn't suffer from earthquakes. Can you imagine the men that survived have become the most valuable commodity on earth – far greater even than oil. The world took a giant step back in time that day. It will take generations to replace the knowledge lost.'

'What about you, Dad? You aren't in hiding.'

'No. But I'm just a computer geek. Your mother was the brains behind our little group. I'm not that important.'

Bill got to his feet. 'Come on; let's get some dinner on the go. And tell me more about this theory Jameson's come up with.'

By the side of Scott's bed stood a small photo frame: in it the picture of a woman and a baby. It was the only picture he had of his mother. Everything else had been lost in the freak wave that had engulfed California and the western seaboard as far north as Vancouver. His father never spoke of it, the previous night had been an exception brought about by the debate in class. And the photo survived only because Bill Anderson had, absentmindedly, stuck it in his suitcase before leaving for the airport.

According to the legend on the back, Scott had been just over a year old. Now it was the first thing he saw when he woke up – a tall, slim young woman. The fingers, curved round the toddler, were long and tapering, her collar-length hair shaded blonde. The photo was quite small, only postcard size, leaving Scott to imagine the grey of the eyes smiling at him. The baby was just a baby; it didn't interest him much even though he knew it was him – it was always at his mother's face that he stared.

He, Scott, had survived the disaster because he'd been with his grandparents in Sacramento and there had been sufficient warning for most of the residents to reach the Sierras, far enough away from the coast to escape drowning. Redwood City, where his parents worked, had been only three miles inland.

Every morning, when he opened his eyes and saw his mother he wished he'd known her. Although to be honest, he didn't miss her because she'd never been there and he had no experience of what it was like to have a mother. Besides, he had a great dad who had done his best to fill the role of both parents. He could cook and keep house, he read a lot, taught Scott to swim, pitch, play chess and poker, kick a ball, climb and ride a bike; although that was more about Scott, it didn't really tell him much about his dad, except that he was pretty fit for a person nearing fifty. Scott touched the glass – still it would have been good to know his mum.

The house was quiet but it was light outside, so his dad would be about. He always got up at daybreak, incapable of sleeping longer. Scott wandered into the kitchen and grabbed some juice. His dad was reading the day's news on his laptop.

'Anything I should know about?'

'You could read it yourself. Pancakes on the side.' Bill nodded in the direction of the hot plate.

Scott loaded his plate and sat down. 'No time, anyway I prefer the potted version thanks, Dad.'

'Well, let's see. A ban is in place to control the movement of pigs, sheep and cows. Radiation levels are being checked, yet again. Chickens are up in price. There's the usual warning to stay away from contaminated areas when on holiday. They've even supplied a list – which means no seaside this year, by the look of things.'

'So could we use the spring holiday and go to the mainland? I'd love to visit Holland and see the flowers.'

'Wow! The Keukenhof? Would you really? Rather an unblokish thing to do.'

Scott grinned. 'We've done all the bloke things, Dad, and I've got the blisters to prove it.' He held up his hands, the flesh across the palms still showing pink, the result of a week's trekking and climbing in Wales at half term. 'Besides we've never been to the mainland.'

He took a mouthful of pancake swimming in syrup, chewing happily.

'Isn't there ever anything besides contamination reports in the paper – you know stuff that's actually interesting. We know about contamination – can't they give it a rest?'

'Okay, so ... a monarchist rally in Brussels. Crushed, of course, and ten dead. Does that grab you? There's sport? Money Markets?'

Scott shoved his stool back and stood up, hastily stuffing the last of his pancake into his mouth. He picked up his bag. 'I'll go to school, thanks.'

'Bring some milk on the way home.'

Bill crossed the kitchen to fix himself another cup of coffee. The view through the window, over a spotlessly clean sink, was across the yard towards the door of his workroom and the gate into the lane. Amused, he watched his son, balanced precariously on the thin rims of his bike, attempting to shut the gate without dismounting. Having succeeded, he flashed a grin at the window aware his dad would be watching, before disappearing from view.

Scott freewheeled down the track. He'd even surprised himself about Holland. The only reason he could come up with: in the photo a vase of tulips was on a table next to where his mother was sitting.

Halfway down the lane he stopped. A navy blue van, marked with the Ministry logo – a dark blue circle motif with the words *Radiation Assessment* encircling gold laurel leaves – was attempting to park on the grass verge opposite a field full of sheep, and blocking the entire lane.

I could park better than that, thought Scott indignantly, waiting for the road to clear.

George Beale, a local farmer, together with a couple of helpers, was busily erecting a series of temporary pens, so his sheep could be tested before being released back into the field.

Scott called out, 'Hi, George. What's going on?'

'Mornin', young 'un.' The farmer ambled leisurely across the lane just as the doors to the van opened and the driver and his mate, both in navy-blue overalls, got out. 'Bloody Ministry. I want to send me lambs to market. Can't do it without a red tick. Look at them – fit as fleas the whole ruddy lot of them. Interferin' busybodies.'

Scott gazed across the field, the grass bright green in the sunlight, where the lambs from the previous autumn were happily grazing. Colour was nothing to go by. Radiation leached through the soil whenever it rained and was taken up by the roots, into the stems, and then into the lambs as they munched the new grass.

'B'ain't no contamination in my flock,' the farmer continued. 'In fifteen year there's never a lamb showed positive, but I still 'ave to go through the same ruddy rigmarole every time. You'd think they'd 'ave learned by now – b'ain't no contamination in my flock.'

'They were talking about it in the news, this morning.'

'Were they then? Not my flock, they weren't talking about. 'Ere, you ready?' He called out to a third man, who had emerged from the rear of the van and was now busily hauling out metal boxes with long cables attached. 'Bloody foreigners, too,' he muttered out of the corner of his mouth. 'Gets on my wick sending a foreigner to do an Englishman's job and they're that cack-handed, you'd think they'd never done this job before.'

'Yes, sir. We are almost ready to begin.'

'About time, too.'

Scott glanced back up the hill, the studio in plain sight; the propellers of the wind turbine, which supplied enough electricity to run the computers, clearly visible behind it. His father was probably already hard at work, although you'd never know it; the blinds in the studio not only keeping out daylight but also masking the artificial light his father worked by.

That was another of those puzzles that dogged Scott's waking hours. His father had designed and built the studio when they first moved into the cottage. It couldn't have been cheap even then, filled as it was with state-of-the-art computer equipment. But the financial side of the project didn't particularly interest Scott; that formed part of a more general question: *so where does our money come from?* The question he couldn't answer was: *if his dad didn't want daylight, why had he built so many windows?*

Setting his bike in motion again, Scott carried on down the lane heading for the main road. On days like this it was pleasant riding the five miles to school. It was only when there happened to be a downpour of rain or snow that his father got out the Four by Four and drove him.

The Ministry van was still there when Scott cycled home again. No sign of George Beale or the lambs; the field, at the far end of the lane, empty of livestock. Despite that, the three men continued to range over the ground, scratching around in the hedgerow with their machines.

'What are you doing now?' he called.

The man nearest to him stopped his machine and stood up, rubbing his back. 'This field is contaminated so now we 'ave to recheck every field.'

'That's shocking.' Scott leant over the handlebars, adjusting the clip on his front light. 'Poor George. But what about his sheep? Were they clear?'

The man laughed. 'That farmer was so lucky,' he said, his accent quite strong. 'If 'e 'ad kept the animals in this field,' he pointed back up the hill, 'we could not 'ave moved them.'

'So what are you going to do about it?'

'Nothing!' The man tugged at a piece of twig caught in the front wheel of the bulky machine. He flipped it casually into the air. 'We will test them. If they are radioactive, we will test them again in a year. In the meantime, they will be closed off.'

Scott watched the fragile sliver drift back down and land on the machine again. 'It's very hard on the farmers,' he said, trying to conceal a grin.

'Radiation is very 'ard on the 'ole of Europe.'

'I guess – but you said the sheep were fine?'

'Completely safe,' the man flexed his fingers, as if they were stiff from working the machine. 'When you go to the supermarket, you can buy lamb in full confidence.'

'That's good.' Scott set his bike moving. 'Okay, then – see you,' he called back.

He rode off up the track, putting his energy into climbing the steep gradient. He didn't look round though it took real effort not to. He wasn't mistaken. After all, he went up and down the track every day and it was definitely that field the sheep had spent the better part of the winter. So how could it be contaminated if the sheep weren't? He pounded the pedals, panting slightly. George would know; he was the person to clear up that particular mystery. Scott pushed the puzzle to the back of his mind. Tomorrow was the river trip and he hadn't asked his dad yet. Idly, he wondered what Hilary would be wearing.

'So what's the news from the real world?' Bill glanced up from his computer. 'Anyone new in town?'

Scott kicked the door of the studio shut behind him, closing out all traces of natural light. 'Dad, you really ought to get out more. It's bad for you to spend every day in here.'

'I get out enough, Scott, when you're at school.'

'No, I mean meet people.'

'Okay, so whose invitation is it this time?'

Scott grinned, somewhat shamefaced he'd been so transparent. 'Travers,' he said, handing over a cup of tea. His hand froze in mid air. 'The milk! Damn! I forgot it.'

'Remind me to buy you a book on brain training. We can make do tonight; I'll get some in the morning.'

'Sorry.'

'So?' Bill knuckled his eyes.

'Travers's parents are taking a party up-river in his cruiser and we're invited. His dad said he needs you there to save him from boredom,' Scott adlibbed.

Bill laughed. 'I'm flattered, only met Doug Randal a couple of times. I must have made an impression.'

'Can we go?' Scott said. 'It's an early start but you won't mind that.'

Bill screwed up his face. 'Don't think so, cocktails on the river aren't really my scene. Don't get me wrong, I like Doug, good bloke. But the company he keeps – media celebrities.' He shook his head. 'No, you go and enjoy yourself. I'll probably take the bike out.'

Scott fiddled uncomfortably with his spoon. 'Dad?' he said, keeping his gaze firmly fixed on his saucer.

'What?'

'Well, I'm nearly sixteen. Isn't it about time you told me some things?'

'You mean stuff like sex? I thought you knew about that.'

Scott's head jerked up his eyes sparkling. 'I do. No, it's not that – it's everything else – such as why you never mix with people? I mean some of the rules you've given me are pretty weird and yet you say you aren't in danger, but are you? And what are you working on? And why everyone knows me as Scott when my name's really Sky.'

Scott peered into the sheet of mirrored glass tucked behind the door, the only thing to decorate the workroom's plain cream walls beside two life-sized posters of his dad's bike.

The first was simply the bike in a blur of red speed. Its caption read: *So take the High Road.* In the other, the Suzuki had stopped by the side of a lake. Mountains appeared in the background, snow decorating their peaks, with a biker's helmet lying on the ground. The caption: *That'll do nicely.*

Since they were the only things hanging on the walls throughout the entire cottage, Scott had spent time studying them, not certain whether his dad had first seen the posters, and been persuaded to buy the gleaming red monster parked in the garage, or whether the purchase of such a beloved object as his bike, had prompted the posters.

He examined himself in the glass, seeing an ordinary face surrounded by almost shoulder-length fair hair – Sky? His eyes were grey.

'Were they ever blue?' he said.

His father looked up, a wry smile on his face. 'I don't remember. But to answer your question … I'm an American and, in view of what's happening in the world today, it makes good sense to take a few precautions.'

Scott wished he could say: *I hate being American, Dad. I hate keeping secrets and I hate being the dumb one at school. All I want is to be like everyone else* – except that was stupid, because they never would be like everyone else. Instead he said, 'Dad, when I spoke to George Beale, he told me he'd not had a single lamb show positive, yet the Ministry still ban all movement; so he can't shift his lambs until they're confirmed as clear. Don't you think that's a bit weird? Although to be fair,' Scott added more cheerfully, 'George was more upset they'd sent a foreigner to do an Englishman's job, than he was about having his lambs tested. He was going-on about how useless they were ...'

A buzzer rang out, cutting across their conversation, the television screen abruptly erupting into life with images of the lane.

'*What's that?*' Scott said, sounding startled.

His father moved to the window. Pulling back the blind he peered out, his face completely expressionless as if he were wearing a mask. To Scott, this was more alarming even than the buzzer.

The only things to be seen were a scattering of sheep in the distance and the blue ministry van; the men packing their instruments away, their work over for the day.

'Why the buzzer, Dad?'

'Front door bell,' Bill said, his tone casual. 'I like to know if anyone comes up the lane when I'm in here working – like double-glazing salesmen, for example.' The rigid lines in his father's face began to relax. 'So they were testing George's sheep, were they? I expect they triggered the beam by accident. It's happened before.'

That's when Scott should have told his dad what the men had said, about the field being radioactive when the lambs weren't. It was after all the sort of thing he asked to hear about. *Tell me if anything unusual happens, Scott.* That's what his dad always said. Still, it would be better to check with George first; no point worrying him for nothing.

Bill smiled, answering Scott's earlier question. 'George will never accept that England is simply a part of Europe. He's the type to have a photo of the last king hanging on his wall. Come on – let's get some supper.'

Bill wandered round the workroom, clicking off screens and backing the computers down into safe mode.

'Why did the king go?'

'Not only ours, Scott – they all went. Parliament voted for a Presidency.'

'You mean the European Parliament, right?'

'Hell, yes! Ours lost its teeth and was demoted to council status years ago. Come on.'

He closed and locked the door, handing Scott his specs from the table. 'After dinner let's go for a spin.'

'On the bike?'

'*On the bike* and I'll ride pillion. But first it's your turn to cook, so wha'dya want to eat?'

'I'll do stir-fry and pasta, if that's okay.'

'You *always* do stir-fry and pasta. Surprise me one time by cooking something else.'

Scott washed the vegetables while his father chopped them, but even though they were chatting about things that had happened at school that day, things that concerned Scott, the image of his father's face, the moment the buzzer sounded, refused to vanish. For a moment there, his dad had been scared.

Why do you need to know if anyone comes up the lane, Dad?

That was another question he should have asked – but didn't. And once they were roaring round the country lanes, eating up the miles on the menacing red monster, its immense power controlled by a fingertip, Scott forgot about it. The bike swooped into bends, their combined weight laying it almost horizontal before he opened the throttle to accelerate out again. Now it was simply another puzzle to be added to the list and hopefully, one day, solved.

THREE

Bill watched Scott wheel his bike across the yard – no lights – but he'd only get an argument if he insisted; Scott swearing that any animal on the path would have felt the vibration in the ground and vamoosed, long before his wheels appeared. Bill knew only too well his son would free-wheel the slope all the way down to the main road, a mile away, and not using lights was part of the game.

He clicked the kettle on for coffee, watching light creep into the sky. It wasn't long after six, Scott had left in plenty of time to catch the tide, and it looked like being a fine spring day – the birds already beginning to sing, a good sign.

Moving across to the breakfast bar he plugged in his laptop, networked to the main computer in the studio, in case there was anything he wanted to check after he'd closed up for the night, and settled down to read the day's news.

The Iran fiasco had been responsible for a great many crazy laws; in hindsight, proving the perfect opportunity for Europe to flex its muscles. Rabinovitch, their President, had stormed to power on a tide of hysteria, which had resulted in the sweeping away of the monarchies. When protests followed, Rabinovitch had responded by creating a European strike force answerable, so it appeared, only to him.

The continuing erosion of civil liberties, forced through parliament under the guise of radioactive fall-out, had been misguidedly welcomed with open arms. How else had the wearing of spectacles come about? A blanket publicity campaign, highlighting the need to wear special lenses designed to deflect radioactive beams and avoid tumours and melanomas, had left the entire population of Europe clamouring for the product; despite research proving the government's safeguards to be a knee-jerk reaction. A dozen years later, with radioactivity now mainly confined to small areas of Europe – Turkey and Greece in particular, plus more generalised mountainous regions – the wearing of glasses still remained mandatory, with a fine for a first offence and imprisonment for a second.

Bizarrely, the practice of presenting a child with its first pair of regulation specs, on its eighth birthday, had become a ceremony almost as meaningful as the Bar Mitzvah or first communion.

After a couple of hours, Bill closed the laptop down. Stretching, he stood up and tucked the case out of sight in the cupboard, housing the ironing board and electric cleaner. Clicking on the coffee machine, he had opened the fridge to take out the milk before remembering there wasn't any. He picked up the empty carton, a drizzle of semi-skinned milk still lingering in its corners. Making a mental note to keep a spare carton in the deep freeze, he switched the machine off again and, grabbing his jacket, headed for the garage; his hand automatically reaching down to pick up his specs from their case.

The day had carried out its promise of early dawn, the sun warming steadily. It wasn't far to the village and, if Bill hadn't been denied his second cup of coffee, he would have walked across the fields. Now, with a blur of red movement he zoomed down the lane; the roar from the bike's twin carbs still capable of startling the sheep however often they heard it, vociferously protesting the interruption to their grazing, before making a panicky dash to the far side of the field.

Swinging into the high street, he dawdled along and stopped outside the supermarket. He was surprised to see the figure of George Beale push open the door, a large box of chocolates held in one of his work-scarred hands. He was wearing his town clothes and appeared to have both bathed and shaved, a far cry from his usual getup; a thick piece of string keeping his trousers in place, several moth-eaten sweaters and a bright yellow plastic jacket, with a green bobble hat and mud-caked wellingtons.

Bill dismounted and took off his helmet, smiling. 'You must have been their first customer.'

The farmer ambled over to the bike. 'Ay – off to Falmouth, the bus'll be along in a minute,' he muttered conversationally. Bill was amused to see the occasion also warranted the wearing of a denture, the farmer's usual smile missing everything from the canines backwards.

'Special occasion?'

'Always go to me sister's once a year arter I sell me lambs. I take her chocolates and she gives me a bite of dinner, then I has a bevy in the pub on the way home. It's a nice day out, I looks forward to it. Time was ...' George's voice took on a more serious tone, his friendly good nature vanished. 'When this bloody radiation malarkey started, I wondered if I'd ever sell a lamb again.'

'That reminds me.' Bill leaned comfortably against the black upholstered seat of his bike and crossed his ankles. 'I wanted to ask. Scott told me you'd never had any contamination?'

'That's true enough. Only last year the ministry sends me a letter with one of them exemption stifficates, to say my farm be free from contamination for ten year. So I thought no more testing. Then this bloody ministry man shows up – polite as you please – asks if I farm the fields at lower Oddisham 'cos they want to test 'em. I showed 'em my paper ...' the burly farmer glowered, his lower lip pursing with indignation. 'An' I pointed out where it said I'd be exempt. But he told me the flock had to be tested. Bloody foreigner telling me my business.'

'And did they know *their* business?' Bill said, a knot of unease beginning to stir.

'That's just the point. Proper rubbish they were. I began to wonder if they knew which end was which. Bloody ministry people. I've a good mind to make a fuss.' The hum of a distant engine came within earshot and a single-decker bus swung round the corner. 'There's me bus.' He stuck his arm out, seemingly oblivious to the pulsing amber light indicating the driver's intention to stop. 'Nice chattin' to you, Bill. So long.'

Bill watched as the old man paid his fare, collapsing into the first available seat as the bus lurched into motion again; the day's ration of buses to Falmouth already half-full with eager shoppers.

George Beale could be an awkward customer but despite his oddities of speech and dress, there was little wrong with his powers of reasoning. The childless widower would most likely leave his nephews and nieces a tidy inheritance. But a newcomer, meeting the country farmer for the first time, was presented with an awkward and frequently truculent character. From there it was but a small step to getting on the wrong side of him, the friendly chat something that appeared only after several years' acquaintance.

Bill pushed open the supermarket doors. Still, it was curious that George should comment on their inefficiency, as if they'd never done the job before. To his knowledge the same tests were repeated each year. He'd been there more than ten and, in the early years, had frequently watched the whole process. They used the fields at the bottom of the lane, where the sheep spent the summers. Even if they were double-checking the fields, there should be no need to stray on to his driveway at the top. Bill made a mental note to check the ministry website as soon as he got home.

Five minutes later, clutching eggs, milk, fresh bread and a delicious-looking Brie, he was back on the pavement. More people were about now, the bright weather encouraging local residents to get their chores done early and make the most of the day. He wandered across the road to where Jean, the landlady from the pub, her long hair in curlers, was taking in the morning's papers.

'I'm not on public display,' she growled at him. 'Come back at eleven.'

'Mrs Roper, you always look fantastic.'

Jean laughed. 'Flattery, Bill! Coffee?'

'Great idea! My wretched son forgot the milk, so I haven't had my usual quota,' Bill said with an amused grimace. He followed Jean into the restaurant which, geared for night-time entertainment, appeared shabby and neglected in daylight.

Jean bustled about behind the bar and, within seconds, a steaming cup of coffee was perched on the table in front of Bill. He eyed it covetously.

'By the way,' she called over to him. 'Someone was asking for you.'

Bill's head jerked up but he kept his voice relaxed. 'When?'

Jean frowned. 'Yesterday. A reporter? Hang on I've written it down somewhere.' She disappeared. Bill fingers unconsciously beat a tattoo on the table.

The door opened, Jean wafting a slip of paper. 'No number. Sean Terry, *Exeter Chronicle.*'

'Important?'

She shook her head. 'Didn't say. Weedy bloke – scruffy – looked like he needed a damn good wash. Still most reporters look like that, don't they? Never get enough to eat, I s'ppose.' She smiled. 'See you tonight?'

'Not sure, yet,' Bill got to his feet. 'Scott's gone on the river with some school friends and might be late, so I'm celebrating my freedom with some sandwiches and a trip to a coastal pub.' He lifted his hand in acknowledgement. 'Thanks for the coffee – lifesaver.'

Leaving the pub, he strolled back across the road to the bike, carefully stowing away his groceries. The kernel of anxiety remained. He could feel it struggling to expand, to overtake rational common sense and become paranoid. *Why should a series of unrelated incidents still, after almost fifteen years, create such a furore in his guts?* It was no good he'd have to go back and check, he'd get no peace until he did. He glanced down at his watch. It was still only a little after nine, plenty of time to go out afterwards.

Bill headed back along the main road and into the lane, the

powerful engine making light work of the steep gradient. Switching off the engine, he cruised up the final stretch of slope towards the gate. Nothing stirred; only the odd crow or magpie foraging for food and a wandering sheep in the lower field – the house and yard basking in the spring sunshine. Still, his feeling of unease refused to abate. Dismounting, he rolled the Suzuki into the garage and parked, pulling the heavy machine onto its stand. Despite knowing no one ever came near the house, he still moved cautiously and, leaving his jacket and helmet on the saddle, hurried into the kitchen, dropping his shopping on the worktop. Pulling the laptop from its cubby hole, he flicked up the Internet searching for Reuters – the only independent news site left. It took him a few minutes. Finally the column flashed up; its heading, "*Ministry Warns of Surge in Radiation Levels.*"

Bill scrolled quickly down over the paragraph. He had already seen the report in the newspaper. In any case this was Reuters' usual opening – something dull that few people would persevere with.

He scrolled down again and gasped, his face becoming ashen under its tanned skin. An obituary – dated that morning, April ten. He read it carefully. This time his antennae had not played him false. For years he had scanned Reuters every day, making sure he wouldn't miss the warning when it came. The relief, when the page remained blank, leaving him drained. Now they'd been found. At least, *one of them had – and dealt with.*

Momentarily, Bill stared blindly at the screen: a friend dead, a man asking questions in the pub? Was he the forerunner of those they'd been watching for all these years? Bill didn't know, but he had to find out before the man located their hilltop sanctuary. Or had he already done that, wrapped in a neat package of idle gossip in the pub?

'Bill Anderson? Got a boy, Scott?'

'Of course I know them. My girl goes to the same school; Falmouth comprehensive. Nice chap. Has a cottage on the hill overlooking the village.' And the interested and well-meaning individual, no doubt encouraged to talk with a pint of best bitter in front of him, would jerk his head in the general direction. 'Bill works from home, computers or something.'

The obituary was timed at eight that morning. What a day to pick to damp down his alert module, sandbagging his antennae with platitudes: *it's a coincidence, you're imagining it*. If he had listened, as he had done countless times before, he wouldn't have wasted two hours.

Bill hastily scanned the final report, knowing this was Reuters' signature card; the reporting of something that would make the dailies a little later. It was an eye-witness account of a monarchist rally in Norway; severe enough for the Federation to send in Polish troops from the Strike Force to crush it, the National Guard refusing to fire on citizens of their own country.

It's spreading, he thought. Pulling out his mobile he dialled Scott's number. It was picked up immediately and he felt his racing pulse begin to slow.

'Hey, Dad, changed your mind?'

'No, just checking.' Bill forced himself to adopt his normal casual tone. 'You arrived safely?'

'And how!'

Bill heard the laughter in the background. 'Scott, is Jameson with you?'

'No, he's gone to a family wedding. Why?'

Bill hesitated. 'Thought you'd probably like to spend the night. What time will you be back? I'll pick you up.'

'Okay! Hang on.'

He heard his son's voice in the background repeating the question.

'Sixish, okay?'

'Okay, Scott. And take care.'

'I always do, Dad. Bye.'

The phone clicked off. Bill stood silently for a moment, the mobile still in his hand, staring at the screen. He pressed print then, closing down the laptop, put it away.

Scott would get his wish to see Holland. But first things, first. Remove everything of value. His phone was clean; constantly renewed through a series of clumsy accidents, like letting it slip out of his pocket halfway up a cliff. Still. He took out the sim card, grinding it under his heel. No paper, not a single sheet capable of betraying information about him; only the computer files on his work and he'd deal with those now. After that, he'd get lost in Falmouth for the day.

Closing the kitchen door behind him he crossed the yard, the sunshine warm on his face, the air taking on a tinge of blue that often heralded settled weather. In the distance came the faint sound of a tractor, hard at work. Lambs bleated plaintively in the fields and birds sang about nothing in particular. It was ironic how bad things could happen on such a peaceful day. Yet it had been a day like this, the air warm and friendly, when an earthquake had struck in California. He unlocked the door to the studio and, leaving his specs on the low table in the annexe, pulled open the inner door.

Three men were waiting, one of whom closed the door politely behind the reluctant figure.

It was no good trying to run. Bill's heart slid to a stop and a muscle tightened in his cheek, but otherwise he showed no sign.

'This is rather unusual,' he said, 'to find burglars in daytime.'

'Meester Masterson?'

Bill raised his eyebrows. 'Can't help there. You must have the wrong place. No one of that name here. Name's Anderson – very close – easy mistake to make.'

'You disappoint me. May I call you Bill?'

'Sorry,' he said lightly. 'Only my friends do that.'

Ignoring the man standing behind him, he crossed to the computer console and leaned back, attempting an appearance of nonchalance.

'Meester Masterson – we 'ave been looking for you for fifteen years ...'

Bill relaxed against the console and crossed his ankles, his left hand resting on the keyboard behind. The dormant engine in the processor immediately woke; power surging soundlessly through every corner of its printed circuitry, its screens switched off at night remaining blank and dark. Bill's fingers crept upwards, the span of his hand sufficient to hold down *control,* at the same time depressing two keys on the top right-hand corner of the keyboard with his fourth finger – the number '8' followed by the letter 'l'. Praying the software still worked, after so many years on standby, he touched them lightly once and then twice more in quick succession, allowing the message to flash by electronic pulses across the landscape.

'And now we 'ave found you.'

Bill said casually, 'So Terry phoned you, did he?'

'Terry?'

'Yeah – you probably know him by another name – weedy individual, needs a shave and a bath, or so I heard.'

The three men exchanged glances and the man that had spoken shook his head. 'Now it is my turn to be mystified. We did not 'ave proof that you lived 'ere until yesterday.'

His front door bell! 'You mean you're the Ministry men? *Why did I not guess?* The farmer said you were rubbish at your job.'

The speaker flushed at the sarcasm. 'Stop playing games, Masterson. The name is Gerard Davois. I expect you 'ave heard of me.' Bill kept silent. 'No? No matter. Since we will be accompanying you to your new 'ome, we might as well become acquainted, but first ...' he indicated with his hand, 'Arnulf will search you.'

Bill flinched as the muscle's rough fingers batted his feet into the spread position, spinning him like a top to check his back and shoulders; turning him round again to check under his jacket, sliding his hands down over his hips. Fingers dug themselves into the small of Bill's back indicating they were finished. They pushed him roughly against the edge of the bench, as if contemptuously throwing away a piece of garbage, and knocking him off balance.

'French *and* German – multinational. How politically correct,' he said, trying to keep his tone normal-sounding. 'So where am I being taken?'

'A journey – and one for you, for which there will be no

return – but you may choose 'ow you travel. Give me your word not to escape and it will be in style. But, of course,' Davois shrugged, the gesture typically Gaelic, using his face and hands as well as his shoulders. 'First there 'as to be a gesture of goodwill. The names of your colleagues?'

'Colleagues?' Bill kept his voice bland, camouflaging his relief. So David hadn't talked but that silence had cost him his life. Thank God the electronic traces on David's computer led only to him. He closed his eyes briefly, aware his computer would hand the enemy another link, praying his warning would be in time. 'Don't work with anyone. Should I?'

'But of course you do. Never mind – we 'ave your friends; someone will talk.'

'Sorry, don't have any friends.'

'No, but you 'ave a son.'

'*You touch him and I'll kill you.*' Bill's tone was savage. Instantly anger flooded over him for being so gullible.

While they'd been talking the third man had left the room. He reappeared, shaking his head. 'No sign of him, boss.'

'Meester Masterson – where is your son? 'E was with you last night and we 'ave been watching the house since daybreak. We would 'ave seen him. We saw you.'

Thank God for Travers's invite. 'What a pity – he's away for the week. Try again later,' Bill said lightly. This was the time – the time he had been preparing Scott for; hoping it would never happen but fearing it would. All the lectures and drills, the climbing of the mountains, surfing, riding his bike – all of them preparing Scott for just this situation. And how many times, in the course of fifteen years, had he said to his son, *remember this and you'll stay safe.*

'Thank you,' Davois said with a mocking bow. 'We will. Meanwhile are we to 'ave your word?'

'Sorry … can't give my word unless I know where I'm going. Now you tell me that and I'll think about it.'

'Meester Masterson, you think we are born yesterday?' His hand moved.

Bill struggled automatically as he felt his arms gripped tightly. He took a deep breath, knowing what was going to happen, and aware he could do nothing about it – not one against three. It was of some comfort, though not much, that he wouldn't be nursing a bullet like David. He felt the needle enter his arm, and he had just time to hope that help would come – then there was nothing.

'Bring the van.' Davois instructed the two men as they laid the unconscious figure on the ground. 'Load this stuff in.' He indicated the bank of computers. 'You will stay 'ere and wait. 'E can't 'ave gone far.'

FOUR

The motor launch had taken them way up-river; Doug Randal insisting the chill factor cruising the open bay would be quite significant, since the sea hadn't begun to warm up yet. They had idled along, the day fine enough to festoon the fore and aft decks with a collection of bodies; his wife, out of long habit, consulting the radiation monitor in the cruiser's cabin, before agreeing to her charges sunbathing.

The monitors, one of the more expensive knee-jerk reactions to the Iran blast, had been declared obsolete three years earlier; nevertheless the population as a whole remained nervous about exposure to sun. Catherine Randal anxiously checked her four charges for sun block, before allowing them to lie around and absorb the warming rays, so inviting after a long cold winter.

It was full spring, the trees not yet at that bloated, slightly flat look of summer, and the sunlight created delicate patterns of dappled shadow on the moving water. The river bank bristled with willow and poplar, their supple stems elbowing one another out of the way in a pursuit of light and space; while tightly curled leaves adorned the polished bark with fresh green frills, like a muslin tutu bursting out of a paper bag.

'I love rivers,' Hilary trailed her hand in the water. 'We had nothing like this where I lived before.'

'I thought you lived in London. That's got a river right slap-bang in the middle of it.'

Hilary's hand jerked. She stared at Scott with a guilty expression. 'Forgot the Thames,' she hastily amended.

'Honestly, Hilary,' Travers murmured lazily. 'How can you forget something as big as the Thames, even I'd find that difficult?'

'Don't know, just did. Shame your dad isn't here, Scott,' the girl said changing the subject.

'He hates water.'

'But I thought he taught you to sail.'

Scott flushed, annoyed at being caught out in such a stupid lie. Except – how would Hilary know he and his dad went sailing, unless she'd been asking questions about him. The thought made him feel instantly more cheerful and his eyes brightened. 'It was a joke,' he said. 'He hates parties.'

'Pity, he sounds interesting. Travers said he rides a bike.'

'So do I! So you'll have to make do with me,' he said, preparing to flash his best smile but her face remained resolutely turned in the direction of the water.

'Come off it, Scott,' Mary smiled kindly, aware of his efforts. 'Poor Hilary, I invited her for a nice day out.'

Scott fixed his gaze on the river bank, wracking his brains for something to say; wishing, and not for the first time, that he could be like Jameson whose garrulous chattering could jump-start a dozen conversations. He began chasing sentences round his head, hoping to come up with something dynamic, only too aware that dynamic was impossible at the best of times – *and ten times harder today*. Hilary had arrived at the Randal's house looking totally stunning; her skin and hair polished to a fine silky sheen, which had left him with spaghetti for brains. Why couldn't it be Mary he was talking to. With her it was easy. It might not be scintillating but at least words flowed out of his mouth, no problem.

'So what's it like, living in London?' he managed, hoping the sentence wasn't really as boring as it sounded.

'It's a town – you know like living in a town.'

Scott winced and hesitated a second before adding, 'But London has to be different. I mean there's so much history.' He leaned forward eagerly. 'Did you ever go to the London Eye? I've always wanted to do that.'

'No!'

'Well, what about Tower Bridge? Do boats still go underneath?'

'Madame Tussauds?' Travers raised his head from the deck. 'Trafalgar Square?'

'*Oh, for crying-out-loud, give over on the third degree, can't you.*'

Mary, who was sitting next to Travers her arms clasped round her knees, made eye contact with him. She raised her eyebrows and shrugged her shoulder in the direction of his mother. She was standing by the rail enjoying the placid scene, after handing out Cokes and crisps for elevenses – even though it was only ten o'clock. With breakfast served at seven, she knew only too well Travers would already be hungry again.

'Mum?' Travers, taking the hint, called across the deck. 'What was it like before the blast?'

Catherine Randall looked up from her inspection of the river. 'Seriously, Travers – on such a nice day?'

'We're studying it in school, Mrs Randal,' Mary explained. She prodded Travers with her elbow to stop him dropping into a doze, before his mother had a chance to even answer the question.

'We still wore sun block, if that's what you're getting at.'

Catherine Randal was dark like her son but tall and finely built; her clothes giving off an appearance of extreme elegance, the colour of her tailored cut-offs mirroring the stripes in her jersey, with matching rope-soled shoes. She sat down and crossed her legs. 'Global warming was talked about, so was the hole in the ozone layer. Both were regarded as a threat although, at that point, all they'd done was cause freaky weather – you know like drought and floods.'

Travers sat up and rubbed his thigh where he'd been prodded. 'Not that stuff, Mum, ordinary life.'

'Surely you don't want me to get profound, it's a bit early?'

'My dad can get profound at any hour,' Scott said, without thinking. Glancing up, he caught the interested expression on

Hilary's face. What *was* her problem? She liked older men? He'd read about girls like her in magazines. Besides his dad was real old too, years older than Travers's, and she didn't appear interested in him.

'You should have dragged him along.' Catherine Randal smiled.

Scott returned the compliment and smiled back. Mrs Randal was definitely far too attractive to be anybody's mother. Jay's mother was nice but not in the same league. Anyway he'd known Mrs Brody forever, ever since he and Jay hooked up at primary. And Mary's parents – they were the original starchy drawers – at least that's what Mary called them. She said they disapproved of everything young people did, constantly going on about how things were different in their day.

'Ok-ay, so life what was it like? M-mm. Seriously? So … it was simpler … easier … better … yes, definitely better – except I wonder if all generations believe their time was the best. What do you think, Doug?' she called out.

Doug Randal, catching the sound of his name, stuck his head round the cockpit; the face which had adorned television screens for twenty years still handsome, although now showing traces of a decade away from sport.

'What?'

'Life when we were young – was it better?'

'Yeah – definitely – I weighed a hundred and ninety-six then. I weigh two hundred and twenty now.' He laughed and stuck his head back inside.

'*Dad!* So what Mum?'

'Leaving aside the rose-coloured specs, we had the monarchy which made things very stable. Although the monarch had no actual political role, they acted like a fulcrum.'

'What's that?'

'Thank God you can play rugby, Travers.' Catherine Randal smiled mischievously. 'It's the pivot around which both sides of a lever balance. The monarchy was held in high regard and politicians lived in fear that, if push came to shove, the people would back the monarch, not them. That's what made our country so stable. Great Britain, as it was known then, had tremendous influence around the world. Partly because of its history as an industrial nation, but also because the monarch was head of the Commonwealth – a league of a hundred and fifty-one nations – all independent – rather like a large, squabbling family of brothers and sisters.

'The years after the blast were bad, pretty chaotic. And, as a result of radiation, life has changed. There weren't as many rules; like not being able to leave England, even to visit the mainland, if you're an ex-con. To-day the Federation controls every aspect of our lives. For instance, the company making our protective glasses ...' she put her hand up to touch the lenses, which had now darkened in the sunlight. 'They have a monopoly and have to be making trillions of Euros. In the olden days there would have been action groups besieging parliament. Now we don't even have much of a parliament. Some years back, when they were contemplating rebuilding the UK's nuclear programme, there were huge protests. Since the Federation came into existence, no one bothers.'

Scott, remembering the monarchist rally in Belgium, could have disagreed but as usual he kept silent.

'I know we never talk about the USA,' Catherine continued, 'but lots of people in this country have really fond memories of the Americans. Nice people – lousy leaders.' She got to her feet in one graceful moment. 'Now I'm going to join the grown-ups for some adult conversation, such as the price of an elegant blue number I saw in a boutique on the way here.'

With a grimace, she vanished into the cockpit, where a clinking of ice cubes showed that the party had got down to the serious business of the day.

'She's beautiful,' said Hilary, smiling round as if apologising for her outburst.

'She used to be a model,' Travers said proudly. 'Do you believe that stuff about each generation ...?'

'Thinking their youth was best?' Mary completed the

sentence and, rolling over, gave him a peck on the cheek. 'When we're old and grey, Travers, we can ask ourselves.'

'By the time *you're old and grey*, he'll have forgotten the question. Look at him,' Scott prodded the comatose figure, half asleep already. 'Sorry about before,' he apologised to Hilary. 'I mean I've always wanted to go to London.'

'And I hate talking about myself,' she said. 'So why not tell me about you. For instance, what about your family?'

'There's only Dad and me.'

'Oh yes, sorry. I heard you lost your mother. So what does he do?'

'Some boring job,' Scott said. 'He's pretty boring, too. I made up the bit about him being profound.' Scott wanted to say: *change the record can't you.* Instead he said, 'He's always doing housework or gardening – that's why he didn't come today – you know pruning roses.'

Mary leapt up. 'Come on, Hilary, I want to explore below. Come with me in case we meet up with any spiders on the way.'

Travers grinned. 'Rats.'

'What do you mean, *rats?*'

'You get rats on boats not spiders.'

Mary grabbed Hilary by the hand and dragged her to her feet. 'In that case you *have to come.*'

Scott gazed after the two girls making their way along the deck. 'What's with her? She isn't like this at school.'

'I expect it's some girl thing. Leave it to Mary, she'll sort it. But she certainly snapped about London. She obviously doesn't like talking about herself.'

'No, she prefers talking about my dad. I only wish she wasn't so great looking then it wouldn't matter. Help me out here, Travers. Give me something to talk about.'

Travers shrugged. 'You've got the wrong person, I never bother. If they don't like me as I am, that's their problem. I don't care.'

Scott glared. 'You don't need to care. Every time you set foot on the blasted rugby pitch half the girls in the school fall into a dead faint.'

Travers gave a shout of laughter. 'No, they don't and Mary wouldn't let them. You're good at plenty of stuff – you know – like climbing. I'd never get off the ground. Talk about that.'

'Knowing my luck, she hates mountains too.'

Scott flicked a glance towards the twisting lane, not much more than a pot-holed track that wound down through woods from the main road; a long line of parked cars ample proof of the popularity of that particular stretch of water.

He prayed his dad had brought the bike, desperately in need of a head rush, like driving fast to lift him out of his gloom; the Four by Four simply one of a dozen dotted about. Scanning the queue of vehicles, he searched for the familiar face among the gawping pedestrians, as the cruiser slid silently and efficiently into its berth. Barefoot, he and Travers leapt athletically onto the quayside, securing the heavy ropes to the solid brass capstan, the boat swaying slightly as it pulled against its restraints.

It had been a lousy day as far as impressing Hilary went and, halfway, Scott had stopped caring. He had really tried too; thought up all sorts of subjects – her family, friends she'd left behind, what sort of house she'd lived in, music she liked, her favourite shops – only to have her shut up tighter than a clam. Okay, so she'd been quiet at school but he'd put that down to being new. Besides, she'd not had any bother talking to Mary. But with him … She might be pretty with a dazzling smile but they were wasted on her. He groaned miserably facing the obvious, that her acceptance of the invitation *had* been to go out on the river and not because she fancied him. Well, if she did, she had a funny way of showing it.

Doug Randall ambled up while Scott was putting on his socks and shoes. 'Dad not here?'

'He's probably got delayed. I'll give him five minutes.' He grinned cheekily. 'You know dads.'

'I sure do.' Doug patted the teenager on the shoulder, his six-foot-four-inch frame looming over Scott's slight figure by a good five inches. 'We'll load up, take your time.'

Scott stared at the broad back, wondering what it would be like to exchange places with Travers, and not have to follow such crazy rules. What he'd told Mr Randal was true all right. He did have to wait five minutes before phoning. It was part and parcel of all the mysteries he had buried deep inside his brain – never to be forgotten.

'If you can't raise me on the phone, Scott,' his dad had instructed, 'you don't go home. Remember that and *never* forget it. *You don't go home.* Go to a friend's house. I'll find you.'

It had been tested, too. One day his dad had simply not appeared at the school gates and, after hanging around for half-an hour, Scott had gone home with Jameson. But since that day his dad had never been late, never once; at least not more than a few minutes.

Only a few vehicles remained parked on the slip road now, most people having left for home as soon as the sun began to drop. A car appeared but no sign of the bike or Range Rover. Impatiently Scott dialled the mobile again, then the house.

'Dad pick up,' he muttered. The phone clicked into life. Scott jumped and yelled, '*Dad*, where are you? I'm sitting on my backside at the docks.' He was met with total silence; then the answer-phone, designed to come on line after eight rings, responded by asking him to leave a message.

An irrational sense of fear swept over him at the thought of the message playing to an empty house. He quickly closed the connection, shoving his mobile deep into his jacket pocket and looked up, to find the normality of the scene unchanged. Travers and Mary, arms entwined, were still gazing out over the water; Doug Randal, one arm round the shoulders of his wife, was shaking hands while Catherine blew kisses in the direction of the last of their guests to leave. Nothing but an ordinary Saturday afternoon.

A cold breeze from the river wafted in his direction and he shivered, noticing that the sun had vanished behind some ominous-looking clouds. His line of sight levelled to see Hilary staring in his direction; *watching him like a hawk* was the phrase

41

that sprang to mind. Scott hoped he hadn't gone white.

'Bill not showed?' Doug Randal called over to him.

Scott shook his head, not trusting his voice.

'So what's it to be?' The ex-rugby player split away from his wife strolling back to Scott's side, his imposing presence attracting curious glances wherever he went; most people recognising the face even if they couldn't always put a name to it. 'Travers and Mary are going with Catherine. I'll drop you off if you like, on the way to Hilary's. Plenty of room for your bike.' He indicated the spanking new vehicle. 'I wanted a word with Bill, in any case.'

Hilary was talking into her phone, her gaze still fixed on him. As her glance met his, she hurriedly broke eye contact turning away. Scott flushed angrily. *What was her problem?* Couldn't wait to tell her girlfriends what a let down Scott Anderson had been? No way was he sharing the back seat with her, every pothole a stabbing reminder of a perfectly miserable day. The thought made him feel sick. He shuddered, saying politely, 'No, thanks, Mr Randal, I'll head for Jameson's if that's okay. He'll be back by now.'

'Everything all right?' Doug's amiable tone vanished, his brown eyes serious.

'Course,' Scott lied. 'It's easier for Dad to get me from Jay's. I'll probably stay the night, anyway. Thanks, Mr Randal, it's been a great day.'

'Glad you enjoyed yourself. Tell your dad to give me a ring sometime.'

Scott smiled automatically, his brain barely registering the friendly message, more concerned with willing his mobile to ring, rehearsing the words: *Dad where are you*, over and over again.

FIVE

Scott repeated the same words, speaking into his mobile twenty minutes later, only the name was different.

'Jay,' he said, his voice sounding panicky, 'where are you? I'm sitting on your doorstep and there's no one home.'

'What the devil are you doing sitting on my doorstep?' Jameson said. 'I'm not there, I'm here, you wal.'

His friend's voice sounded extra-exuberant; something he generally reserved for earth-shattering occasions – like meeting a new girl. But so infectious, it immediately reduced Scott's nagging worries to a figment of his own imagination. His dad had gone out and forgotten – it happens. It didn't last. His burgeoning optimism nose-dived at the idea of riding the ten miles home in the dusk. 'You're not coming home?'

'Got it in one! Met this great girl. She is ... What are you doing on my doorstep?' Jay repeated.

'Dad forgot to pick me up at the boat. Thought I could stay with you?'

'Well you could but you can't,' his friend laughed. 'Dad's decided to stop on for a few days. *I'm trying for a week.* Unlikely though with the Haybarn,' he said, referring to the restaurant in Falmouth that his father owned. 'She only lives next door to the house where we're stopping. Isn't that great? What was your day like?'

'God awful! Whoever decided to make a friend of Hilary needs their head sorting out.'

'You did, Scott, remember?'

Scott sighed. 'I guess! Never again! I've definitely gone off girls with doglike or bovine tendencies.'

'Go home.'

Scott hesitated. 'Jay?'

He heard a burst of laughter in the background; Scott recognising Jay's younger brother and then his friend's own boisterous tones.

'What?' The voice sounded distant, not attending much.

Scott bit his lip. 'It's okay. Have a good time.'

'I intend to.'

Scott closed the connection, immediately wishing he'd spat out what he'd been trying to say: *Dad's not home and I'm worried*.

He stared down the long drive, the grey stone house one of several recently built on the edge of Falmouth, its perimeter marked by billowing rose-coloured trees, on the point of bursting into blossom. Its driveway of red brick reminded Scott of a chess board and his old habit of solving problems, setting out a single chessman for each problem. Marshalling his thoughts into order, he began placing them in the small squares – half a dozen to be gradually and logically reduced to one, representing the action he was going to take: Dad had taken the bike out, it being a good day he had ridden a long way; he'd had a puncture; his mobile had failed or the battery run down and he couldn't find a phone; his instruction to stay away from the house only applied when he was a young kid not now; and he was getting hungry. It was probably … Scott eyed the clouds … definitely going to rain.

If he didn't go home, the alternative was Travers's house, eight miles further on, and he didn't fancy that in the wet. He groaned aloud, wishing he'd never set eyes on Hilary because now he could be sitting down to a warm meal in an elegant house, containing six bedrooms, constant hot water and a plentiful supply of snacks and DVDs.

Scott got to his feet, his decision made. He'd go home.

A light drizzle had started, adding to the doubts in Scott's head.

It wasn't as if his dad laid down rules just for the fun of it. It had never occurred to him to question anything before; you learned that when you were dangling at the end of a rope, facing an awfully long drop off a mountain. So why this time? What was different?

It felt a long way in the dusk and drizzle. Each time lights approached along the far carriageway he prayed it would his dad's bike or the four-wheel-drive – bitterly disappointed when the vehicle swept past without even slowing. He had frequently done the ride from Jameson's but rarely in the dark. Now he was aware of cars bearing down on him, their front bumpers sitting right on his tail, only swerving round at the last minute. It was scary stuff with ten miles beginning to feel like twenty.

A ribbon of light loomed out of the dark. Thankfully, he swung into the secondary road that looped through the village, rejoining the dual-carriageway a mile further on. Visibility had dropped steadily and the fine, misty drizzle had begun to lie; beams of light from the street lamps reflected in the puddles at the side of the road. The high street was deserted; even dog walkers, their duty done for the night, back home and watching television. A light flared deeply orange as a door opened and shut again. On impulse, Scott pulled to a stop outside the pub.

Not bothering to lock his bike, he pushed open the door. A blast of warm air, laden with smells of food and beer, welcomed him in. In a corner of his mind, he half-expected to see his dad leaning up against the bar chatting. He scanned the room eagerly, recognising the cheerful face of George Beale.

Jean, a ton of make-up now hiding the lines on her face, was standing behind the bar nursing a well-earned drink, after preparing several dozen meals. She smiled cheerfully, welcoming the boy in. 'Not often we see you in here at night, Scott.'

'Can you fix me a sandwich, Jean?'

'Sandwich? Do better than that. How about chicken wrapped in bacon, served on a bed of mashed celeriac and parsley, with a mushroom sauce?'

Scott was hungry and yet the thought of food … He glanced

at his watch. It was almost nine. He needed something to eat, whether he wanted it or not. 'A sandwich will do fine,' he said. 'The chicken sounds good but no money.'

Jean gave a smile and waved her hand in the air, magicking the problem away. 'Don't worry, your dad's credit's sound. When's he back?'

'Well, *now* I hope.'

'So what are you eating here for? He's a great cook.'

Exactly what was he eating there for? He'd be home in ten minutes and could get something then. The reason was obvious. Scott gave a half smile. 'Dad's gone walk-about,' he said, hoping his casual explanation would stop any further questions.

Jean laughed. 'He was in here this morning – chasing coffee.'

'You've seen my *dad*?' Scott heard the tone of his voice, it sounded desperate.

Jean noticed it too. 'That sounds like you're worried, Scott. No need to be. He said he was going off for the day. I was talking to him about that reporter.'

'What reporter?' Scott said, scarcely listening now his sense of relief so overwhelming. Dad was okay. He *had* just gone out.

'Sean Terry, he said his name was. I thought it was probably about you. You know – outstanding achievement in your exams or something.'

'As if,' Scott rummaged up a grin.

'Well, anyway, I expect your dad'll be back shortly. Right, I'll get you some dinner.' Jean said, disappearing through an archway into the kitchen.

Happy now he'd made the right decision, Scott wandered over to the farmer, an orange juice clutched in his hand. 'Did your lambs get off?'

The farmer dragged his eyes away from the screen, a premier-league football match in full swing. 'Ay, young 'un, they did. Got a good price for them, too. Bloody foreigners, tryin' to tell me my business. Knew them lambs was as right as rain.' He beamed at Scott. 'Me dad farmed this land and me granddad, afore me. There ain't much I don't know about it.'

'Can I ask you something?'

The farmer, his face lined and weather-beaten – his cheeks a slow purple after fifty years of getting up at dawn and working outside whatever the weather – nodded.

Scott hesitated. 'You know last winter; the sheep were in the top field, next to our land – the one with the stone water trough. That's right, isn't it?'

'Ay, lad, always do. Land drains real quick there. The spruce to the west draws out the water and gives shelter. If they lamb early I don't have to worry about losing lambs to the wet. New borns can stand cold but not wet.' He took a sip of his beer. 'Why do you ask, you ride past it every day, you saw 'em.'

'I know, but that man from the Ministry, I saw him checking that field. He said it was contaminated and they'd have to retest them all.'

'Rubbish.' The old farmer's tone was dismissive. 'How come he never said nothin' to me about it? It was like I told your dad ...'

Scott's eyes flew round the room. 'When did you see Dad?'

George chuckled, his glance speculative. 'Avoiding him, are you? Well, don't worry, I won't tell him I've seen you. It were first thing this morning. I was on the way to me sisters. He was ridin' that bloody-great red bike of his. How he doesn't have an accident ... He asked me about them radiation tests.'

'Did he?' So at least two people had seen him.

'Ay, he did. I told him straight. I'd got a stifficate of exemption and I couldn't see no reason for them radiation testers to be there in the first place. Bloody useless lot they was too. Never seen a sheep before. You take it from me, lad. That field's not contaminated. Bet my life on it. So don't you worry your head none, young 'un. My sheeps are just fine.'

A huge shout erupted from the crowd watching the game. The farmer swung hurriedly round to the television, anxious to catch the replay of the goal just scored.

Scott wandered back to his table, which had miraculously acquired a red and white checked tablecloth in his absence, a plate, knife, fork and spoon, and some bread. He wasn't mistaken. But George's answer hadn't cleared anything up; made it worse, if anything, for now he needed to work out why those men were interested in that particular field.

He gazed down at the tablecloth, absentmindedly tearing chunks off the bread and placing the pieces on the cloth.

'Here you are.' Jean stared at Scott's hand poised over one of the squares, a crust of bread in it. 'What's with the bread?'

Scott said embarrassed, 'I sometimes work out problems this way.'

'Okay, everyone to their own. Mind you eat it now.'

'Thanks, it looks really good.'

He picked up his fork eagerly trying to decide which bit to taste first. Ten minutes later he stared down at his empty plate. He must have been hungry.

'Sorry,' he said, as Jean came to clear the table.

'*Sorry*! Your plate doesn't even need washing! You'd better have pie for afters – that might fill you up.' She plopped a dish down in front of him. 'God, the appetites you kids have – good job my customers aren't all like you, I'd be out of business in a week.'

'That's why I said sorry.' Scott eyed the large piece of pie, covered in fresh cream, with gratitude. 'We've been on the river – it gives you an appetite,' he explained.

'Good day?'

'Great – thanks.' Well it would have been if Hilary had been friendlier.

Jean moved back behind the bar.

Automatically, Scott glanced down at his watch. Aware he had a decision to make, he pulled out his mobile and dialled the number. It was still dead. Reluctantly he tried the land line, counting off each ring, imagining his dad dashing in from the garage to grab it before the answer-phone clicked in. His heart lurched wildly as he heard the recording and he spoke without thinking, 'Dad – if you get this message, I'll be home shortly, okay?'

Weird how things can change from normal to total devastation in the blink of an eye – an image of the phone ringing endlessly in the cottage seared Scott's brain. Sometime in the past twelve hours, something bad *had* happened to his dad.

Two things were clear as day. His dad's warnings had never been about having an accident or breaking a leg. An accident wouldn't have stopped him phoning unless he'd been killed, which was pretty unlikely when he stayed at home all day. And the buzzer to warn Bill of people coming up the lane? The constant questions about new people in the village? That wasn't only about being an American and lying low; there were people searching for him.

And the second thing? Whoever it was – they'd found him.

Scott lifted his hands away from his face, the decision made. Somehow he had to get to the house and without being seen. The thought of riding that last two miles in darkness, all the time wondering what was waiting for him, was not pleasant, but it had to be done and the sooner the better.

Reluctantly he got to his feet. 'Thanks, Jean,' he called, 'I feel heaps better now. I'll come by tomorrow with the money.'

'No rush. I know where you live.'

The door swung to behind him severing all connection with people and light. Now he was on his own. He gazed up and down the forlorn-looking street. He could see no one about, the street dark, even the light from the street lamps diminished by the fine drizzle into a small well of brightness.

His bike, well maintained by Bill Anderson, made no sound, an occasional swish of water floating up from the puddles as he rode through them. Away from the main road nothing moved; the road silent. He cycled past a lay-by a single car parked up – its driver most likely sleeping off his Saturday night visit to the pub. He slowed and listened, the overhanging trees up ahead obscuring all sight of the lane that led up to the cottage. Not a sound. He changed gear as the gradient began to bite. He'd not bothered with lights after leaving the pub, knowing the way blindfold and, now his eyes had adjusted, it wasn't that dark even with the moon hidden behind rain clouds.

An owl hooted, its mournful cry floating into the rain-sodden air. A fox barked, a threatening sound that spooked the sheep in a neighbouring field, making them move restlessly. A dark shadow scuttled across the lane in front of his wheels. He swerved but didn't slow, knowing full well the badger had already seen him and wasn't particularly bothered about it. They were nice creatures and he was glad they were sensible enough to have their sett well off the beaten track; somewhere cars couldn't get at them. He detested the carnage on the main road in the mornings when he rode to school, the tarmac resembling a charnel house and littered with corpses.

He slid his bike to a halt, near where he'd seen the Ministry van parked the previous morning. Looming above him, no more than three hundred metres away now, was the shadowy silhouette of the house – its oblong shape densely black. He dismounted carefully aware that any sound would carry across the still air and leant his bike up against the gate. Then, using the stile, dropped down into the field. From here up to the house there were no sheep to startle, the field empty. Cautiously, keeping close to the hedge for cover, he crossed to the far side.

His stomach griped and he stopped – exhaling slowly through his mouth – as he'd been taught. That had been on the mountain when he had slipped and, after a heart-stopping rush downwards, had jerked to a halt, held only by a rope.

His dad's voice had never changed. 'Scott – take some slow breaths,' he had said, his tone as calm as if they were standing by a window gazing out at the view. All Scott wanted to do was grab at the nearest rock, but his dad's voice had stopped him. He did as he was told, breathing slowly and steadily, concentrating on that alone, and trying to ignore his swinging body until he felt the panic begin to subside. Only then had he reached out to the rock, to search for a hand hold. He felt the rope slacken as he took control once more. 'Atta boy,' his dad had called out.

Now, Scott felt his muscles begin to relax, that terrible

sensation of cold fear leaving him. The slope drifted up towards the back of the garage, the field separated from their small garden by a low wall. He was close enough now to make out the windows at the back; his bedroom with his dad's on the far side, both overlooking the garden with its pastoral scenes from countryside calendars of fields and wooded copses.

A narrow path hugged the walls of the garage, circling round into the yard at the front. Here, the double wooden doors were in constant use, either by the four-wheel-drive or the motorbike. In summer, when the lawn needed mowing and borders weeding, the narrow doorway at the back was left open, but always locked at night.

He paused, hesitating. He might be familiar with its layout better than anyone except his dad, but how was he to get in without being spotted? He frowned, the realisation that he was on his own suddenly hitting home. *Still, I can find out, can't I*, he thought, *then get help*.

The slope increased, the grass greasy under the rain. Wishing he was wearing his climbing boots instead of trainers, he gripped the long grassy tufts with his hands to stop his feet slipping. He moved even more cautiously now covering the final ten metres, a heavy stone wall barring his view into the garden. Keeping tight to the rock, he shinned over and dropped to the ground, a flowering currant bush shielding him from anyone watching from the window.

Without warning, a hand clamped itself over his mouth, another tight across his chest. His fingers flew up, clawing at the hand pressed against his nose and mouth, but the arms of his attacker were like steel. Scott couldn't move, his lungs gasping painfully as they were denied oxygen.

A voice hissed in his ear. 'Not a sound! If you move or shout, you'll find yourself dead.'

SIX

Scott froze, his arms dropping down to his side. He could do nothing anyway, his attacker far too strong. *How could he have been so stupid?* Climbing over the wall on top of someone watching the house! Of all the crazy … why had he come … his dad had warned him to stay away … useless … how could he possibly help Dad now … he was a prisoner too!

His head tightened as waves of dizziness swept over his body. He fell forwards and put a hand down to the ground to steady himself. The fingers, gripping his mouth and nose, relaxed slightly and he dragged in a life-saving breath.

'Listen to me carefully,' the voice whispered in his ear. He didn't recognise it – but why should he?

'The name's Sean Terry.'

Scott started. He'd heard that name and just recently but who …? He tried to clear his head, to think, to remember, but found nothing there beyond the need to keep breathing.

'I'll let you go – but listen first. There's somebody inside the house, waiting for you, I guess. I don't know who they are but until we have them safe, not a sound, okay?'

Scott nodded and touched the hand, pulling at the fingers. Immediately, the band of iron clutching his arms and chest vanished, allowing him to breathe deeply sucking in the welcome air, his straining pulse already beginning to steady. Silently, he massaged his forearms, feeling the bruises well up from the force of the man's grip. Inching round sideways, he tried to get a look at his attacker's face, staring instead at the outline of a gun.

Scott was as scared as he had ever been in his life. It was like falling off the mountainside again; although then he'd simply been frightened. Now, to his surprise, excitement was jumbled up with fear. He swallowed; the sound in his ears so loud they could have heard it in the house. But how did the man with the gun know there was someone in the house?

'Who are you – the police?' he whispered at the black silhouette.

'All in good time. Stay down and don't move.'

As far as Scott was concerned, they were alone in the garden. He couldn't see anyone else, but then he'd never spotted the man with the gun, had he?

He heard a muffled whisper, '*Go!*' Two bushes changed shape, elongating into dark figures. In a crouching run, they disappeared round the corner of the garage towards the front of the house. They made no sound. All at once a blaze of light appeared, the cottage and workroom as bright as day. A voice cut across the silence.

'*Inside the house* – come out – your hands held high.'

At that instant memory hit a home run. Jean at the pub had spoken about someone making enquiries about his dad, a reporter called Sean Terry. Scott swung round, the words: *But you're a reporter,* on the tip of his tongue, when the man beside him stirred. He caught the whispered words, '*Use stun.*'

The night sky exploded. One of the windows in the cottage burst outwards in a shower of glass and a figure hurtled out, somersaulting to its feet. The sudden crack of an automatic followed – its jagged-staccato beat criss-crossing the night sky. Scott nose-dived into the ground, the flare from the bullets arcing from one side of the garden to the other. Another flash – this time from the yard – and then, shouting. The figure charged down the garden. Sean Terry took careful aim and fired, the noise blasting a trench in the sky. The figure leapt into the air and, from a great height, crashed to the ground and lay still.

A black shape emerged from under the wall and ran across the garden towards the body. Scott caught the thumbs-down gesture.

'*Goddamn it!*' The man beside him stood up. 'All over – it's safe now. Your place is probably a bit of a mess but we'll get it cleaned up as soon as possible.'

Scott leapt to his feet. Faint sounds came from the yard, but otherwise the night was silent again. In the distance the fox barked sharply.

'Dad!' he yelled. '*Dad*! *Where are you?*' He dived for the path, praying it really was safe and no more bullets were flying. A fleeting glance round the yard showed the garage doors still shut. As far as he could see the studio hadn't been touched either. But the front door into the kitchen – or what was left of it – stood open. The remainder, blasted into long painted slivers of wood, decorated the paving stones in the yard. Two men dressed in black flak jackets and dark trousers appeared, a third man bundled between them. From the distance, headlights approached up the slope.

Scott tore through the kitchen door, shouting as he ran. He returned to the yard, his face ashen. 'He's not there,' he said in disbelief. He glowered at the prisoner. 'Where's my dad?' he yelled, pummelling his fists against the man's chest. 'If you've hurt him, I'll kill you.'

The man's head jerked upright. 'Your dad's fine,' he protested. 'We only wanted to talk. No need for all this.'

'But why? What do you want him for?' Scott peered at the man closely. 'I know you,' he said, his voice trembling, close to tears. 'You were driving the Ministry van.'

'Ministry van?' Sean Terry said from behind him.

Scott swung round to find the reporter almost treading on his heels. He flinched and stepped back a pace. 'Yes, they were checking the farmer's sheep for radiation, only yesterday.'

'Were they now! That's interesting. So where is he?' Sean Terry demanded.

'I don't know. We were waiting for the kid. I told you.' The man yelped loudly, as his arms were roughly pulled back. 'Okay! *Okay*! Take it easy. Set me loose. I'll talk but let me go.'

'Talk first. Then we'll see.' Sean Terry spoke to the men guarding him. 'Take him back to headquarters and find out what he knows. Come on, Scott – let's get in out of this wet.'

'But what about the garage and studio, he might be in there. Have you searched?'

A third man, his face streaked with black lines, was leaning comfortably against the wall, adjacent to where the front door had been, an automatic propped up next to him. He nodded in a friendly fashion to Scott.

'Name's Pete. Sorry, kid, our prisoner told the truth. There's no one here. We checked the house first of all – it was empty, so was the garidge,' he shrugged. 'The studio's locked and I figured I wouldn't win any popularity contests if I bust down two of your doors in one night, so I was kind'a hopin' you had a key?'

'Yes, there's a spare.' Scott said eagerly. He hurried back into the kitchen pulling open the door to the cupboard, where they kept the vacuum cleaner and iron. He lifted the key from its hook and hesitated, his hand in mid-air. *Holy crap!* He had to get a grip. What *was* he doing rushing to help, when he didn't know if he could even trust them? He spun round to ask the question and found Pete right behind him. Scott caught sight of the man's feet. He was wearing trainers but even so he had to move like a cat.

'Relax, kid.' Pete took the key from Scott's grip and gave him a friendly grin. 'We may not look it but we're actually the good guys come to save your bacon.'

'But …'

'You'll get your answers, but do it the boss's way, okay?'

Scott hesitated. 'Okay,' he agreed reluctantly. 'But I'm coming with you. Can we check the garage again?'

'There's nothing to see, I told you, your dad's not here. Those men were foot soldiers. The prisoner told the truth. They were waiting for you.'

'I still want to see for myself,' he insisted stubbornly.

Pete tilted a finger in acknowledgement and led the way back into the yard. Seeing them, Sean Terry immediately broke-off his conversation with one of his men, following on behind. Like I'm

55

a prisoner, thought Scott, trying to conceal a shiver; Pete's friendly words of little comfort when he'd just seen a man killed.

He pulled open the double doors, his eyes swivelling from left to right exploring deep into the shadows. It struck him as being unusually cavernous, as though his dad's disappearance had created an enlarged area of space. But nothing had been touched, everything exactly as should have been. Then he noticed the helmet, jacket and gloves still draped over the bike. He kept his face expressionless, aware that his father had planned to go out again almost immediately. But why? Scott didn't have the answer to that, but it didn't take a genius to work out that intruders had broken in while his dad was out and had been waiting for him.

'You're right,' he said, 'nothing's been taken from here.'

He backed out quickly, hoping no one else had picked up on the jacket and helmet. Hurrying across the yard to the studio, he waited impatiently while Pete fitted the key into the lock. The man turned it, pushing the door open his gun at the ready. The neon tubes flickered and jumped into life as he clicked the switches.

'It's okay.' He beckoned them in.

Automatically, Scott bent down to leave his glasses in their holder. He stifled a gasp. His dad's specs were still in their usual place on the table. For a brief second hope flared. It didn't last, the workroom obviously empty.

He hung back in the doorway, acutely aware that it was from this studio his dad had vanished. Reluctantly the thought began to take shape; the prisoner had lied. There could have been nothing friendly in the way his dad had been dragged away – it was as a result of something so violent he didn't even have time to pick his specs up from the table.

Scott began to feel sick. If only he could curl up on his bed and go to sleep and not have to think any more. If he did, perhaps in the morning everything would be back to normal. Except it wouldn't. This time it wasn't him hanging from the rope but his dad – and it was up to him to get them safe back onto the rock. Scott stared about him, trying to keep his face blank, his actions casual. If any clues existed, they would be here. He swivelled on his heel to inspect the door for signs of a forced entry, knowing it to be a waste of time. If there had been even the faintest suspicion that something was wrong, his dad would never have walked into the trap.

At first glance the room appeared much as usual, each piece of equipment, highlighted by powerful lights, emerging strangely stark and solitary, their overlapping brightness wiping out any shadow. The posters leapt out of the wall, as if they were new and he had never seen them before; the scarlet Suzuki jarring incongruously against its background of plain cream emulsion. The monitors were still in place but the box containing the hard drive had vanished, leaving a large gap where it had once stood.

'The computer's gone.' Reaching behind him, he quickly picked up his dad's specs, slipping them unnoticed into his pocket.

'Anything else?' Sean Terry asked, restlessly prowling round the room. Drawing back the blinds he peered out.

Scott hesitated, Pete's words still ringing in his ears. 'You expect me to tell you stuff when I don't even know who you are? Or how you knew Dad was missing, when I didn't know it myself?'

'That's not strictly true, kid.' Pete grinned at Scott, the wall keeping him upright. 'Unless that's the usual way you enter your house?'

Scott flushed.

'I asked if there was anything else missing?' Sean Terry repeated, in a voice like sandpaper.

'I don't think so.'

'Pete, get one of the boys to check for prints. There won't be any but you may get lucky. Come with me, Scott. Nothing more you can do here.'

Scott followed the long, thin figure into his own house, kicking off his muddy trainers at the door. None of it felt real, not even the man walking in front of him. From behind he resembled some species of stick insect, the weedy *before* bloke in an ad-campaign for protein supplements designed to build muscle; his jacket and trousers flapping loosely against his bony frame. Except he wasn't. Scott winced, vividly recalling the arms clutching him, with their tendons of steel.

The kitchen was a mess. Whoever the men were, they'd been waiting there a while. Cupboards had been raided and empty crisp packets lay on the floor, dirty cups by the kitchen sink. His dad would never have left it like that. Scott checked round the small house yet again, the bedrooms, even the bathroom – still hoping. Reluctantly, he returned to the kitchen.

'He's not there,' he said, as if the reality was only now beginning to sink in.

Sean Terry picked up the kettle carrying it to the sink to fill it. 'Okay, if I make us a drink, the guys could do with it?'

'But …?'

'It's okay, Scott. I heard. Your dad's missing. Get dry first, we'll talk then.'

Angrily Scott headed for his room and slammed the door. Crashing down on the bed, he buried his face in his hands. Who were they? A reporter that carried a gun? And the others? They weren't English police – so who? And how did they know his dad was missing even before he did? Scott raised his head, staring blankly at the wall. *Exactly*! How *did* they know? Where had they come from and how did they know how to find the cottage? And how many were there? There'd been three in the garden, their faces blacked out and two in the yard.

Scott closed his eyes vividly recollecting the time he'd been surfing and his board had been caught in a strong current, sweeping him out to sea. There'd been nothing he could do about that, either. Calling for help had been a waste of breath; no one on shore able to hear him. Only one possibility – ride the current till it petered out. By then he was way out, the people on the shore minute dots, like ink spots on a sheet of paper. Still, he hadn't panicked. Instead, he had set a parallel course to the shore, freed himself from the current's clutches and, taking control, slowly paddled back in. This was the same. Somehow he had to get back to shore.

He leapt to his feet, for the first time aware he was both wet and muddy. He stripped off his jacket and trousers – at the last minute remembering to change over the contents of his pockets; his phone and some money.

A knock came on his door. 'You decent?' The door opened and a stubble-bound chin, preceding a pair of tight blue eyes, appeared. 'Okay?' Sean Terry looked enquiringly at the boy sitting on the bed. Scott nodded. 'Did they touch your room?'

'They've been in but I don't even know what they were looking for, Mr Terry, so how can I tell if anything's gone?' Scott's caught his voice – even he could hear its whine. It sounded as miserable as he felt. And right now he didn't have time to feel sorry for himself.

'No good pounding your pillows and feeling sorry for yourself,' his dad used to say, when he had a bad day at school. 'Get angry and take it out on your bike or the swimming pool.'

'Name's Sean. I've made coffee … interested?'

It was hard, like acting in a play. He clenched his teeth, pumping himself up to sound angry and frustrated, looking the reporter straight in the eye. 'I'll get some tea, thanks.'

SEVEN

Scott wandered round the kitchen, tidying the mess left by the intruders. Dad would hate it if he came home and saw it. He glanced back at the open doorway where Pete – once again propping up the wall – was drinking a cup of coffee, his attention directed across the yard.

'Sentry,' Sean explained, catching the direction of the boy's gaze.

'You think they'll come back?'

'Nope! Not tonight anyway! That sort cut their losses; the men they use are expendable.'

'The man you shot, is he dead?'

'Yeah, a real drag. I could have done with talking to him.'

Scott heard the twang in the voice. 'Are you an American?' he said, trying not to sound astonished.

'Officially I'm Irish, but hell – yes, I'm American.'

'Jean at the pub said you were a reporter.'

'That's right, the *Chronicle*.'

Scott retorted, unable to stop himself, 'But English reporters aren't American. And they don't go round with guns and blacked-out faces, killing people. Well, not in our village anyway. So why ...'

'So why am I an American, who happens to carry a gun and turns up in your backyard in time to save you from the bad guys?'

'Something like that,' Scott tried to smile but his face felt as if it had been dipped in concrete.

'I work for the American Secret Service. My badge.' A wallet appeared. Inside was a card sheathed in plastic, covered with official-looking stamps.

Scott tried to read the scrawled signature, over the words *US Department of Justice.* He'd only ever seen that done in old movies. Now it had been done to him and he was none the wiser. Flashing a piece of card didn't make it genuine, he thought indignantly.

'So why are you living in England disguised as a reporter?'

'I've been trying to find your parents.'

'I don't understand,' Scott felt himself sway. He grabbed the edge of the breakfast bar. 'But my mother died in the tsunami,' he said a bewildered expression on his face. 'There's only Dad and me.'

'Here, sit.' Sean pointed to an armchair, one of two that had somehow found their way into the kitchen; a narrow table, big enough to hold a couple of glasses, standing between them. After a hard day's hiking, it had been so much simpler to collapse in one of those, rather than shower and change in order to use the more formal sitting room.

'You won't be going to bed yet awhile so we might as well make ourselves comfortable.'

Scott sat down. The shock of being taken prisoner was beginning to disappear, genuine anger rapidly becoming his overriding emotion. Anger at the people who had taken away his dad; anger at the thousand questions jumping round in his brain, which one to ask first; and anger at not knowing whether he dare believe the answers or not.

'So what is the American Secret Service doing in England? I mean after what the United States did to Iran, I thought all communication had been severed.'

'We didn't do anything to Iran.'

Scott opened his mouth to protest.

'Look! This is going to be one hell of a long night if I say something and you dispute it. How about I fill you in; then if you have any questions you ask them at the end – sound fair?'

Scott's head whirled. He'd listen but that wasn't to say he'd believe. Sean Terry was beginning to irritate the life out of him, acting as if he owned the house and giving orders; and his tone of voice – that made him feel like a young kid, not even big enough to wipe his own nose. Besides, if he really did belong to the American Secret Service, then he was operating illegally. One call to the police and he'd be arrested.

'So let's see,' Sean began. 'Fifteen years ago the Iran nuclear blast happened and on the back of that came the earthquake that destroyed California. Okay, so far?' Scott nodded. 'The Iran fiasco wasn't altogether unexpected. The Atomic Energy Commission had been monitoring the process for years, warning that staff needed better training, safety practices were being ignored, and some of the processes were unstable.

'I'm making some more coffee. The lads need it, they'd been waiting awhile. Is that okay?' Sean Terry ranged round the room while he talked, collecting coffee cups and rinsing them under the tap.

Scott counted them carefully. Only three now; two of the men must have left with the prisoner. The kettle steamed madly then clicked off. 'There's a tray.' He got up, taking it from the cupboard. The coffees were black, without milk or sugar.

'Thanks, I'll give these to the boys.' Pete wandered off the wall, collecting the tray. He crossed to the doorway and whistled.

'Okay, so let's go on,' Sean said. He hooked a stool out from under the breakfast bar and perched on it. Scott opened his mouth to protest. It was the one his dad always used and, right at this moment, he could hardly bear to see someone else using it – which was pretty stupid, it was only a stool.

'When America was blamed, we looked to the Commission for vindication. The earthquake struck and so did a bomb, destroying the Commission's offices, while the commissioner, invited as guest speaker at a conference in Paris, was never heard of again.'

Sean paused and took a sip of coffee, steam still rising from the cup. 'I was a young FBI agent at the time, part of a team despatched to discover what had happened to the boffins attending the conference. Most had died but those still alive we gathered up, escorting some back to their homeland, the rest – our own – we took into protective custody.'

'Why ...?' began Scott, unable to stop himself.

Ignoring the interruption, Sean Terry picked up a spoon, stirring the hot liquid thoughtfully. 'No one stateside believed for a moment the quake was an act of God.' He leaned back and, stretching out his arm, dropped the spoon into the sink. 'Hundreds of attendees to the conference remained unaccounted for; among those your parents. It was the very devil of a job sorting it all out – took the best part of a year. We had so little to go on; a mass of photos, which we circulated round the county – hoping to find at least some alive in hospital. The description we were given of your dad; six feet, fair, with brilliant blue eyes to die for.' The tight line of his mouth relaxed as if contemplating a smile; like a light bulb trying to ignite and failing. 'That touch was contributed by an ex-girlfriend who, I reckon, still fancied him.'

'Slight, good athlete, played ball for his college,' he droned on. 'Not much, but we followed it anyway. Your mother died, you say ...'

Scott dashed into his bedroom to fetch the photograph, quickly returning. 'That's her,' he said, passing it over. 'It's the only photo I've got.'

'Yeah, that's Sarah Masterson. We have a photo of her taken at about the same ...'

'*Who?*'

'Sarah Masterson, your mother.'

'My name's not Anderson?' Scott blinked, wishing he could see through the fog clogging his brain. Despite the tea, he felt desperately tired and a blur of names were jumping about in his head, refusing to stay still and be sorted: Anderson – Masterson – Scott – Sky? None of it made any sense.

'No, your father changed it, not a lot though which is surprising. Still, it did the job. Kept him hidden for fifteen years.'

'*So why didn't you leave him alone?* If no one knew ...'

'Someone did, Scott,' Sean said interrupting him. 'The radiation experts, remember? We don't know who they are yet, but we're working on it.' The thin figure got to his feet and paced the floor, his coffee forgotten. 'It's rather like a jigsaw puzzle. Occasionally we find a piece that fits – like tonight – we took one of the men alive. But *someone* set off that earthquake.' He slammed his hand against the breakfast bar making Scott jump. 'And we're going to discover who. It doesn't matter how long it takes.' He spun round, his eyes piercing, as if he was the prosecuting counsel in a courtroom and Scott the guilty party. 'The world believes the US destroyed Iran and set off earthquake by accident. We intend to prove it was the other way round: Iran was the accident.'

'Can you prove it?' Scott asked, breaking the tension in the air.

'Pretty much,' Sean Terry said, his voice sounding quite calm again. 'Too many coincidences. Take, for example, the computer experts. Those unaccounted for were mainly working in the same specialised field. Then the business of the Atomic Commission; offices bombed so all proof of the Iran fiasco vanished. Now it's youngsters – mostly to do with computers, disappearing into thin air. It's like someone is gathering together every computer expert in existence.'

'But my dad wasn't into computers,' Scott blurted out.

'Sure he was,' the reporter's tone was abrasive. 'He was a world-renowned expert on viruses. So was your mother. They were part of a team working on a virus that could penetrate any computer system in the world, collect its data and disappear without a trace. If you're a terrorist organisation, or rebels trying to overthrow a government and take over a country, you can no longer do that by simply raising an army and marching in. Plans have to be documented and communication is by computer or mobile phone. The work they were doing was vital for world peace.'

'*That can't be true*, you're making it up,' Scott shouted wildly. Pete glanced across at the reporter – neither man speaking. 'Dad told me he was just a computer geek – nothing important.'

'He did that to protect you,' Sean said, dismissing Scott's outburst. 'What else did he say?'

'Nothing much.' Scott put on the brakes, shrugging. And if he did, no way am I telling you, he added silently.

'Okay, we can come to what you know later.'

'So who's behind it?'

'I told you, we don't know. But we're getting closer; the trail has led us to Europe.'

'And you?'

'I've worked for the *Exeter Chronicle* for two years.'

'But how did you get here so quickly?'

'I thought I was doing the talking.'

'You are, but I'm not much interested in the problems of America,' Scott's voice sounded rude even to him, but he didn't care. 'The only thing that's important to me is finding my dad. And if you want my help, I need to know some things – like how you got here so quickly – with armed men – and ready for a fight.'

'We'd been closing in on your dad for weeks now.' Sean looked down at his watch, a workmanlike chrome affair with a series of buttons decorating the side.

Scott found himself needing to check the time, too. It was the same when someone scratched their nose or head, your brain picked up on the electrical impulses and you found yourself copying the action. He looked down. It was just after twelve; surprising really, considering everything that had happened. He'd been up since before six; no wonder he felt shattered. If only he could fall into bed and go to sleep.

'I was planning to see him tomorrow. Then this evening our agent tipped me off that your father was missing. We came prepared. Found men – not your father – making free with the house.'

The man seated opposite looked tired too – grey shadows of exhaustion tracking down his cheeks. Momentarily Scott felt sympathy, wondering what it was like to kill a man. He squashed it, still unsure of whether to trust him or not. What had Dad always said? *Before deciding on anything, turn it upside down and look at it another way.* How could anyone know his dad was missing? He hardly knew it himself. Scott replayed the scene at the marina and the pub. He'd told no one; so if no one knew … were Sean Terry and his team, with their stun guns, the enemy? And the men in the house simply a decoy? But why? To capture him, too? They'd done that in any case. And the man in the garden, the one that had dived through the window? Had it all been an act?

'So, how did I give myself away?' he said.

'You didn't. We posted a car at the entrance to the lane. He missed you. I guess you were riding without lights?'

'Yes.'

'He radioed up that he'd seen something but didn't know what; then nothing more till you shinned over the wall and came to rest beside me. Scared the hell out'a me … hence my welcome. Sorry about that.' A bleak smiled crossed the agent's face.

Scott made up his mind. 'Look, Mr Terry, I'm not yet sixteen. I'm at school all day and when I get home, I get Dad a cup of tea. Every day I say to him, *hey what are you working on* and every day he replies, *so what's new in the outside world?*'

Scott felt the piercing look, as if a laser was drilling into him.

'I don't buy that for a second.' There was more warmth in a block of liquid nitrogen than Sean's voice. 'You know stuff; things that will help us find Bill Masterson. And I need to know what they are, whether you like it or not.'

A thrill of pure excitement, like he experienced when riding the Suzuki at full throttle, spun through Scott. He was glad now his dad had never confided his thoughts.

'So what are you going to do, *beat it out of me?* A lot of good that would do you! I promise, my dad was the most cautious man alive. I thought I knew his name – but I didn't, *did I?* And if I tell you his age, you'll probably say I'm wrong about that, too. *I didn't even know he was into computers.* Anyway, even if I did know anything – which I don't – *why should I trust you?* I thought the only Americans in England were refugees. Now I know for a fact, there are at least six over here, armed to the teeth, telling me they belong to the Secret Service.'

Pete, still on sentry duty, flicked his cigarette into the yard.

'*And don't mess up my dad's yard.*' Scott's voice cracked.

The two men exchanged glances.

'Is Stone here?'

'Just arrived.'

'So what are you waiting for?' Sean snapped. 'Okay, Scott, I don't blame you for not believing me – it does sound pretty far-fetched. But there is someone you might believe.'

Scott glanced up at the door. Pete had disappeared. Someone else was standing in the doorway – someone he recognised. Scott's mind felt groggy with exhaustion. What on earth was Hilary Stone doing there and why had she changed her clothes? On the boat she'd been wearing jeans and a sweater, like the rest of them. Now she was dressed in a flak jacket, black sweater and trousers, a gun belt and holster around her waist.

'This is agent Stone,' Sean Terry said. He passed a weary hand over his face. 'I think you've met before.'

EIGHT

Scott's brain seized. He could feel the gears grinding but not a single coherent thought passed through its cogs, as if he'd been knocked out in a fist fight. He shook his head to clear it and flashbacks of their miserable day on the river swam into view. He glared at Hilary.

'*That's just great*! With her in the Secret Service you'll have the world sorted out in no time – they give in 'cos she'll bore them to death.'

Hilary flushed scarlet.

Scott felt the adrenaline rush. He'd never been in the habit of using sarcasm, *but boy, did it feel good!*

Sean got to his feet. The youngster wasn't kidding. He had meant that – and then some – total anger and dislike poured into one sentence. 'Stone – a word,' he clipped, his voice as glacial as the blue of his eyes. He led the way into the yard. Hilary flashed a hurt glance at Scott, reluctantly following.

'So what the hell was that?' he snapped. 'I thought your job was to get pally with him. If it was – you failed miserably.'

'What about my phone call; saving his hide you called it?' Hilary retorted.

'You were doing your job. That's what we pay you for. And if you're that good at it, how come he hates you now?'

'I don't know. It would have been easier making friends with an oyster,' Hilary defended herself. 'Wouldn't say a word about his family. I did try. God knows.'

'You did *what!*'

Hilary flinched and took a step backwards. 'My instructions were to learn as much as I could about Bill Masterson.'

Sean groaned. 'Goddamn it, Stone, don't they teach you anything in training school about boys, and how to get on with them? You don't get on their right side by talking about their dads.'

'So what else was I to do?' The girl's puzzlement sounded genuine. 'I told you; when he did finally open his mouth all he did was ask stupid questions about London. Whether I'd seen the Eye and the Tower; like a kid of ten, only they're brighter than that. So how could I answer him?' she said defiantly. 'I've never been to London.'

'So you say: *wonderful, great, fabulous, stupendous, you must go, perhaps we can go together sometime.* Make something up, for crying-out-loud. *Hell!* Why send a girl to do a man's job? Anyone with half a brain could have done better than you.'

'I'm sorry,' Hilary's voice was tight. 'I'll sort it. I promise.'

'You betta had. I need you to babysit him till we get hold of his dad. So let's get back in and I'll give him the good news.'

The adrenalin charge remained. Whoever they were, good or bad, and at this stage Scott didn't much care, they were seriously put out. Well, his dad had spent his entire lifetime teaching him to fend for himself – and that's precisely what he intended, starting right now.

Swiftly pulling open the kitchen cupboard, he yanked the laptop out from behind the ironing board and headed for his bedroom, closing the door silently behind him. Somewhere safe? His eyes were drawn to the drawers in his divan bed. By day they were covered with a bedspread. Trying to make as little noise as possible, he swung the bed round. It moved easily on its castors and he snatched the pillow, tossing it to the far end. Stuffing the laptop under some sweaters, he pushed the divan tight to the wall flicking the cover back into place. Now, unless someone took it into their head to search his room, it was safe.

He closed the door behind him and tiptoed back up the

corridor into the kitchen. Angry voices still wafted in from the yard. He sat back down in his chair and closed his eyes, only opening them when he heard the two agents enter the kitchen again, the expression on their faces neutral, revealing nothing.

'I was going over some details with Agent Stone here,' Sean explained. 'She's going to stay. I'll leave one of the men, too. But first I need you to tell me everything you can about your father's work.'

'Sorry about before.' Scott smiled at Hilary, keeping his voice casual sounding. 'It was all a bit much. Do you get to carry a real gun?'

Hilary's hand automatically dropped to check the holster against her right hip. 'Of course. Colt M-Nineteen eleven, Service issue.'

'Did you bring your gun to school?' he said, knowing the question was bound to annoy her and glad of it. He tried again. 'Good disguise by the way, I'd never have guessed. Have you been an agent long?'

Hilary flashed a hurt glance at Sean. *See*, it said, *what I had to put up with*.

'Not long,' Sean said, answering for the girl. 'Now, about your dad?'

Scott twisted round to stare at the reporter, still lounging in the doorway. He came all the way in, perching once more on the stool, leaving Hilary to stand.

'I told you, you know more about Dad than me – even his real name. All I know, he's a great dad,' Scott's voice broke, his resolve of the moment before vanished. 'And if you really are the Secret Service, you'd better find him.' Or I will, he added to himself. 'Look,' he stood up. 'I can't think anymore tonight, I've got to sleep, and you're losing time. Shouldn't you be following whoever took him?'

'We are,' Sean's reply was brusque. 'Okay, I know when I'm beat. Get some sleep. We'll talk in the morning.'

Pete came into the house, a key dangling from his hand. 'You want this?'

Scott nodded. 'I'll put it back. Thanks. Find anything?'

'Prints, but I expect they're your dad's. The door's arrived. And we boarded up the window at the back with some cardboard we found in the garidge.'

Scott was impressed. It was almost one o'clock. He listened to the gears grinding their way up the steep incline towards the gate into the yard. How do you get a door in the middle of the night? 'How ...' he began.

Pete grinned. 'Pinched it. We left an IOU. It's not painted though, only primed – still it'll do for now. Tell you what, boss,' he said to Sean Terry. 'Why don't I stay? You can take the girl back with you. I'll be hanging out in the kitchen anyway, fixing the door.' He pointed to the chair where Scott was sitting. 'I can doze in that. It'll be fine. I'll keep the kid safe.'

Sean Terry took a sip of his coffee, pouring the remainder down the sink. 'Nice of you to offer, Pete, but no deal. I can't afford to take chances with Scott. I'd feel happier with both of you here.'

'Okay. Get some sleep, kid. It's surprising how different you can feel after a night's kip.'

The muscles in Scott's face relaxed enough for a reluctant smile to take over. There was something about this black-clad agent, who appeared to find standing on his own two feet impossible, that filled him with confidence. Sean Terry certainly didn't, an impenetrable sheet of steel, you'd never second-guess him. And Hilary? Patronising and opinionated – and what was worse, it looked like he was stuck with her.

NINE

Scott slept; the noise of hammering, accompanied by a dull thud as the door was hung and a lock fitted, mingled with the abrasive tones of the reporter's voice, except he wasn't a reporter, and the softer, broader, more casual speech of Pete. Scott caught the sound of a vehicle revving its engine – the sounds meshing together inside his brain, as he dived headfirst into a deeply exhausted unconsciousness.

He was awake again before seven, nagging his eyelids at their refusal to cooperate and stay open. For a moment he lay there half-expecting to hear the radio or even the sound of his dad whistling. The cottage felt eerily silent and empty. Then he remembered. *Dad!* A wave of misery stormed over him.

Wide-awake now, he tiptoed down the corridor and peeped into the kitchen. Pete was asleep, stretched out between the two armchairs, facing the new door. Its rough-hewn rawness, with its pile of wood shavings awaiting a dustpan and brush, jarred angrily against the elegantly smooth surface of the surrounding frame. Pete's arms were crossed over his chest, a handgun clasped in his right hand, his automatic in plain sight tucked in the angle between his body and the chair. He didn't stir; his breathing slow and regular.

Scott returned to his room and stood by the window, staring out – trying to unravel the events of the day before and arrange them in sequence. The morning was grey, as different from the previous one as only England could be, and a wet mist hung low over the ground, making it seem cold and desolate. He shivered and, climbing up on his bed, tucked his legs back under the duvet.

Why had his dad phoned him at the river? It had already been agreed that Scott would cycle home, so his dad could go out if he wanted. And was that before or after he went to the village? Scott picked up his mobile from the bedside table and checked the time of the call: nine forty-nine. So what had happened to change things? He pictured his dad at the breakfast bar sipping his coffee while he read the news on the laptop. Was that it – something he'd read?

He jumped out of bed and slid the divan away from the wall, anxious now to boot up the laptop. Not bothering to shut the drawer again, he plugged it into the computer terminal next to his desk, watching the familiar pattern of icons appear down the left-hand side of the desktop, waiting impatiently for the egg timer to cease fluttering. He clicked into *Network Neighbourhood* before remembering that the hard drive had gone. Without it, the laptop had access only to its own operating programme. Wretchedly, he stared at the square-framed message that had appeared on the desktop: *unable to access*. So now what? He was about to close the machine down again when, in the corner of the screen, a white post-it flashed: *Printer's Folder. Paper Jam.*

Paper jam! So his dad *had* come back to check something – something that was important enough to print out. Not bothering to shut the laptop down, Scott left it hidden under the bedcover; anxious now to get into the studio and access the printer – without being seen. He needed a shower but that had to wait. Dressing rapidly, he grabbed his padded jacket from the wardrobe and, flipping open the top of the laundry hamper, stuffed in his other jacket – covered in mud and grass stains – on top of his jeans and underwear.

The new lock clicked loudly. Instantly he felt eyes – and possibly a gun – trained on his back.

'Going somewhere?'

As casually as his pounding heart would permit, Scott swung round, sketching a brief smile. 'Sorry, did I wake you? I wanted to check – you know?' He kept his voice light.

'In case somehow your dad's turned up?' Scott shrugged. 'Mind if I go with you?' Pete was already on his feet, no longer requiring a handy wall to lean against, his gun steady in his hand.

Damn!

The muzzle of the automatic poked its nose into the yard. Nothing stirred, everywhere quiet, not even the sound of a tractor or the whoosh of a speeding car, everyone that could grasping the opportunity for a Sunday lie-in.

Scott's bike stood against the kitchen wall. For a moment he wondered what it was doing there. 'So much going on, I forgot about it,' he admitted.

'I guess.' Pete smiled amiably. 'Midge brought it up before they left.'

'That was kind. I'd have remembered eventually.' Scott wandered across the yard. A brightly shining padlock and chain adorned the upper rail. 'You locked us in?'

'No,' Pete scooped up a piece of wood from the pile in the yard. 'We locked them out.'

'Oh, okay.' Scott leaned over the top rail facing out towards the fields, tracing his route of the night before. 'But no one would come here in the daylight,' he said, naively forgetting it had been daylight when his dad went missing.

Pete didn't reply, seemingly inspecting the fields spread out before them, a low mist still hanging about the hedgerows.

'Can I go in?' Scott indicated the studio.

'Why?'

'Habit!' He passed Pete the key from his pocket.

'You okay this morning?' The lean figure propped himself up against the diagonal length of planking that formed the crossbar. Propping his automatic against the gate, he pulled out a penknife and began whittling at the sliver of wood.

'I slept. You were right, it helps, but I still feel pretty helpless. And whatever Mr Terry says, I have to inform the police – and school, but that can wait until after half-term.'

'You on holiday?' Pete looked up.

Scott nodded. 'A week.'

'Don't worry with the police. We'll find your dad. For what it's worth, I'm sure he's okay.'

'How can you possibly know that?' Scott said angrily. Noticing the black streaks on Pete's face were smeared and partially rubbed off, he added, 'You need a shower. Dad'll kill you if you got that black stuff on his chairs.'

Pete grinned, his smile twisted up as if chewing a straw. Closing the penknife, he slipped it back in his pocket, tossing the strip of wood away. 'You have a strange way of saying, *thanks for keeping me safe*.' He unlocked the studio door. 'I'll go and drag Stone out of bed. She can keep you company, while I shower.'

Flicking the light switch, he poked his gun into the main room, then stood back for Scott to enter first.

Trying to conceal his frustration, Scott took off his specs and placed them on the table. 'But why? I'm okay on my own and there's no one about, you've checked.'

'I know Sean might seem like a tight bastard ...'

The change of subject startled Scott.

'But he really is one of the good guys. You can trust him to find your dad, only he's going to need your help.'

The words sounded casual, without importance. Scott didn't react, recalling the innocence of his dad's feints while playing chess, almost always unexpectedly ending in checkmate. 'He's got an odd way of showing it,' he said, his tone almost apologetic.

'Yeah! Hasn't he just – lips sealed tighter than a clam. Still, give it a whirl. Just talk, doesn't matter how trivial; let the big guys sort out what's important. You'd be surprised how much kids pick up.'

Mimicking the action of the secret service agent, the night before, Scott wandered over to the window. He pulled back the blinds peering out. The countryside felt like him – empty.

'Pete?' Dropping the curtain back into place, Scott picked up a pencil rolling it aimlessly backwards and forwards across the empty desk. 'If there really is someone stealing computer geeks, I could understand them wanting somebody like my pal

Jameson, 'cos he's the greatest, but why were those men waiting for me? I know nothing about computers – I told Dad that.'

'That what?'

Scott's hand froze. *Damn!* Hiding his anger at his own stupidity as best he could, he said casually: 'Dad read about kids disappearing. He told me to warn my classmates.'

'So you do know stuff,' Pete propped up the door frame. 'Read where?'

Careful now! 'An internet site but don't ask me which one.' Scott shrugged. 'Anyway, it makes no difference, the computer's gone. You're right; it won't hurt to wrack my brains.'

'Okay then on your own for a couple of minutes?' Pete smiled. 'I'll get Hilary. And just in case you're wondering, she took first watch.'

Scott stared in astonishment. 'But you were sleeping when I came through the kitchen.'

Pete grinned. 'Like hell I was! I heard you first time round. I only opened my eyes on your second visit.' Tipping the barrel of his machine gun towards Scott in a friendly salute, he disappeared through the door.

Minutes – it had to be enough. Leaving the door ajar, he hurried over to the mirrored glass, pressing his fingers firmly against the surface to release the hidden catch. There was a gentle click and the mirror swung open to reveal a shallow cupboard, piled high with the paraphernalia associated with computers; books of technical data, ink cartridges, spare discs, and wires – feeding in and out of the small server connected to both printers – one coloured, the other black and white – its on-off switch flashing indignantly.

Scott opened the machine, carefully teasing out the tangled piece of paper and clicked the printer into life. For a second or two nothing happened then, with a gentle swishing noise, a sheet of paper appeared, the printer reproducing line by line the last instructions of his dad.

Reading upside down, he transcribed the headline: *From our Reuters Correspondent.*

Impatiently he waited for the page to finish printing. It seemed to take forever. There – it was done. Snatching it up, he quickly folded the A4 sheet into four and slid it carefully into his pocket.

'She's in the kitchen making coffee.' Pete's voice sounded from the annexe.

Scott started nervously and hastily clicked the mirror-door shut. It was like a game of cat and mouse – with him as the mouse. How much easier it would be, if he could hand the sheet over and let Pete do his thinking for him. He wanted to, desperately, yet something held him back. He could almost hear his dad's voice: *Trust only what you know for definite, Scott.* So what did he know? Nothing – except they didn't want him contacting the police.

'What's up? Find anything?' the agent said, his glance penetrating.

Scott shook his head. 'You never said why I'm so important?'

'I guess if you went along too, your dad would find it that much easier to co-operate.'

After a big breakfast Scott disappeared off to his room, making the excuse that he had to get his jacket and trousers washed from the previous night. The talk had been general, Pete asking questions about his daily life and Scott glad to answer them. It helped pass the time but it didn't make him feel any better. Nothing would, until he found out where his dad was being held. And was anyone actually looking? It was all so frustrating – this waiting.

'Thanks, Hilary,' he said politely. She had made quite a good job of breakfast and kept the kitchen tidy, putting away the eggs and bacon in the fridge and wiping the surfaces as soon as she used them. But he still felt uncomfortable with her about. How could you think of Hilary, the new girl at school, as a Secret Service Agent? It was ridiculous and, under any other circumstances, laughable. But with Dad missing, nothing was laughable. He still didn't like her, though, not after the way she had acted on the river.

'Glad to help.' She was back in ordinary jeans and the shirt she had worn the day before and looked quite normal, except for the gun at her side.

'You still expecting trouble?' Scott's eyes were drawn to the cylindrical black dullness of the gun barrel. One like that had killed a man, the night before.

'Not really. It's just routine. If you're washing, mind if I add stuff?' Hilary pointed to the stain on her shirt, where hot fat from the frying pan had splattered her.

She was being friendly all right – no doubt under orders.

With the laptop once again hidden, Scott nervously unfolded the last message sent by his dad. It was a Reuters' article. Puzzled, he read the opening paragraph. Radiation levels up again. He gazed at it in bewilderment, quickly scanning the second paragraph. An obituary? He read it carefully.

Sudden Death of Famous Writer

It is with sadness and regret that we learned early this morning of the death of Damon Runyon, aged 62, at his home in London. Damon Runyon, well known both as a journalist and writer, rose to fame through his sketches on daily life amongst the gangster community in New York, peopled by a motley collection of characters with such colourful names as Harry the Horse and Nathan Detroit. His most famous work, Guys and Dolls became both a stage play and a motion picture.

Runyon died in the milieu in which he had lived and worked, a single gunshot wound to the head, following a struggle with an unknown assailant.

What was so important about an obituary? Scott read on, hoping there would be something there – something obvious.

A violent monarchist rally took place in Oslo last night. Protestors stormed the old parliament building demanding the return of their King and home rule. The National Guard, called out to quell the riot, disobeyed orders to fire on the people,

remaining in barracks. Acting swiftly, the Federation has sent for
troops from Poland. They are expected to land within the next
two days. Meanwhile the protest has spread to neighbouring
Sweden and Denmark, with people taking to the streets in
Brussels in sympathy.

Nothing struck a chord. So which one was it? The obituary or
the rally?

He heard footsteps, followed by a knock on the door.
Panicking, Scott shoved the sheet of paper under his bedclothes
and grabbed the laundry basket.

It was Hilary. 'Sean's on his way up the lane.'

'OK, a minute.'

Slipping the folded sheet back in his pocket, he followed her
out to the garage, where the washing machine lived. An old black
Citroen drew up alongside and Sean Terry slid out from behind
the wheel. He looked as if he hadn't slept – his face ravaged with
fatigue, his stubble speckled with grey.

'Pete?' he bellowed, ignoring Scott.

The rangy figure stuck his head round the kitchen door. 'Yo?'

'Give Stone that stuff.' Sean indicated the hamper of washing
clutched in Scott's arms. 'I want to talk to you.'

'Did you find my dad?' Scott dumped the washing basket
down. 'Use programme E.' He followed the thin figure into the
house.

'No!' The tone cut through the air, like a guillotine through
paper.

'But what about your prisoner? Didn't he tell you?'

'When we got to headquarters, he was dead on the floor of
the van.'

'Oh!' Scott subsided into a chair, and a feeling of utter
helplessness swept over him. 'So there's no clue.'

'Not unless you give me something. Pete?'

'Yes, boss.'

'Tulsa and Arizona said they searched the prisoner. Did they?'

Pete nodded – his eyes hidden behind their reflective lenses, his lean frame lodged against the nearest wall, automatic by his side. 'I watched. They searched him thoroughly; did a good job.'

'Not good enough,' Sean spat back. '*Damn*! And I thought we were getting somewhere. What a bloody waste of time. Now it's up to you, Scott.' He rounded on the boy.

'I keep telling you, I don't know anything,' Scott protested.

'Well, if you don't know anything you might as well forget your dad – *you won't be seeing him again*,' the agent snapped savagely.

Scott gasped and ran out of the room.

'Nice going, boss.'

'It's true though.' Sean Terry passed a hand over the stubble on his chin and sighed wearily. 'I've no time to be nice, Pete – that's your role. Doesn't the boy know he's in danger?'

'I told him. I also happened to mention that you're one of the good guys. After this, I'm not sure he'll believe me.'

Sean stared across at the empty chair, his expression bleak. 'Hell!' he said.

Scott lay on his bed. He'd been crying. He heard a murmur of voices as Sean and Pete talked. He sat up rubbing his eyes, and clicked the intercom.

That was another thing they didn't know about. His dad had installed it so they could talk from one room to the other. At the time it seemed stupid. After all, the cottage only had four rooms and you could easily shout from one to the other. Only the studio really needed it. Now he was grateful, the voices sounding as if he were standing next to them. He kept the volume low.

'Where do we go from here?' Pete's voice.

'Not sure. Not sure neither about Tulsa and Arizona. I've sent Midge to check them out.'

'No, boss. They wouldn't.'

'Someone did or they got careless and missed the cyanide.'

Scott heard the outside door open and someone enter the house. He heard Hilary's voice.

'What are you planning to do with Scott?'

'He's an okay kid, boss,' Pete added. Scott gave a half-smile, feeling grateful for the compliment. 'Doesn't say much. Thinks more. Go easy on him; he's just lost his dad.'

'He's almost sixteen, for Pete's sake, and says he doesn't know anything? All kids know more than they let on. There's nothing for it, if he's only prepared to come up with one answer a day, we'll be here months. We'll have to take him in. I can't afford to waste all that time.'

Scott gasped aloud, thankful the intercom switch was down – incoming only. He had to get out before he became a prisoner, like his dad.

Sliding open his dressing table drawer, he pulled out a bankcard and some cash: *for emergencies*, his dad had said. Well, this was an emergency. He checked his keys – the house, his locker at school, the garage key – same for both front and back doors. Of course he knew they were there – but with so much going wrong, they could easily have gone missing. He'd used the key before, too; after rows with his dad when he wanted to slip out of the house without being seen. Out of the bedroom window, into the garage through the garden door, grab his bike – easy.

No time for clothes. No time for anything. He caught sight of the photograph of his mother and slipped it into his pocket, staring wildly round the room. *Laptop*! He needed that. Grabbing it from the drawer, he slid open his window and dropped to the ground. The washing machine gurgled noisily, absorbing the dull thud of his feet landing on the path. He knew the key would open the door okay. Everything his dad used worked properly, but his hands were shaking so much he could hardly turn it. Then he was in the garage, the double-doors to the yard ajar. Closing the garden door quietly behind him, he quickly pulled on his dad's jacket and helmet. He tugged at the driving gloves, his hands still shaking, his glance constantly flicking towards the yard. The drum from the washing machine began to spin, slowly at first, then faster and faster, the machine lurching against its concrete base with a noise like thunder.

Rocking the bike off its stand, Scott stepped it to the entrance. The gate stood open, left like that after the black car's appearance. Praying they were all too busy talking, to notice anything above the throbbing of the washing machine, he switched on the ignition. There was instantaneous contact, followed by a roar as the massive engine burst into life. Now he was committed; no turning back.

A spur of excitement flashed through him, like an electric shock. He held up one of his gloved hands and smiled. It was no longer shaking. Gunning the accelerator, he tore towards the gate and into the lane, confident that no one could follow him, not even bullets from a machine gun. Then, he was out of range and halfway down the lane.

TEN

The Suzuki loved speed and at sixty purred along like a well-fed cat, offering constant reminders that it really would like to go a little faster. Scott resisted the temptation, anxious not to invite attention. The events of that morning continued to replay over and over again, like a damaged groove on a disc repeating the line of a song. He was still wondering, a grin on his face, how on earth he'd pulled a stunt like that – and got away with it – when the suburbs of Falmouth appeared. He throttled back to a gentle thirty, the bike rolling smoothly along the asphalt surface.

The lending library in Helston had been rejected as being too small; Penzance, the superior by far, was ignored on the grounds that it led nowhere except the Atlantic; Falmouth was part way to wherever the puzzle led him.

On both sides now appeared lines of elegant bungalows, their neatly-pruned shrubs artistically placed amongst borders of flowering daffodils or dropped into lawns, cut with military-style precision.

Ahead of him a line of cars were patiently inching forward, waiting to join the traffic circulating round a flower-filled island. Scott neatly side-stepped his way to the front of the queue, searching for a break in the traffic piling in from the right. The driver of the approaching vehicle slowed slightly, as if unsure which way to go. Scott opened the throttle then, with a sudden change of direction, swerved across the bonnet of the car next to him, hearing its horn blast out indignantly. Next moment he was accelerating along the by-pass. Crazy not to have thought about it earlier; Falmouth would be the first place they'd check. He flew the bike past a column of cars heading for St. Austell. There, he would be twice as safe with a choice of roads, north towards Exeter or north-east to Plymouth.

The miles disappeared, the road only moderately busy with local traffic and the occasional tourist who, braving the variable spring weather, was en route to one of the numerous attractions of south Cornwall. Scott swooped past a curtain-sided artic, plastered with gaudy advertisements for yoghurt, on its way to restock a busy supermarket. Despite wearing his dad's windproof jacket over a thick sweater, the wind chill factor at sixty was significant and Scott was glad to feel the sun break out from behind the low cloud base.

Ten minutes more and a proliferation of road signs, multiplying faster than rabbits in a warren, heralded the outskirts to St. Austell. Scott slowed. Moments later the streets of the old town closed in, forcing the bike to slow even further. Nervously, he picked his way into the town's centre, searching for the main library. Almost directly in front of the library building, he noticed a small space between a large van and an illegally parked car, its bumper sticking out into the roadway. He squeezed the bike into it, trusting to the bulky shape of the van to shield him, only too aware that its sleek lines and brilliant colour made it a magnet for idle eyes, even mums with small children stopping to admire it. Worse, it was illegal. He might have been a competent rider since he was thirteen, but he couldn't take his test for another six weeks – not till his sixteenth birthday. Still, he looked of age and, so long as he didn't draw attention to himself, there was no reason for the police to pick him up.

Overhead a blue metal sign, embossed with black letters, authorised thirty minutes free parking, with no return under one hour. Scott switched off his engine and, placing his feet flat on the ground, bounced the bike strongly back on to its stand. Remaining seated, he removed his gloves, turning round to drop them into the box. Moulded into the framework, part seat and part support for a pillion rider, it had scarcely enough room for a jacket and helmet. His hands were stiff after so long a ride and he flexed them, rubbing at his wrists and forearms to restore their circulation.

Behind him, the traffic was beginning to back up along the street. Scott threw a pitying glance at the driver of a bus, stationary in front of an impossibly narrow gap, who was making his frustration felt by furiously banging on the steering wheel and swearing loudly. Thank heavens for two wheels. Four would be a nightmare in this town of narrow streets.

Grinning at the expression on the bus driver's face, he tugged at the Velcro strap on his helmet. He stopped dead, his hand plastered against the front of his visor. He'd only gone and left his specs in the kitchen. Scott collapsed back against the saddle, picturing his glasses in their holder by the kitchen door. Walking the streets in a visor was a dead cert for anyone trying to get arrested. His hand strayed towards the pocket of his jeans, and he patted it triumphantly, pulling out his dad's pair. Dismounting, he slipped the keys into an inside pocket and, with his helmet slung over his arm, headed up the shallow stone steps, and pushed open the polished brown door.

'Damon Runyon?' The woman flicked the screen. She shook her head. 'Out of date, I'm afraid.'

'Is there nowhere I can get a copy?'

'Exeter, most likely. There should be a copy in the Reference Library. Would you like me to check?'

'Please.' With a sudden spurt of unease, Scott strove his keep his voice calm, not wanting to display his anxiety to a stranger. Had he left home for no reason? If the book was not in print, then why?

The librarian scrolled down reams of printed text. After a few minutes, she raised her head from the screen. 'Sorry, it's not listed.'

'But I need it – *for school*,' he insisted.

She pursed her lips, peering down at the screen again. 'History or English?'

'History?' Scott said, with a puzzled frown. 'Why history?'

'Well, Runyon's not your contemporary writer, is he? Most of his stuff was written early in the last century, between the two great wars, if I remember correctly. He wrote about prohibition in America. Sue?'

Her colleague looked up from her computer. 'Yes?'

'Damon Runyon?'

'Who?' the young woman raised her eyebrows enquiring.

'See!' The middle-aged woman nodded at Scott, an expression of pleased triumph on her face. 'Nobody knows about him any more.'

Someone does, thought Scott. 'Would there be a biography?'

'Wait!' More clicks and more screens. 'Bingo!' She looked up and beamed, her pleasant face breaking into a wide smile. 'Have you got a code?'

'Yes, somewhere.' Scott pulled out his wallet, searching for his library card.

'You can access it from here.'

The librarian indicated a bank of screens, only one of them in use by an elderly man reading the day's news, and handed Scott a pencilled slip of paper, the reference already written on it.

Scott noticed the clock on the wall. Already twenty of his allotted thirty minutes' parking time had gone. He couldn't afford to draw attention to himself by being late. 'Can I print it out, I'm short of time.'

'There's six pages.'

'That's okay.' He pulled out a twenty-euro note and the librarian pressed the print key.

Seven minutes later, clutching a handful of change and a-half-dozen loose sheets of A4 paper, he dived out of the library and made for his bike, sneaking a glance at the busy street. Both the bus and the offending car had vanished and been replaced by a white delivery van, its driver in the middle of a heated argument with a motorist, who appeared determined to squeeze his car into a space built for a tricycle. Scott grinned ruefully and, replacing his helmet, started the engine; a brief glance in his wing mirror sufficient to identify the familiar black jacket of the traffic warden, heading purposefully up the street towards him.

A double-cheeseburger, purchased from a drive-through fast-food restaurant, lay forgotten on his plate while Scott studied the pile of paper. He had parked the Suzuki out of sight of the main road but within view, so he could keep an eye on it; dumping himself down on one of the bench seats, provided for motorists that didn't want to dirty-up their cars by eating in them. Only a couple were occupied, but no one appeared the slightest bit interested in him, which suited Scott just fine.

From the moment the librarian mentioned that Damon Runyon wrote his books almost a century ago, Scott guessed there was a riddle waiting to be solved. Anchoring the pages with the fingers of his left hand, he started with the Reuters' article, the text still insisting that Damon Runyon had been shot, two nights ago, in London. Somewhere, in those precious sheets of paper was a clue – there had to be.

He sighed, took a bite out of his cheeseburger and began to read. On page four he stopped.

The musical Guys and Dolls was based on two Runyon stories, "The Idyll of Miss Sarah Brown" and "Blood Pressure". Like all of Runyon's short stories this play celebrated the world of Broadway in New York City, during the Prohibition era. Runyon spun a tale of gamblers, petty thieves, actors and gangsters; few of whom go by "square" names, preferring instead to be known as "Nathan Detroit", "Big Jule", "Harry the Horse", "Nicely-Nicely", "Good time Charley", " Dave the Dude", and so on.

In the film, made in 1955, the Oscar Award winning stars, Marlon Brando and Frank Sinatra, played the lead roles of Sky Masterson and Nathan Detroit, with Jean Simmons in the role of Sister Sarah.

He didn't read on.

Scott stared into space – his mind a blank. After the shocks of the last two days, this was the worst; learning your dad had, for the whole of your life, been living a lie. He felt sick and knew he looked it, too.

He read the article again – slowly. There was no mistake. His dad had belonged to an organisation that communicated by means of the Internet, hiding behind characters neatly provided by the American author, Damon Runyon. Only the person using that name had been murdered two nights ago. And if his mum had been Sister Sarah, someone had killed her, too. His dad was *Sky* Masterson, that's where the name came from. No wonder he'd never been allowed to use it. So, had Dad been kidnapped or murdered? He was alive, *he had to be.* Scott repeated the phrase again, refusing to let the nightmarish thought take root.

But the names? "Nathan Detroit", "Big Jule", "Harry the Horse", "Nicely-Nicely", "Good time Charley", "Dave the Dude". He didn't know any of them. But then he wouldn't, would he? His dad had never mentioned he had friends.

Except …

Far off a memory lurked. Scott frowned, trying to tug at it and prise it loose. Was it something his dad had talked about when they were having breakfast? Scott thought back to recent conversations – but nothing stirred. Or had he read it? He searched his memory banks, everything he'd read at school and at home. He tried the alphabet trick, ploughing through the letters one by one. Had he seen it? He visualised the cottage, searching through it room by room and into the studio. He felt a blast of recognition, the picture painfully vivid. The silent room, decorated with its two posters, an ominous gap where the processor had once stood – *the posters!*

"*That'll do nicely.*"

"*So take the High Road.*"

It had been staring Scott in the face all the time. Nowhere in the cottage was there a single picture – only the posters in the studio. Now he came to think about it, they were totally foreign to his dad anyway. He hated anything modern – including pop music. His tastes were classical music and nineteenth-century art. He would never have had a poster of the bike, never in a million years, however much he loved it. If he'd had a poster at all it would have been Monet's *Water Lilies*.

So all he had to do was take the bike – along a high road – to find a character who presumably answered to the name of Nicely. It seemed simple enough but which high road? There were thousands in England alone. Scott hurried across to his bike and, unlocking the box, pulled out the laptop. Returning to his seat, he flipped open the top and booted it up.

A waiter appeared clearing glasses and debris from the tables.

'I don't suppose I could have another milk shake?' Scott said his voice a little tentative, aware that although waiters might react pretty sharply if an adult asked, they preferred a more direct response to kids; such as: *you've got legs, haven't you.*

'I don't want to carry all this lot into the restaurant,' he explained, pointing to his helmet, gloves and laptop.

'No problem.' The waiter leant across to pick up his empty glass and plate. 'Anything else?'

Scott concealed a grin, cock-a-hoop that the bike and laptop had elevated him automatically into the league of adults. 'No, I'm fine.'

He typed in the words *High Road* then stopped. Too vague. Adding the words *Take the,* he pressed *Search.* Twenty-two thousand and thirty-one hits in less than two seconds and he had to go through all of them.

It wasn't that difficult to find. By the time he had waded through his chocolate milk shake, sucking up every last drop, the words of the ancient song were printed on the page.

Oh ye'll tak the High Road
An' I'll tak the Low Road
An' I'll be in Scotland afore ye.
But me and my true love will never meet again
On the bonny, bonny banks of Loch Lomond.

He even knew where in Loch Lomond. The website had the same view as the poster; the lake with its snow-capped mountains in the background.

He searched the route maps, trying to memorise which road led where: motorway all the way to Glasgow, a little over five hundred miles. And if he was followed?

Scott groaned loudly, before remembering there were people nearby. He squinted across at the nearest table and was relieved to find no curious eyes staring back. Being followed was way down his list of problems. The theory of riding up to Scotland might sound simple; but putting it into practice? He'd never ridden fifty miles in one go, never mind five hundred. He groaned – more quietly this time – before closing the laptop, reluctant to take the first step into the unknown.

ELEVEN

He had to stop, both hands so cramped and stiff he daren't stretch them; his fatigue so overwhelming that the slightest shift in weight distribution and the delicate machine would veer out of control, with him unable to stop it.

The motorway had taken him through the sunny pasturelands of Devon and Cornwall, populated mostly by sheep and cows. Scott concentrated on maintaining his speed and staying safe among motorists that found it amusing to play *dare* and *catch- me-if-you-can*, staying dangerously close behind him. At Taunton, the debris from road works – a heap of dust-ridden, weed-infested shale, broken concrete posts and barren landscaping – accompanied the motorway inland through to Shepton Mallet, before heading north towards Bath. Hastily constructed to replace the pathway over the Somerset levels and the Bristol Channel corridor, which had been destroyed by the giant wave, it remained in a constant state of repair.

Now he was nearing Birmingham. A slip road swung left round a light-controlled traffic island. Frozen to the bone he followed it, heading for an outcrop of concrete and glass buildings set back off the road, where rows of shiny new cars were displayed under a vast concrete canopy. Throttling back to twenty, he inspected the conglomeration of motorcar sales, DIY, carpet and bed stores that usually clung to the outskirts of towns, where taxes were less onerous. Among them was a more modest building, heavy plate glass protecting its stock of two-wheeled power machines from creative shoplifters.

Leaving his bike tucked out of sight of the road, Scott entered the shop. Twenty minutes later he emerged feeling a mile high, wearing black leather trousers over his jeans and a blouson jacket, which made him appear all at once older and heavier; grateful that the assistant in the shop had been more interested in selling the expensive outfit, than analysing the age of his customer.

Cramming his dad's jacket into the box with the computer, he headed back towards the motorway. In the distance a police post appeared, guarding the approaches to a motorway exit. Scott had heard about them but this was the first he'd seen. It had a pitiless air about it; a forbidding mass of black reflective glass stretching from one side of the motorway to the other. He wasn't exactly sure of its powers; only that its flashing lights and klaxons were there to alert the traffic below to an immediate and rapid descent of steel curtains, designed to drop down over all-six carriageways, if necessary, and block them off. As terror alerts had become more frequent, so had these barriers. Firstly, surrounding only major cities, their function had been to isolate and prevent any escape by road, by closing all major arteries in and out of the city. Now, they were gradually spreading across the landscape.

He shivered, feeling himself under inspection, as he swooped under the black bridge. Ahead was Junction three – Halesowen. The next signpost – coloured dark green – displayed the symbol for a hotel with a restaurant attached. Watching out for the one-hundred metre sign, he slowed slightly. Then, taking the slip road, ran down onto an urban freeway, heading directly into the densely populated area of the Midlands metropolis.

The *Stop and Rest* chain of motels operated comfortable rooms based on any six, twelve or twenty-four-hour period; a team of domestics on hand to service vacated rooms, quickly and efficiently, in time to accommodate the next exhausted traveller. With modest rates and a fast-food restaurant next door, the formula had quickly spread countrywide. To some self-confessed enthusiasts, the chain had single-handedly been responsible for lowering the accident rate on major roads and motorways.

Scott booked a twelve-hour stay, figuring he could leave again by eight in the morning. He set the alarm, courtesy of the management, and an integral part of a bedside console that also contained a reading light.

Before checking in, Scott had eaten and taken a long walk to stretch his legs. There wasn't much to see, only the paraphernalia of suburban living; streets of houses and rows of parked cars. But a picturesque view was not part of the deal. In any event, Scott was only interested in restoring circulation and working out his next move, not gazing at ponds with swans floating on them or glorious vistas of ruined castles surrounded by moats.

He felt exhausted, the excitement which had spurred him into action long since drained away. Now inside him was a deep well of misery, mixed with bewilderment. The realisation that this could be a wild goose chase was not long following. He might well be … Scott frowned, as the clichés: *"barking up the wrong tree", "jumping to the wrong conclusion"*, sprang to mind. For that's exactly what he might be doing if he pinned all his hopes on the hypothesis that somewhere, on the banks of Loch Lomond, he would find a huge sign: *this way to the next clue*. Still, it was all he'd got. Besides this fragile kernel of hope, he had no one and nothing. If he didn't find his dad, that would be the situation that existed for the rest of his life. How would he manage when he could only cook stir-fry with pasta?

Scott paused, his foot hesitating in the middle of its step, struggling to accept the premise that his father had taught him the skills necessary to survive, because he had anticipated just such a day.

His room had been created for sleeping; a neat cell with a single bed, its shower and loo enclosed in a polystyrene bubble, a style of furnishing which represented a significant departure from more traditional hotels. Here, everything possible was built-in or bolted-down to minimise vandalism and deter petty thieves; some guests still believing that payment for a room justified stealing anything that could be carried in a suitcase. And, since towels, sheets and bath mats were pretty much the only things not bolted-down, these were of a plain-white commercial quality, unlikely items for souvenir hunters.

The hundred or so rooms were identical, except for those on the first floor overlooking the car park. These possessed a small balcony, screened off by heavy net curtains. Scott had pulled them aside glancing down at the neatly parked cars in their white flagged bays. In theory, it was perfectly possible to step outside and take the air, in practice rarely done; the noise and fumes of passing traffic bestowing the air with an unpalatable opaque quality. The Suzuki was nowhere in sight. Had he been too cautious? Scott had even surprised himself by arguing for greater seclusion. The manager, courteously agreeing that his bike was probably considerably safer in a neglected underground staff car park, rather than a high visibility area with both lights and cameras, had even permitted Scott to use the staff elevator to access the space.

He crashed into oblivion, ahead of him hours and hours of blissful slumber, so that the key card swiping the door lock to gain entry, failed to waken him. Neither did the first intruder.

He glanced down at the boy deeply asleep and grinned across the room at his colleague, who was leaning back against the closed door. He wore overalls – the words Service Personnel emblazoned on the breast pocket. One of the sleeves had a small tear in it, where it had caught on the wall in his struggle with its original owner, now helplessly pounding on the laundry room door, in the forlorn hope that someone, in a building designed for guests to sleep undisturbed, would hear him.

'Don't you just love it when they're already sleeping like babies,' he said. He yelled, '*Wake up!*' directing his voice at the sleeping boy and roughly shaking him.

Scott heard the sound, struggling upwards against a tide of sleep into consciousness. 'You want something?' he muttered. 'I've paid for twelve hours, it can't be checking out time already.' He gazed wearily at the window. It was pitch black outside.

'Yes, you! Get dressed. We're taking you to see your father.'

Instantly wide awake Scott stumbled out of bed, checking that his helmet and leathers were still where he'd left them, on the floor near the door. He glanced up at his attackers, forcing himself not to react at the sight of a gun loosely clasped in the second man's hand. Not having pyjamas, he'd slept in his underwear. Now, he fumbled his way into his jeans, pulling on his shirt and sweater; making each movement clumsy and slow, his mind frantically racing round and round. He forced himself to slow down, breathe deeply, watch and wait.

Wait for a chance to get away. He had no doubt that's what he was going to do – even with a gun pointing at him. Slowly and carefully, he checked his few belongings and slid them into his jacket pocket; loose change and the keys to the bike. Thank God he'd left his laptop and the photo of his mother in the Suzuki.

Judging it was about time he asked the question, Scott said: 'Where is my dad?'

There were four violent bursts of ear-splitting noise. The door crashed open and jagged slivers of light and sound echoed round the room. The light bulb in the ceiling exploded, plunging the room into darkness but not before Scott had seen the man at the door knocked sideways clutching his arm, his gun spinning across the room; while the man at the bedside collapsed in a messy heap on the floor.

A hand tugged at his sleeve and a voice whispered, 'This way.'

Hesitating only long enough to grab his precious leathers, he was running. The door slammed shut behind him, the corridor dark; the burst light bulb triggering a trip-switch that controlled all the lights on the first-floor.

'Your bike?'

'Basement garage.'

He ran, spitting the words out between breaths, heading now for the service elevator. It was stationary on their floor, clearly the mode of entry for the men in the grey polyester jackets. The figure beside him punched a button. Then safety lights swung into action, flaring dimly, but sufficient for Scott to recognise who had saved him.

Hilary Stone!

Speechless, he glanced down at the gun that had wreaked so much damage. The girl tucked it away in her holster, smiling at the shocked expression on Scott's face.

'Don't look so surprised, Scott. Don't forget I'm supposed to be looking after you.'

'How …?'

The elevator juddered to a halt, the doors opening into the silence and eeriness of a deserted car park, only a handful of cars belonging to night-staff dotted around.

'Later. Where's your bike?'

He pointed. Echoing footsteps, taking the stone stairs three at a time, came from the stairwell behind them.

'Run!' Scott fished in his pocket with his free hand and pulled out his keys. 'No helmet!' he gasped.

He heard a crack of noise and the plaster in the wall beside them exploded, showering them with white concrete dust.

'No time!' came the breathless response. 'Just get away.'

Scott tore round the pillar and leapt for his bike, fumbling for the ignition; his hands shaking so much the key jerked sideways in the curved aperture and jammed. He swallowed nervously, beating his clenched fists against his knee. Taking a slow and deliberate breath he tried again, inching the key into place against the ignition.

Another crack of sound! He winced as fast-moving air brushed his cheek. Hilary, behind him on the bike, ducked.

'For Pete's sake, hurry,' she hissed.

He ignored her, concentrating on sliding the bike off its stand. The engine fired, its roar of noise muffling the sound of a third bullet, which twanged against the hubcap of a nearby car. Then, they were moving. He accelerated towards the ramp and felt Hilary's arm clutch at the fabric of his jacket. A dark figure had appeared from nowhere barring their exit, his arms extended at chest height. The man took careful aim. An earth-shattering blast resounded in Scott's ear as Hilary fired, the motion of the bike spinning the bullet harmlessly over their assailant's head.

Scott braked and swerved; his foot skidded against the concrete floor, as he swung the red monster round in a half-circle. The returning bullet bit into the space where the bike had been less than a second before and he heard the sound of glass shattering.

'For crying out loud,' Hilary yelled, both arms clutching him round the chest. 'You'll get us killed.'

Scott laughed excitedly. 'You concentrate on shooting and leave the bike riding to me,' he yelled over his shoulder.

Pulling the bike back upright he paused, gunned the engine and headed at top speed for the shooter, already poised to take his second shot. Scott didn't care. He'd back his bike against a bullet any day. And the man had better get out of the way, if he didn't want to get killed. Hilary screamed and pulled on his arm; Scott ignored her. At the last moment, the figure cartwheeled to one side and then they were racing up the ramp and out into the road, too absorbed in their flight to hear a car start up and begin to follow.

The bike accelerated along the empty road, flying over the bumpy patches in the camber. Scott caught sight of a large blue metal sign overhanging the side of the road.

'Where to?' he shouted, half-turning his head.

He caught the muffled response, the wind quickly blowing away any sound. 'Not the motorway! Lose them in the town.'

Ahead, in the distance, he could already make out the dark shape of the police control post. From here it resembled an eagle, its wings outstretched as it hovered menacingly over the lighted carriageway. He cast round for an alternative and spotted a narrow lane, almost completely hidden by a car-lot, on the far side on the road.

'*Hang on!*'

Pointing the nose of the Suzuki at a stretch of grass on the central reservation, he wove the bike through a narrow gap in the bank of accident-absorbing shrubs. He heard a screech of brakes and a car door slammed. He ignored it, more concerned with avoiding scratches to the scarlet paintwork, that would land him in trouble with his dad, than their pursuers, who he knew were stuck unable to get through the bushes.

Clumsily, he bounced the bike back on to the roadway and opened the throttle. The front wheel, heavily coated with mud from the wet grass, shifted sideways and, without thinking, Scott braked. The rear wheel locked and the bike slid round in a half circle, spinning out of control. Hilary screamed. Scott felt a spur of fear as, almost in slow motion, the bike slewed across the carriageway and veered towards the oncoming traffic. There came the sound of tyres squealing and the car that had been accelerating away from the slip road screeched to a halt, the driver's fist thumping the horn. Scott heard the horn and the abuse that followed but ignored it, more concerned with regaining control. He rammed his feet hard into the ground, struggling to manhandle the bike back upright. Its tyres gripped and they stopped.

'Oh you beauty,' he murmured and let out the breath he'd been holding.

Slowly he opened the throttle and moved off again, carefully checking the bike's reactions were back to normal. He accelerated and, with a burst of speed, they were into the lane, the bike gobbling up metres of road as if they were chocolate drops.

'Jeez, you can ride,' Hilary spat out.

'Told you, I could,' Scott said, feeling his face break into a grin.

The road was unlit and, surprisingly, in such a densely populated area, ran through an area of scrub. A minute later they emerged into an elegant avenue, with mature homes on one side, their double-garages surrounded by low walls and neatly mown grass. Opposite, coloured flags hung limply from tall poles, and a brightly-lit hoarding announced a forthcoming, *luxury* housing development. Street lighting was already in place, shining down on mud-strewn paths, connecting a row of dark skeletal structures in the early stages of becoming new homes.

After five minutes they found themselves, once again, facing the dual-carriageway and, like a homing pigeon coming back to roost, with the motel only a few hundred yards away. Scott gazed at the flurry of activity in dismay. Police cars were milling about in the parking area and, above the sound of early-morning traffic, he detected another siren heading purposefully in their direction.

'No ambulances,' Hilary said. 'So whoever it was left before the police arrived. Let's leave them to it. You fit?'

Scott said firmly, 'Sorry – *not us*, m*e!* This is where we part company. Thanks for saving my life and all that, but I'm going on alone.'

Something sharp dug into his backbone making him flinch.

'*You forget I've got the gun.* So I suggest you start thinking in terms of *us* from now on, because I'm going nowhere.'

Scott shrugged. 'You'll regret it; you've not even got a helmet.'

'Neither have you. And I'll get one.' Hilary's voice sounded crisp, emotionless.

'But not at four in the morning. Besides you'll freeze,' Scott argued, half-heartedly wondering if it really was possible to escape with a gun digging into your back.

'So I'll freeze, but wherever you're going, I go too. Understand.'

He shrugged again and, pulling the bike off the road, cut the engine. Dismounting, he motioned Hilary to get off, her fair hair blown wildly about her face with the speed of their escape. He saw her carefully holster her gun before moving. This was the opportunity he'd been waiting for. He hesitated then, making up his mind, unlatched the box at the rear of the bike. 'You'd better wear Dad's jacket, I don't want to be responsible for you catching your death,' he said, tugging at the material tucked round his laptop. 'At least it'll protect you from the wind.'

'What about you?'

He picked up the bulky leather top, which he'd sat on to stop it blowing away, pulling the trousers on over his jeans. 'I'm organised,' he said. He hastily closed the box lid, adding, 'But we have to keep away from main roads till the shops open. And, if you really are determined to come with me, I want some answers.'

'Okay – sounds fair. I'll tell you what I know if you tell me what you know. So which way are we going?'

'North,' he admitted reluctantly.

'So head towards Birmingham, we'll stop off at an all-night café somewhere. Okay? But even if we did have helmets we'd have to stay away from motorways.'

'Why?'

'You don't know? *God, you Brits!* You're so naive!'

Scott flinched, furious with himself for not riding off while he still had the chance. If that's what Americans were like – thank heavens he no longer was one. Gun or no gun he'd ditch her at the first opportunity. 'If I knew, why would I ask?'

Hilary spoke over his shoulder. 'Police posts – like the one you saw near the hotel. They're computer centres. They tag every vehicle passing beneath them. If it's stolen, or the owner wanted for something, the computer picks up on it and informs the police. I expect that's how they traced you. The bike must have been reported stolen.'

'So how did *you* find me?'

'I bugged your bike.'

TWELVE

The all-night eatery alongside the northbound carriageway of the Shrewsbury road was packed with shift workers. After an eight-hour stint in one of the factories, sited in a nearby industrial park, they enjoyed an early breakfast before heading home to sleep; although mostly it was the long-distance lorry drivers, who ploughed from north to south along the main arteries of England, that kept the eateries open. Five days a week, large men with protruding bellies occupied their own personal table, an early-morning edition of a tabloid newspaper spread out in front of them; bare boobs and long legs competing for attention with plates piled high with bacon, eggs, fried bread, tomatoes and sausage; a mug of tea at their elbow.

It wasn't a particularly salubrious place. Years of frying had coated the light-cream walls with a dirty yellow sheen, while dark-brown nicotine stains encircled the lights. Even at six in the morning the air was blue; no one in the least bit bothered about laws banning smoking in public places – and the owner of the café realistic enough to admit that had he insisted, ninety percent of his clientele would have vanished overnight. The toilets, too, were a health hazard – at least the Gents had been – Scott not daring to ask such a personal question of Hilary.

Scott had kept going, finding his way around the vast suburban metropolis, the majority of residents still asleep, only an unlucky few facing an early start up and about. Finally, they had stumbled across a road that mirrored the route of the motorway, passing through an unending sprawl of main road housing, occasionally broken up by blocks of small shops – a bookie, a fruit and veg, an undertaker. For the next hour, Scott had followed it, his bike the solitary occupant of a road where, almost the only other things moving were stray cats on the prowl.

A straight run through to Worcester, only to see a black tower barring their entrance to the town of Kidderminster. Escaping round a traffic island, they had backtracked along secondary roads before rejoining the Shrewsbury road again. It was slow going. In desperate need of sleep, Scott had to will his eyes to stay open, fighting against his brain and body's desire to shut down. No way could they stop, at least not until they'd put a few more miles between them and their pursuers, and while it was still dark.

The bacon, eggs and fried bread were good, the tea hot and strong. No one took any notice of them and gradually Scott began to relax, his breakfast all at once tasting fabulous. But not too much, he told himself sternly. Find out all you can, make an excuse to go to the Gents and leave.

He kept his voice low, leaning forward to talk, although he needn't have bothered. Loud crashing sounds, capable of drowning out anything less than a full-blown rocket attack, constantly erupted from the kitchen, augmented to a deafening quality by blasts of bellicose laughter from men, for whom the words *softy spoken* belonged to a foreign language.

'So why are you travelling north? Know something I don't?' Under cover of the plastic tablecloth, Hilary casually removed the clip from her gun, checking it before clicking it back into place.

It was a neat trick and one, Scott knew, designed to keep him in line. 'How many bullets does it have?' he said, peering over the table.

'For Pete's sake, you're doing it again!'

'What?'

'Asking questions! It drives me nuts.'

Scott grinned – his face all of a sudden lighting up, his grey eyes springing to life. He took a large bite out of the crispy-brown sausage dangling on the end of his fork. 'Does me too.'

Hilary glowered then laughed. 'We did get off on the wrong

foot, didn't we,' she said, her tone frank. She held her hand out across the table.

Scott put down his knife resting it on the edge of his plate. 'Thanks for saving my life,' he said, and shook her hand.

'*But?*'

'I still don't know if I dare trust you.'

'That's *crazy*. We *have* to be on the same side. Why else would I go to all that trouble?'

'I overheard Sean Terry saying he was going to lock me up.'

Scott stretched his arm for the ketchup. He shook a large dollop on to the side of his plate, admiring the neat way Hilary was eating, cutting her food into small squares before using her fork. She'd obviously done the same at school and no one had noticed. Or if they had, not realised this was an American habit – at least they always did it in American films.

'No, he wasn't. It might have come out like that. He wanted you safe, that's all.'

Scott studied the girl's face. He wanted to believe her. After all they'd been schoolmates for the last month. 'What happened after I left?'

'The boss was furious. He stamped off with Pete, leaving me at the house in case you came back.'

'You didn't tell him about the bug?'

'After being bawled out. No thanks. Anyway, I wanted to impress – you know – by finding you first.'

'So how did *you* get here?'

'I used my car.'

'*Car!* But you're too young to drive,' Scott protested.

Hilary pursed her lips frowning. 'That's rich, coming from you,' she accused.

'Sorry.'

The girl laughed. 'So you should be. So what's it going to be? You going to let me in on what you know?'

Scott hesitated. He could tell her enough to keep her happy – but that wouldn't stop him ditching her. 'Are you going to tell the others?'

Hilary shook her head, her ponytail flipping from side to side. 'Not if you don't want me to. I only hope I don't live to regret it.'

Scott made up his mind. 'Dad left clues,' he said and briefly outlined the various connections that were sending him north.

Hilary gaped. *Is that all?* She pointed her fork at him. 'You're going to the north pole based on a couple of posters?'

Scott flushed angrily. 'So you'd have stayed at home and done nothing?'

'No! But I'd have told my boss and let him handle it. That would have been the sensible thing to do,' she snapped back. 'It's a long way to go if you're wrong.'

Scott glared at the table. 'I know. But then it's not your dad that's missing.' Defiantly, he shovelled in a large forkful of egg and began to chew. There was a moment or two of silence. 'But I'm *not* wrong so I'm heading for Scotland,' he said boldly. 'What you do is your own business. If you still want to come … I can't stop you, you've got the gun.' He paused and the tone of his voice changed. 'You know those men?'

'The ones at the hotel?'

'Yes, those! They weren't cops – they came along later, so who were they?' He picked up his fork again, scooping up a large portion of savoury toast covered in egg yolk and bacon, the extreme corners of his empty belly beginning to fill up.

'I don't know – that's been puzzling me too.' Hilary leaned closer her hands spread out on the table. 'How did they find you?'

'You said it was the tower south of Birmingham,' Scott reminded.

'So it might have been,' Hilary said, sounding irritated as if Scott were a six-year-old who kept repeating the same question. 'But that doesn't totally explain it. As far as I know, all the computer does is relay info into a central office. If the vehicle's stolen,' she continued, 'local police follow it up – tracking it on CCTV. But …' She paused. 'No one knew you'd taken the bike, only us. And the boss never works with your police, so why would they believe it stolen?'

'Don't ask me. You're the expert. All I know is they weren't police. Still, if the information can only be accessed by government agencies ...' Scott sat up straight and stared at Hilary, his breakfast all of a sudden forgotten. 'Does that mean they were ...?'

Hilary drummed her fists furiously on the table. '*No way! That's silly! They can't be government, can they*? Oh,' her tone changed. 'Hang on, before I forget, I found your specs.' She fished in the pocket of her jacket. 'I must have left them in the car.'

'That's okay,' said Scott. 'I don't need them. I've got Dad's.' He patted his pocket.

'You've ...'

Hilary stared over Scott's shoulder, her pupils dilating with shock. The colour drained from her face. Silently, she stretched out her fingers and touched his hand.

'*Don't look round*,' she warned. 'Get up and leave by the side door. But casual.' Her eyes flicked towards the fire door at the back of the café. 'I'll follow.'

Scott didn't argue. He slid from the table, trying to stop himself breaking into a run; to get out, to be safe. Fighting his panic, he walked at a steady pace between the crowded tables, saluting the man behind the counter, to say *thanks* and *cheers*. He reached the narrow door that led out into the yard behind the café and pushed it open. The plate glass swung to behind him.

Pulling his keys from his pocket, he hurtled round the corner to where he'd left his bike; safely tucked out of sight between two giant plastic-recycling bins full of bottles and tins.

Hilary appeared. 'Go – go – go!' she screamed and leapt for the pillion.

Scott hesitated. It was pretty stupid riding out at full blast, when you didn't know what was waiting for you. Cautiously, he rolled the machine softly forwards until they reached the corner of the building.

'What are you doing?' Hilary's voice was sharp and he felt her fist dig into his back. 'I said *go*!'

'Who's riding this bike, me or you,' he retorted.

Dropping his feet for balance, he peered round the brickwork. Three men were standing at the café entrance. They were staring in through the glass window their car, with its engine still running, left in full view outside the eatery. The door opened, forcing them to step aside as a twenty-stone trucker, busily hitching up his trousers, appeared. He paused, his vast bulk blocking the doorway. Ignoring the three men, trying to get past him, he turned and called something over his shoulder. His riposte was rewarded with a burst of raucous laughter.

A loud roar came from the car park as an engine started up. The three men spun round to inspect its driver, the café forgotten. They watched intently as he manoeuvred the cab of the forty-foot trailer in the narrow space, slowly pulling out towards the road. Reassured, one of the men leaned into the car to switch off its engine, before following the others into the building.

Scott also watched the artic pulling out. It was moving at a snail's pace and in a few seconds the entire building, with its length of glass frontage, would be masked by its great bulk. For anyone looking out, that was all they would see. He slid the Suzuki silently into its shadow, screened from curious eyes.

Hilary prodded him in the back. 'Your specs quick,' she said.

'But …'

'But nothing!'

He fished in his pocket and held them up. She grabbed them out of his hand and leapt off the bike.

'Where're you going now?' he hissed impatiently.

Not bothering to reply, Hilary darted across to the lorry, patiently waiting for a long column of approaching vehicles to clear, before turning into the dual-carriageway. Quickly hooking the frames through its webbing straps, she sprinted back to the bike.

'Now *go!*' she shouted, grabbing hold of his jacket.

The forty-footer pulled out into the roadway, making a wide turn. Scott, on its near side, opened the throttle and, with a roar, allowed the bike to do what it was built for – nought to seventy in a couple of seconds.

A few minutes later he swung on to the by-pass skirting Shrewsbury and pulled the bike to a halt in a lay-by, camouflaged by a vehicle-transporter that had parked up for the night. He watched the steady stream of traffic thundering up the adjacent road. Finally the artic passed them, its sides a blur of speed, making it impossible to check if the specs were still in place. Seconds later it was gone and another had taken its place.

'I don't understand,' he said.

Hilary followed the line of his gaze. '*You Brits*! You can't even see what's happening in your own back yard.'

Scott flushed angrily. What gave her the right to insult him and his country whenever she felt like it? She might have saved his life but she was still patronising and opinionated – that hadn't changed.

Hilary felt the muscles tense in Scott's back. 'Sorry, that was a stupid choice of words. Put it down to being tired and cross and an American. I so wish we had my car, I really ache.'

Scott opened his mouth to retort.

'Yeah, I know – the place was full of cops,' she recited. She eased her legs, tapping him on the shoulder by way of an apology. 'I'm surprised you actually bought that stuff about government-issue specs giving the only genuine protection against radiation. I bet your dad didn't.'

Scott blushed. He had.

'It's rot – it's a lie – pure and simple. Any transitional lenses will do the job. It was the Federation's way of ensuring everyone carried identity cards, without knowing about it. Every piece of info about you is stored in those frames. There's even a coded signal with a ten-mile radius. It started off as a means of tracing illegal immigrants. Then, shortly afterwards, the towers began to appear.'

'But why?'

'Because the Federation is fast becoming a totalitarian regime. Every other nation in the world knows it – except Europe. Radio, TV, newspapers – they're all censored.'

Scott pulled off his gloves, listening.

'Scott, we're not safe yet,' Hilary objected.

He ignored her. 'Go on.'

Angrily, Hilary climbed down off the bike and began swinging her arms vigorously across her chest, stamping her feet to get warm. The early morning air was biting, made worse by the absence of anything remotely resembling a tree or bush; the vast concrete platform of the adjoining motorways creating one long wind tunnel.

'It might not look that way, if you live in England, but from outside you see things differently.'

'So,' he said slowly, staring at Hilary. 'If you're right – and I'm not saying you are – when a car passes the tower, the vehicle is logged but so is the driver. That means, within seconds, there's confirmation that the car is stolen or whatever, and it can be tracked. I was wearing Dad's specs so ...' He paused, staring at nothing. 'But that still means ...'

Hilary nodded. 'Whoever's behind this has access to government records and that, to be honest, freaks me out.'

THIRTEEN

Scott slept, his mind cleansing itself of the detritus of the day, tossing out a string of jumbled phrases and meaningless numbers: A49 Whitchurch, avoiding the A534 – wrong way – goes to Crewe. Tiverton, Tarporley, stay on the A49 – safer. Hilary to buy helmets and sunglasses – easy for a girl. Pick up the motorway at junction twenty-two. Nearly caught at junction twenty-eight. B5253 – where does it lead? It has to go somewhere. A582 through Preston – pick up the motorway again at junction thirty-two.

The list was endless: Lancaster, Kendal, Penrith. Need money. Hilary tired – not saying anything though. Have to stop – eyes blurring. Need a shower. Carlisle – Glasgow. Towers blocking the road! Get off – *get off*!

He murmured in his sleep, replaying once again the nightmare scenario of the last few miles; the black eagles, with their wings outspread and hovering, eager to pounce, controlling every slip road in and out of Glasgow. Forced to turn back, worrying about how long they could keep going in the wrong direction.

The day had been grey with low cloud producing a light drizzle, making it necessary for motorists to keep their sidelights on for safety; and dusk had fallen early under the thick pall of cloud. Scott fixed his gaze on the vehicle in front, his speed slowing as he tried to control his fatigue. He blinked and a myriad of lights, from oncoming traffic, blurred into a single circle of brightness. He had to stop before they had an accident but daren't, not until they were safely past the towers.

'Scott!' Hilary cried out. 'Cones! Look! There's a digger, too, and lorries. There's got to be a way off.'

Scott had seen the cones merging four lanes into three, but only as something to avoid. He slowed, squinting through the gloom towards the area under repair; a digger left with its jaws open, in the middle of devouring its next mouthful of earth, its driver presumably unwilling to give his job a single second unpaid.

The dense rush-hour traffic passed him with a monotonous swish of tyres as he slowed still further, zigzagging his bike through the long line of cones onto the hard shoulder, now a dumping place for hard core.

Hilary thumped him on the back. 'There!'

In the poor light Scott had not noticed the hastily constructed mud track, deeply scored with tyre marks. Gratefully, he swung the bike round and, slowing right down, bumped it carefully over the rim of the carriageway and on to the track, trying to avoid the worst of its rain-filled puddles. Two hundred yards later they emerged onto a minor road.

He stopped, resting his head on the handlebars. 'I've had it,' he said, his voice barely audible. 'I've got to stop.'

Hilary rubbed his back; her brain continuing to create a sensation of movement. She daren't get off and stretch. If she did, she wouldn't be able to get back on, her muscles screaming with tiredness.

'We'll stop at the first place and get you some tea, it can't be far now. On the map Loch Lomond's just the other side of Glasgow. We can do it, Scott.'

They had, but it had been very late by the time they turned into the drive of the Youth Hostel, close to Arden village.

'Only dormitory accommodation, I'm afraid. Girls on the first floor, boys on the second. And you'll have to get food out. Dinner's finished. But there's a great view of the Loch at dawn, if you're interested.'

They weren't. Hilary, white with fatigue after two long days travelling, walked slowly up the stairs, her only wish a desire to snuggle up in a warm bed and go to sleep.

Scott, too weary to remain upright any longer, had one coherent thought before he crashed into oblivion. They'd done it. They'd arrived at Loch Lomond.

FOURTEEN

Full wakeful consciousness was difficult to grasp, like a thread of cotton jerked away from fumbling fingers. Twice Bill rose up towards the surface, waking sufficiently to become aware of his surroundings and gradually he began to recall some isolated incidents from his journey; smooth roads, silence and blackness, the smell of the sea, his head dizzy with its topsy-turvy movement, grateful when the blackness took over again.

Now he was awake and very thirsty. He opened his eyes, focussing on a jug of water on the table by his bed. Next to it was a glass.

At least they want me to survive, he thought, an expression of genuine relief on his face. He drank, returning to a position on his back and closed his eyes, feeling the room spin out of control. He knew the drill. It was horrid – but it would pass – an imbalance in the inner-ear caused by the powerful opiate. Food would help. He stretched out his hand towards the table, unwilling to sit up until the dizziness had subsided, and patted its surface. His fingers immediately knocked against a plate on which were some biscuits. He grabbed a couple and munched them slowly. Tentatively, he tilted his head and drank some more water, then lay back down again and closed his eyes, waiting for normality to return. There was not the slightest point in hurrying it, nor in leaping to his feet to check out the room and find a way out, he comforted himself sleepily, there wouldn't be one. Whoever had issued the invitation wanted him to stay – and would make certain of it by bolting his door and barring the window.

He woke naturally some hours later, feeling energy beginning to return to his body. He was stiff and had bruises in strange places but he'd known worse. He padded into the small bathroom. A change of clothing, towels and a razor waited. Bill gazed at his unshaven chin, rubbing his hand over several days' worth of bristles, inclined to leave it and cultivate a new look. He recalled the face of one of the hired help at the cottage, a weedy outcrop clinging to his cheeks and chin, his smirk as he saw the needle go in. Bill's face darkened with anger. Filling the basin with hot water, he picked up the razor.

Twenty minutes later he emerged from the steam-filled bathroom, feeling halfway human. His watch had gone, a faint white mark on his wrist where the strap had been. And his shoes were nowhere to be seen either. Carefully controlling the expression on his face, he gazed round the room, knowing it was likely he was being observed, yet unable to prevent his fists from clenching angrily.

His survival depended on where, at which point, his shoes had been taken away. If immediately before tossing him into bed, the bleeper in the innersoles would lead his rescuers right to the door. If at the start of his journey, he was lost somewhere in Europe.

He crossed to the window, buckling his trouser belt, and peered out through the bars. Most likely Belgium or Holland. Fields as flat as a green pancake faded into the distance, not a hedge or undulation marking one from the other. He could have been in Legoland for all the clues the landscape offered. He pressed his head against the bars, squinting along the side of the building. No clues there either. A house – red brick – not big – he guessed. It had an ordinary enough garden with neatly pruned evergreen shrubs surrounded by wrought-iron railings – typical of thousands he'd seen on journeys through northern Europe.

The door clicked and he swung round.

'Good morning, Meester Masterson. I 'ope you 'ad a comfortable journey.'

'Oh it's you.' Bill eyed the Frenchman, who had proved so skilful with needles, with dislike. 'I was hoping for a buxom country lass with some breakfast. Where are my shoes?'

'Incinerated; the same for your jacket and trousers. We prefer this to be a bug-free environment, as you will see when we go downstairs. Would you follow me?'

Reluctantly, Bill slipped his feet into a pair of loafers that had been left by the bedroom door. Outside the door another figure he recognised, the German with the bulging shoulder pad. He fell in behind.

He'd been right. It was an ordinary house with an ordinary landing, several bedrooms leading off it, except … The Frenchman pulled open a door, concealing the gated railings of a lift.

'What did you say your name was?' Bill asked as they dropped downwards: ground floor – and not stopping – a long drop to the basement. They jerked to a halt.

'Gerard Davois,' said the Frenchman. 'I am so glad you 'ave decided to be reasonable, Meester Masterson.'

'Monsieur Davois … I need food and for that I am prepared to suck up to any piece of shit that crosses my path.'

Bill caught the fleeting change of expression on the muscle's face – hastily wiped off and changed into a clearing of the throat. The man pushed open the gates, gesturing Bill to go ahead.

They were in what, at first glance, appeared to be an underground shopping mall, its vast central area brightly lit, as if the sun had been planted in the roof space; trees and flowers growing among compost-filled islands, with glass-fronted shops on either side. An electric car, identical to a golf cart, whizzed past on a rubber-tiled pathway – making it less of a shopping mall, rather more an underground city. This was followed by an electric scooter – usually the prerogative of the disabled, a two-wheeled dump bin filled with laundry trailing behind; the only thing missing a London bus.

'This way.'

The Frenchman ushered him through a conglomeration of comfortable chairs and low tables surrounding the lift shaft. Bill glanced across at one of the shop windows, identifying a long, winding counter filled with the paraphernalia of a cafeteria, fruit and coffee machines, tiers of plastic shelving displaying biscuits and croissants. At least they fed their prisoners. He allowed himself to speculate on the subject of food, questions like – so how did supplies get in – filling his mind. Through the heavy plate glass on the far side of the large hallway, Bill could see people working – peering into screens. They were casually dressed, and most of them were young.

A short corridor led them towards an imposing set of double doors in cherry-coloured wood. Davois knocked and entered.

The room was vast, impressive even, its walls panelled in the same polished wood as its doors, with views through a picture window towards snow-covered mountains topped with blue sky. In the centre stood an oval mahogany table; a trolley, groaning with food, nearby. Two men were seated at the table, with heaped plates in front of them.

'Join us, Mr Masterson.'

The voice sounded friendly, welcoming even, yet the atmosphere was tense, almost expectant.

The muscle left the room and closed the door after him, hardly bothering to hide the expression of annoyance that crossed his face. Obviously, he wasn't invited. Bill felt almost sorry, since the food looked good.

Power radiated from every pore of the two men facing Bill. It helped that they were wearing expensive Italian suits with handmade shoes, their hands – held out in greeting – neatly manicured.

'Wayne Seagar,' the voice was American, so was the hair; a crew cut disguising a bald patch on top of his head. 'This is my colleague, Ferdinand Aquilla.' The man nodded his head in a brief acknowledgement, his clothes and hair giving the impression of a single colour – grey. 'Take the weight off, the boss will be with us in a moment.'

As he spoke, a section of panelling at the far end of the room slid to one side, exposing a screen which immediately flickered into life. The silhouette of a man appeared. Bill waited for the digital image to clear and focus. Nothing happened, the figure remaining a blur.

'Mr Masterson? The gentlemen you joined for breakfast …' the shadow moved and a finger pointed towards the two men, confirming that he could see and hear everything, 'are my associates in charge of this operation.'

Bill listened intently. The language was English but heavily accented, possibly Russian, although obviously disguised; the voice swirling in and out, with changes of key making it difficult to pinpoint.

'And that is?'

'Do have some breakfast, Mr Masterson. I am sure you are hungry.'

'Thanks.' Bill crossed to the trolley, helping himself to scrambled eggs and bacon. Davois had seated himself at the far end of the table, and was quietly drinking his coffee. He had not, as Bill had done, helped himself to food although there was plenty. It was reasonable to assume therefore that, although invited to stay, Davois wasn't considered one of the inner circle – however much he thought he should be.

'Monsieur Davois – please.' The shadow waved a nonchalant arm. 'After your really excellent work in finding Masterson, you deserve breakfast at the very least.'

'Thank you, sir.' The man got to his feet joining Bill by the trolley.

The coffee was freshly brewed – the aroma definitely European, with the faintest hint of chicory. Bill poured himself a cup and took a sip. Almost instantly he felt the charge, the caffeine kicking-in lifting his spirits to a feeling of normality, or what might conceivably pass as normal after a couple of days drugged and out of it. He gave Davois an amused half-smile.

'Great reward – breakfast. Try the eggs, they're good,' he murmured and, taking his plate, crossed to the boardroom table and sat down facing the screen.

The voice from the screen was casual as if telling a child's bedtime story.

Except it wasn't a bedtime story, Bill could sense the tension dominating the figures round the conference table, their bodies upright in the posture of men on full alert

'You asked about what we do here, Mr Masterson? Quite simply, my associates' task is to keep our computer scientists safe,' the voice said. 'Our city is almost identical to that built in Virginia after the tsunami. Have you seen it?'

'No, nor likely to,' Bill said, wondering how on earth the bad guys had. He felt no hesitation in believing they were the bad guys, however sophisticated the set-up. Good guys don't go round sticking needles into people, he told himself. He ate sparingly, thankful the meeting had started out in a civilised fashion, although it might be prudent to stock up because, if they didn't like his answers, it was possible food could be in rather short supply afterwards.

'Haven't been near the States in fifteen years,' he offered.

'Yes, we know that, Mr Masterson. Although I would be interested to know why?'

No harm there. 'I didn't know if I could trust the Americans.'

'Quite! I can see your dilemma. They had killed your wife and most of your colleagues – such a tragedy – and so you took off alone.'

'Yes,' Bill said, finding a conversation about death and destruction, while eating breakfast, somewhat surreal.

'But not quite alone, Mr Masterson.'

'My son? Of course, we live together.'

'Don't play games, Mr Masterson.' The shadow's voice sounded terse. 'Some of your colleagues did not die and together you are continuing your work. Don't bother to deny it. Now, we would like you to offer you a job.'

'How flattering to be headhunted.' Casually, Bill got to his feet to refill his coffee cup. He sketched a laugh. 'But why? I'm not in the league you want.'

'That is not worthy of you, Mr Masterson. And I am sure,

when you've been with us a few days, you will see the wisdom of confessing your true ability. Naturally, like our counterparts in America, we are short of technical know-how and are seeking intelligent recruits.'

Bill thought back to the Reuters' news report about teenagers disappearing, but the sentence – well, you'll not get them by kidnapping – remained unsaid. 'So establish a university or put an ad in the newspaper,' he quipped.

'Far too lengthy a process. We need scientists now – starting with you.'

The voice remained calm, not a flicker of anger at Bill's sarcasm, nothing that might present him with clues to the man's identity. What was their real intention? A race for global mastery? Or was the man a philanthropist in disguise and this little set-up all in the name of altruism?

Bill shrugged and sat down again. 'Okay.'

This time his words did produce a reaction; Davois being so rude as to choke on his coffee, Seagar and Aquilla, the sidekicks, staring. Only the shadow failed to react.

'As you see, my colleagues are somewhat startled,' it said. 'It is more usual for candidates of your calibre to show reluctance and take a little persuading to change their minds. Perhaps you can explain your sudden volte-face.'

Bill continued to chew, slowly. It wouldn't harm them to wait for an explanation and, anyway, the food was far too good to hurry. He let his gaze slide over to the view. It was fake, like the rest of the set-up; the portrayal of open air, with its subliminal message of freedom, simply a 3D image. Reality lurked behind it, a wall guarding the edges of an underground bunker.

'There are terms, of course,' he said.

'Naturally and they are?'

'I work for you and you quit trying to get hold of my son. Let him alone.'

The shadow inclined his head. There was a gentle easing of breath.

'So what is it you want of me?'

'To begin with something quite easy – your files – and of course the names of your colleagues. Sadly your files are encrypted and our students are, as yet, not able to unscramble them.'

'You've tried already?' Bill tried to conceal his astonishment but the words escaped.

'We don't waste time. We are in the middle of an accelerating programme and have a schedule to keep.'

'To take over the world?'

A pin dropping would have sounded like the blast from a roadside bomb, the silence in the room suddenly so intense.

'I am sorry to disappoint, Mr Masterson. My aim is solely the dominance of technology. Anything else would cost far too many lives and be far too messy. War has never solved anything; it simply substitutes one problem for another.'

'I'm glad to hear that,' Bill said. 'I happen to agree. Unfortunately, that consideration is rarely shared by our leaders.'

'What world leaders believe is of little consequence. After we take over, they will think what we want them to think.'

'And that is?'

'No wars. The world continuing to move forward, as it has done, except we will control technology. You see, Mr Masterson, it occurred to me that the way to control the world was not by refusing to sell arms to a particular country, or by possessing the secret of nuclear fission, it was simply by preventing the global village functioning. If gas could not flow, nor electricity or nuclear power function, neither missiles be discharged, nor planes or ships sail, because there was no computer to operate them or calculate the percentages for the money markets, then governments would fail and chaos take over. Your programme, a virus capable of infiltrating any computer in the world, could create that. How simple would it be then – for nothing would work unless I told it to.'

'Interesting? And do I conclude that your organisation has been behind the recent blips in the stock market?'

Leisurely, Bill got to his feet, helping himself to croissant, knowing the answer he received would be a *yes*. The sudden failure of gilt-edged companies, declaring losses after years of steady growth, had made the headlines on any number of occasions in the past few years.

'But, of course, Mr Masterson. We like to keep ourselves occupied while waiting for the golden goose.'

'So killing off global corporations is simply a way of passing the time?'

Laughter came from the figure on the screen, the distorted sound so eerie it made Bill's flesh creep.

'We must have a game of chess some time. You would prove a worthy opponent. Shall we say, Mr Masterson, while waiting for the big fish to drop into our net, we amuse ourselves with the tiddlers. And the money we gained has proved most useful in expanding our operation. However, these adjustments of companies' assets have become somewhat tedious. It is time we tested ourselves against a more worthy opponent.'

How dictators loved to parade their ambitions, Bill thought, as if talking could make it happen. It was the desire to show off that was always the giveaway, a constant need to boast of their ambitions. He got to his feet, moving across to the trolley. 'Is that okay?' he said indicating the percolator. 'I'm rather thirsty.' This man, whoever he was, was no different from Stalin, Hitler or Pol Pot who had gone before him. Although to give him his due, he had at least moved his thinking into the twenty-first century, and was not considering ethnic cleansing or mass slaughter as the way forward.

'You will find yourself most welcome here. Unlike the Americans and the Arabs, we don't believe in torture,' the voice continued, its pitch sliding up and down the scale, adding to the nightmare quality of his words. 'You will not find yourself experiencing a Guantanamo Bay lifestyle, deprived of sleep and gazing down at blackened fingertips, where electrodes have been attached to them. No, a quick bullet to the head generally silences any opposition, don't you find?'

Bill concealed a shudder, saying lightly, 'You may be

disappointed when you see my files. The project to create that world-beating virus was swept out to sea in the tsunami. It can't be replicated – I know, I've tried.'

'Mr Masterson, don't take me for a fool. No man hides from the world for fifteen years, unless he has a secret so vast he daren't share it, and doesn't know who to trust. Doesn't that more accurately sum up your life?'

'It might have if your friends hadn't killed David Runyon.'

Let them chew on that. He stood up. 'I'm happy to work on the files for all the good it will do. It was David who was the lynchpin. He encrypted key parts, to stop people like you accessing them. You killed the wrong guy. Meanwhile, I suppose I'd better make myself at home. I sleep where?'

The atmosphere had become glacial, and a distinct pallor appeared on the tanned cheeks of the men in the room.

It was Wayne Seagar that answered, his voice strained. 'Not the room you occupied last night. That's kept for visitors. You will be given a comfortable room in the facility. Arnulf will show you.'

'Mr Masterson?'

Bill looked slowly back at the screen, the statement: *a quick bullet to the head,* running through his mind like a record stuck in the groove; aware that the shadow had the advantage, able to study his every expression, even to the involuntary muscle flicking in the side of his cheek.

'I am sure you will think of someway to unlock the information. After all, you will be here a while.'

'A prisoner?'

'Don't sound so disappointed. What I am offering is not so very different from the way you would have lived, had you accepted the hospitality of the Americans.'

'I rejected that,' Bill said harshly, a sudden surge of dizziness almost overbalancing him. He grasped the back of a chair, quickly sitting down again.

'And escaped fifteen years of imprisonment. Those men, in all probability, are even now asking themselves whether their knowledge was worth the sacrifice. Unfortunately for them, it won't be for much longer. It has taken me almost that length of time to locate them and get an assassin into place.'

The pitch of voice had dropped, becoming low and level, almost pleasant sounding, except for its underlying self-satisfied tone, which the man had used to outline his plans for global supremacy. Bill disguised a shiver of disgust. Governments were frequently corrupt but at least they did, for the most part, represent a quasi-honest if somewhat bungling and ineffective attempt to improve the lot of their people. Crackpot dictators always put the evolutionary process back half a century and cost thousands, if not millions, of innocent lives before the world was rid of their polluting presence.

Bill kept up his casual tone. 'So even they are not safe. Doubtless, I am much safer working for you.'

'Exactly, Mr Masterson. I am so glad you understand.'

Bill pushed himself to his feet and, taking care to keep his head still, walked slowly towards the door. 'Have you any objection to my taking a look round?'

'None at all, Mr Masterson. Is there anything else you require?'

'I'd quite like to have my watch back. It was the last thing my wife gave me before you blew up her hotel,' he guessed and went out shutting the door behind him, hoping he'd called it right.

The silence, palpable as dough, lasted several minutes, not one of the three men left sitting round the table daring to break it.

'Is that true about his colleague?' The voice on the screen still sounded the same, its tone smooth, urbane even.

Wayne Seagar swallowed nervously. 'Yes, sir! I had the report in two nights ago.'

'And you said nothing?'

'In my judgement he was the link man, not a scientist.'

'So who killed Runyon? You know I dislike unauthorised killings.'

'Runyon was armed and opened fire. Despite orders, one of the foot-soldiers shot him.'

The shadow stayed silent, a mere blur on a screen, yet the sense of power emanating from it still controlled the room.

'He's already been taken care of,' Seagar hastily added. 'Got himself captured by the US Secret Service – our agent disposed of him before he could talk.'

The atmosphere relaxed as if the three men had exhaled at the exact same moment. Davois picked up his coffee and took a sip, the large breakfast cup hiding an expression of pure relief.

'So is Masterson lying? Could Runyon have encrypted the files?'

'My guess is he's bluffing.' Aquilla pushed his plate to one side and took out his cigarette case.

'Davois?'

Davois anticipating the next question hastily swallowed his coffee. It headed down his windpipe, making him choke. He mopped his face. 'Yes, sir?'

'Where is the boy?'

''E gave the men following 'im the slip. Stupidly, they did not anticipate 'is companion, who was efficient with a gun.' The words were reluctantly said.

'Careless?'

'Yes, sir, very. They won't make that mistake again,' Davois shrugged. 'We 'ave a new team tracking 'im now. 'E's headed north. They will keep me informed.'

'Why north?'

Davois shrugged, the expression betraying his Gaelic origins.

'We now have both processors, sir.' Aquilla blew a circle of scented smoke into the air. 'Hopefully, within a few days, one of them will give up its secrets and lead us to the next link.'

'Runyon led directly to Masterson?'

It was a question.

'Hence my conclusion that Runyon was simply a link in the chain,' Aquilla answered. 'And that Masterson is the main man.'

'Find the boy and bring him here. Then we shall see if Mr Masterson is lying or not. In the meanwhile ...' the man of power waved his fingers, like the Pope bestowing a blessing, 'he is an honoured guest – make sure he is treated like one.'

FIFTEEN

Scott needed help and for the present he, Bill, was helpless. The boy was bright but how could he keep one step ahead of such ruthless men, who killed on a whim and thought nothing of it? And no way would they stop looking for the boy. His only chance lay in finding a way out or his friends finding a way in.

The biggest problem Bill faced was time. He wasn't particularly bothered about the threat of a bullet, although it was a brilliant piece of psychological brain-washing, transforming seared fingertips into a luxury weekend at a health farm. No, if he really was in the hands of the people that had started it all off so many years before, they had proved both patient and unrelenting. Now they'd caught up with him, they would consider him valuable merchandise, knowing if they couldn't use the virus, neither could anyone else.

So how long did he have? Long enough for someone to rescue him? Long enough for him to escape?

Bill closed his eyes as yet another wave of dizziness overtook him, only too aware of the utter futility of his situation. Yet buried in the darkness was a microscopic gleam of light. David had been their conduit, linking the scattered fragments of research into one cohesive structure, nursing each area carefully inside his own memory, their calculations kept solely on discs; hidden where no one could find them, except him. Even David didn't know the whereabouts of the entire team – no one did. The elaborate method of communication, worked out amidst disbelief and laughter, had finally proved itself. Mobiles or pay phones, no addresses, no friendly chats, communication on a need-to-know basis; mobiles changed over every time someone got nervous, personalised computers with warnings built-in for emergencies. A link back to David; yes, that had been unavoidable – but no one except the person concerned party to the method of communication. *Damage limitation* he had once jokingly called it; none of them really believing they could be traced with all the precautions they were taking. They'd been proved wrong and David had surrendered his life protecting what he believed; a man of great courage, although in doing so he may have saved everyone else.

He returned to the communal lounge, his sense of desperation momentarily overwhelming. He might have been given freedom to roam and, since the best way to divert suspicion was to do exactly that, he would explore every inch of the city.

The place appeared empty. Yet he still felt cornered and pursued. He swung round, Arnulf was leaning against a wall six paces away, his arms folded, his eyes unwavering. It was like the man's face was set in stone, nothing moved; even a robot appearing more lifelike. And yet on some level there had to be something behind that expressionless mask; he couldn't simply be a collection of bones, sinew and muscle. Bill remembered the fleeting look of anger that had swept across the man's face on being excluded from the boardroom. Yes, there was something more.

So the German had been ordered to follow him. Strange in a building that was supposed to be escape-proof. The thought offered a spark of hope and Bill grabbed it with both hands. There had to be more than one way out. Food and water had to come in, so did light and heat, while sewage had to go out.

Eight evenly-spaced corridors revolved round the lift shaft like spokes in a wheel, and he had to check them all. Taking the corridor to his left, he set off. An hour later he was back where he started. He plunged exhausted into a chair, praying he wouldn't be called upon to do anything strenuous – like climb up a ventilation shaft – until he felt fully recovered. He eyed the one above his head, the tall fronds of a palm tree brushing against its grating.

The corridors had held no secrets; his shadow only bothering to follow him as far as the first doorway – a small room where linen was stored. He leant against the wall, his face impassive, watching Bill trudge down their endless length, discovering nothing but bedrooms and bathrooms. Only sheer bloody mindedness had kept him going. He had met a few people, all young and cheerful, dressed in the global uniform of jeans and T-shirt; those busy cleaning sporting the addition of a brown armband. He had interrupted work sessions, with a handful of teenagers peering diligently into computer screens, and watched a game of squash. But apart from having a map of the city indelibly printed in his memory, there'd been nothing.

'May I join you for dessert?' Ferdinand Aquilla stood there, a tray in his hand.

'I had thought the boardroom more your style,' Bill gestured to the seat on the opposite side of the table, his dish of vanilla ice cream already beginning to melt in the warmth of the little restaurant.

Aquilla pulled out a chair, sitting down. 'Normally, yes, but I'll let you into a secret. The chef in the communal restaurant is the most superb pastry cook.' He pointed to the substantial slice of *Tartes aux pommes* on his plate, a jug of cream on the side. 'So when *tartes* is on the menu I eat here.'

Bill laughed, the sound making him feel altogether more positive.

He must have dozed away the remainder of the morning, because when he awoke it was lunchtime, and groups of young people were heading for the cafeteria. The sleep had done him good. He was still thirsty and a glass of sparkling mineral water stood at his elbow, although the dizziness had now abated and he was now only aware of it if he moved too quickly. The food was extraordinarily good too, providing absolute proof – if any were needed – that he was in Europe; mass cooking in the schools and universities of America and England edible – but only just. He spun out his lunch of escalope of veal, salad and sautéed potatoes as long as possible, studying the faces that passed by his table in the hope of memorising the majority of them.

'Are they all devotees to the cause?' Bill asked the question, indicating the occupied tables.

'They will be. Simply a question of grooming. There is no shortage of willing recruits. After all with twenty-seven countries in the Federation, most of them overflowing with the unemployed, they provide a perfect breeding-ground for the discontented. Our policy is to encourage those most strongly adhering to our cause to mingle with the newcomers; it helps the process of assimilation.'

'Drugs?'

'If necessary, although teenage minds are extraordinary pliable. Repeat something often enough and they believe it; not only that, their belief becomes so powerful it remains impervious to argument, however logical.'

Bill closed his eyes remembering the tragedies at the end of the last century, from terrorists who clutched religion to their heart. No different from now, except the cause. 'So what's your role? Your boss ... what's his name ... failed to say.'

'Mine is research and he doesn't have a name, Mr Masterson, so I wouldn't bother trying.' Aquilla tilted his chair backwards and, stretching out an arm, dropped his empty tray on the table behind. 'Wayne Seagar's in charge of security.'

'You don't look as if you have any problem there.'

'We don't and Wayne intends to keep it that way. He's concerned you might try to escape.'

'What with?' Bill grinned, holding up the knife and fork he had just discarded on his plate, a second set already in the pocket of his jacket. His new clothes had fitted perfectly and, judging by their label, had come from a fashionable prêt à porter establishment in Paris.

'You know we've met before.'

Bill looked at him startled.

Aquilla sipped at his coffee, cutting his apple tart with a fork.

'You've changed very little. Our paths crossed at seminars and conferences. You wouldn't remember.'

Bill stared at the man, trying to place him. 'No I don't,' he admitted.

In any other situation Aquilla would have been considered elegant, if not down-right handsome; Bill was certain women would think so. His face was aquiline with high cheekbones, his nose straight with perfect teeth; but knowing he might have been responsible for the death of thousands, in Bill's eyes he was gazing at a monster.

Aquilla relaxed the muscles of his mouth, smiling briefly. 'I would have been disappointed in my plastic surgeon if you had. No, I changed somewhat after the earthquake. I was one of a group offered new lives in exchange for our old; a new and very generous employer, a huge increase in salary with no taxes to pay, a playboy lifestyle ... in exchange for what ... loyalty?'

'There were others?'

'Of course, unfortunately only one from your section – Harry Bentley. He retired this year – but, again you wouldn't recognise him. Pity so many were killed. They should have accepted the invitation.'

'And was ... Oh, for God's sake, he has to have a name. *He who must be obeyed* sounds a bit theatrical to me.'

Bill expected to see an expression of some kind, possibly a shrug, a grimace, but nothing was forthcoming.

'It hardly matters. Schmidt ... Smith ... what you will.'

It was strangely surreal how Aquilla limited the use of the muscles of his face, as if emotion might prove a deadly enemy.

'Okay then, Smith, was he behind the earthquake?' Bill said, immediately regretting the impulse that had driven him to ask the question. Questions led to more questions and *he* couldn't afford the answers. But the Argentinean seemed content to talk.

'Of course, but naturally not the tsunami – that was a by-product created by the forces of nature.'

'And the earthquake?'

'That was Russian technology. With Boris Yeltsin in charge everything had its price.'

Bill could have sat there debating the moral argument about the end justifying the means. He didn't, knowing it to be a waste of breath. 'And, do *you* know who he is?'

'That's all the information I'm prepared to give you, despite knowing you can't get away from here,' Aquilla's tone changed abruptly.

Bill ignored it, pushing on. 'And Seagar?'

'He came along later. A disaffected FBI agent with useful contacts. Now, if you've finished …' Aquilla eyed the pool of cream-coloured liquid on Bill's plate with distaste and got to his feet. 'I'll show you to your workstation.'

'I was hoping for a game of tennis or squash at the local club. At the very least, a stroll in the country to walk off my lunch,' Bill said, joining his host at the door.

'I'm afraid all our scientific staff remain indoors, at least until we're certain they won't stray. Think of it this way; European farmers rear their prize stock in barns to keep them healthy. And we want you to stay healthy.'

SIXTEEN

Scott woke with a start, unsure of where he was. His dream had left him struggling among a city of houses, all identical, trawling his motorbike up and down, row after row, calling out: 'Dad where are you?' Once he'd caught a glimpse of his dad's face peering from a bedroom window, but then the road changed into a maze and he couldn't find the window again.

He rubbed his eyes. Of course he was in Scotland. He leapt from his bed, making a dive for the window, eager for the promised sight of the loch – only to be disappointed, his view blocked by the chimney on a nearby roof.

Anxious now to get moving, Scott quickly showered, his surroundings of no interest as long as there was hot water, for the day was chilly.

Had he been interested in old buildings, he might have noticed the remnants of blue-patterned wallpaper still clinging to the walls, left over from when the bathroom had been the dressing room of some rich person. In an era dominated by global warming, the building, with its lofty ceilings and over-sized rooms, had quickly become both unfashionable and impractical. After standing empty for many years, it had eventually been re-opened as a hostel catering for groups of youthful walkers, eager to pit their legs against the Scottish hills. Six bunk beds fitted comfortably into the second-floor room, its high ceiling and heavy walls keeping the temperature to a chilly maximum; although only four of the beds had been occupied when Scott had fumbled his way in through the darkness.

130

Crashing out in the first available space, he hadn't even heard his room-mates get up.

Scott checked his watch. It was gone ten. They had bought toothbrushes and clean underwear near Manchester, Hilary swearing she might be happy to wear her jeans for a week but not her knickers. She had stuck the tube of toothpaste in her jacket pocket, forgetting Scott might need it. Which brought him right back to the main problem, did he trust her?

He ran downstairs. The man in charge of the hostel peered out through a square-shaped hole in the wall, which doubled as his reception desk. 'Breakfast's finished,' he informed Scott cheerfully. 'You'll have to eat out.'

Hilary was already waiting. Her trousers and T-shirt looked as if they had been freshly ironed, not worn for the past two days, and her fair hair was newly washed and pinned back in its usual ponytail. She couldn't have been waiting long though. Scott eyed the wet hair and decided not to bother apologising for being late.

'You okay?' he asked, pulling open the heavy front door of the hostel for her to pass through first.

'A bit stiff and some clean clothes would help.'

Scott blinked as the sun hit him. Overhead, the sky was a brilliant blue with hardly a cloud in sight, the shrubs in the grounds already basking under its warm gaze, like otters on the shore of the loch.

Relieved their journey was finally at an end, they strolled in companionable silence down the driveway, past wide borders of black earth, in which clumps of heather were still flowering, dotted with the bright whiteness of snowdrops. On both sides of the garden, a weathered and crumbling wall formed the boundary and, in its lee, daffodils were already in flower.

'So what now?' Hilary said as they reached the road running past the end of the drive.

On the wall close by, a black and white sign – sporting a large fist – pointed towards the loch. Scott caught a glimpse of a narrow lane, bordered with gardens on one side. He ignored it, food was much more important.

'Breakfast; the coffee shop should be along here.'

He led the way down the narrow street towards the town square, the buildings on both sides in deep shadow. The air struck cold and Scott shivered. He gazed up at the sparkling blue of the sky, the sun's rays trapped among chimney pots and roof tiles, unable to reach the ground.

A coach, that had been jolting slowly along the narrow road towards them, lurched to a stop. The driver stuck his head out of the window eyeing up the space left by a parked car. Spinning the steering wheel, he bumped the cumbersome vehicle onto the pavement, inching it slowly through the gap. Scott hastily plastered himself against a wall to avoid being squashed, leaving Hilary to fend for herself. She ran back along the road, searching for a shop doorway large enough to hide in, ponderously pursued by the single-decker monstrosity. The granite doorstep of an Italian restaurant beckoned and she darted in. The coach lumbered past, its occupants craning their necks over its high windows to stare down at her, as if a girl in a shop doorway was as riveting a sight as the world-famous loch had been.

'Great,' she exclaimed as she rejoined Scott.

He gave her a friendly grin, continuing to watch the coach clumsily negotiate its massive tyres off the kerb back on to the road. 'I wonder how many people they manage to kill in a year,' he joked.

The village was old, the modern town of Arden extending inland away from the narrow, winding streets; its century-old houses clad in dark-grey granite, as rigid as an ancient kirk, topped by steeply-pitched slate roofs. At ground level, most had been converted into shops and restaurants to cater for a bustling year-round tourist trade and the coffee shop was busy, its tables full of walkers and retired couples on a mini-break. Having risen early, by eleven in the morning they were in need of substantial nourishment, the keen air off the loch whipping the appetite into overdrive. Plates of home-made scones and jam decorated almost all of the tables, while their occupants, with the use of maps and magnifying glasses, checked the next stage of the day's activities.

Seeing them enter, a waitress – carrying a tray piled high with dirty crockery – a smile of welcome on her face, paused long enough to ask what they wanted to eat. She vanished into the kitchen leaving them to find an empty table. Noticing one at the back of the shop, next to an open doorway curtained with strips of brightly-coloured plastic, Scott began to squeeze his way through the narrow space between the tables, muttering a continuous litany of: 'Sorry ... didn't mean to knock you... er ... excuse me,' as he elbowed a pair of glasses or bumped against a table, knocking a newspaper or map to the floor.

They had just sat down when the waitress reappeared, hurriedly placing a pot of tea and two cups down in front of them.

'Your breakfast will be along in a minute. Milk and sugar on the table,' she said and, spotting a man's arm waving frantically at her, dashed off to find out what he wanted.

Almost too hungry to talk, Scott added extra milk to his tea and gulped it down before pouring himself another cup.

'We safe do you think?' he said eventually.

The plastic curtain rattled and a waitress appeared. 'Plate hot,' she informed them, crashing down a plate of egg and bacon, followed by a second one with scrambled eggs.

'I think,' Hilary studied her scrambled eggs on a muffin, savouring their elegant arrangement on the plate, before picking up her knife and fork. 'And we need to talk.'

'What about?' Scott eyed her suspiciously, instantly defensive.

'Everything! Anything and everything that could help us find your dad.'

'But I've told you everything I know,' he protested.

'So tell me again. There has to be more. But if you still don't trust me?'

Scott flinched. Hilary really was the most difficult person to deal with. There he was, looking forward to five minutes of peace while he ate his breakfast, only to be faced with her busy-busy attitude all the time – exactly like a teacher. Wishing he was brave enough to say it, he muttered, 'I didn't say that.'

'You don't have to, it's obvious. What do I have to do to prove it to you – *get shot?*' Hilary put down her knife and fork glaring. 'You hardly ever speak and every time I want to know something I have to take out a spade and dig for it. We're in this together or had you forgotten?'

'*I didn't ask you to come.* Anyway I never talk much,' Scott retorted. 'Besides, I have told you everything. It's just so mixed up,' he added relenting slightly.

'You can say that again.' Hilary picked up her knife again then paused, pointing it at Scott. 'You told me the other day you were good at puzzles. Okay, so try this.' She took a bite of her muffin chewing thoughtfully.

Scott waited nervously, wondering what was coming.

'We believe that whoever snatched your dad is linked to government,' Hilary kept her voice low. 'Or, at the very least, someone that works for the government – allowing them to track you through the motorway computer posts.' She stopped to eat a mouthful of breakfast. 'But if these people – whoever they are – already have your dad, why were they still bothering to look for him?'

'But they weren't looking for Dad, they were after me,' Scott said. 'Like those men in the cottage.'

'That's just the point,' Hilary said. 'Were they? Remember it was your dad's bike and *his* specs. So if it was your dad they were searching for … then they have to be different from the lot that grabbed him, which seriously complicates things. But if it was *you* they were after …' she paused, 'they also knew about you taking your dad's bike.'

Without noticing, Scott began to tear his piece of toast into squares.

'Go on – say it,' Hilary stared, her face expressionless.

'And no one knew about that except – the American Secret Service,' Scott finished the sentence somewhat reluctantly. 'But Pete said Sean Terry was one of the good guys,' he argued. 'And to trust him. Surely … I mean … the person who …' he stumbled and came to a full stop.

'I agree,' Hilary chewed thoughtfully. 'I don't believe it's the boss, either, however much I dislike him. So that leaves the people at headquarters. The staff there knew what was going on.'

'Before you arrived at the cottage, there were at least four other men there.' Scott stared blankly at a picture of the loch on the wall nearby, trying to recall the sequence of events. 'Tulsa was one.'

Hilary raised her eyebrows encouraging him to continue.

'And the man they took prisoner – he died.'

'What do you mean *died*?'

'I think someone murdered him.'

Hilary's eyebrows disappeared under her fringe. '*Murdered – the prisoner*!' She shook her head. 'No! You're wrong there, that couldn't happen. There's two men guarding a prisoner at all times.'

'Well, it sounded like that, anyway,' Scott grumbled, fed up with Hilary always insisting he'd got it wrong. 'You were in the garage so you didn't hear. Sean Terry was furious. He said, when they got to headquarters the man was already dead. Pete said he'd been searched before he was put in the van and he didn't believe it was either of the two agents that accompanied him. He was sure they were okay. *Arizona* – that was the other man's name.' He checked his watch. 'Come on, we'd better hurry up – it's almost eleven o'clock.'

Scott gazed out over the loch, staring blankly at the vast stretch of water. The view was stunning; the water crystal clear, exactly as it had appeared on the website, even to the snow decorating the surrounding hills. Except on the computer the picture had been limited by its edges. Here the mountain range lifted the sky to infinity, as if a lid had been taken off the world.

'The photograph was taken from … er … here.' He leapt on to the man-made flatness of a tree stump. 'The outskirts of the village of Arden – that's what it said,' he insisted, unable to believe there wasn't even a fisherman's hut in sight, but there wasn't. The land belonging to the Forestry Commission had been swept clear of the trappings of civilisation, save for the occasional litter bin cunningly disguised as a tree stump. That morning when he had woken he'd felt so hopeful, as if the fragile strands of his search were at long last beginning to knot together. 'There's nothing here,' he exclaimed wanting to howl like a dog.

'What were you expecting – a banner tacked across the top of a mountain?' Hilary's tone carried a sarcastic tinge to it. Scott flushed – he had sort of.

Hilary scuffed her toe in the dirt, avoiding his eye. 'Those clues – admit it, Scott, they *were* pretty feeble.'

'No! They were clues – *I know they were*,' Scott shouted furiously.

Hilary got up and wandered down to the water's edge, gentle ripples on the shore creating a tide-like effect. 'The man at the hostel said people swim in the loch in summer. I could do with a swim.' Pulling off her trainers she inched her toes into the water. 'Yeow! It's freezing,' she squealed, hopping up and down on the fine gravel. 'They should put up a notice – polar bears only.'

Scott's face broke into a reluctant smile, for the first time becoming aware that trouble was easier to bear if you had someone to laugh with. And Hilary was fun when she forgot to be bossy.

'So, if there's nothing here,' he said, sounding more cheerful, 'we widen the search. All round the lake if necessary.'

Hilary bent down to tie her shoe lace. 'But it's five miles wide and hundreds of miles long. I heard the man at the hostel telling one of the guests. And there's villages all round.'

'So we continue north along the west shore and ask everyone we meet – someone has to know him.'

'It'll take forever,' she wailed. 'I still think it's a wild goose chase. But if you're determined to make a fool of yourself, I saw a megaphone in a shop back there, why not buy that and shout it out loud, it would save time.'

Scott flushed and put on his helmet again. *Girls!* He'd opened his mouth to retort when he caught sight of Hilary's face, her eyes underscored by deep-purple shadows. She had to be feeling as rotten as him; two days on a bike gave you sore muscles you didn't even know existed. He raised his visor keeping his tone light. 'That's okay. I'll drop you off at the bus stop if you want – there's bound to be a bus for Glasgow sometime today – you can catch it,' and flashed a smile to show he was joking.

Hilary ducked her head to pull on her helmet. 'Nice try.' She sketched a laugh. 'But no, thanks. Whither thou goest and all that rot.' She climbed reluctantly back on the bike, her muscles protesting angrily as, with a sudden surge of revs, Scott pulled away from the loch edge.

By late afternoon they had scoured the entire length of the western coastline and nothing had happened; local people shaking their heads, unable or unwilling to provide information to strangers. Scott had surprised even himself, chatting to local residents in a friendly way. And, amazingly, after years of monosyllabic utterances it wasn't that difficult – he simply pretended he was Jameson, copying his eager, trusting manner.

His feeling of desolation reappeared as he directed the bike back towards the village. It couldn't be a wild goose chase, could it? He'd felt so certain. He re-ran the events in the cottage – the posters on the wall still jarring. No, his dad would never have hung them on the wall – not in a million years. They passed the sign for the old town. Scott indicated and swung into the lane, heading for the hostel garage.

Like the main building, this had also lain derelict before being converted into a spacious unit, and a handful of rusty horse brasses still clung to the beams, as a memento of its former occupation. In the rear wall, a narrow doorway, already half off its hinges, provided guests with a short cut into the hostel grounds.

Ignoring the door, Scott and Hilary walked back up the lane towards the town square, where an ice-cream sign beckoned.

'I'm shattered.' Scott collapsed on to a bench seat, thoughtfully provided by the parish council for visitors, and grabbed the ice-cream cone Hilary held out to him.

It wasn't much of a square, a stretch of cobbled paving, enclosed on three sides by shops and houses, a road along the fourth. The post office cum general store occupied a central position, a drinks machine chained to the wall outside. On the pavement white metal signs, displaying brightly-coloured advertisements for daily news and the more popular varieties of ice-cream, clattered noisily to and fro in the wind. On either side, shops with narrow, plate-glass windows, of a style only ever seen by tourists wandering off the beaten track, shielded wilting vegetables from the sun and the usual paraphernalia of a chemist's shop, a bunch of leaflets in a fly-spotted, white cardboard carton. A florist had filled its window with fake Easter lilies, leaving perishable stock safely in a fridge at the back, while a gift shop displayed the flags of all twenty-seven European nations; a solitary dog lying asleep on its doorstep.

From time to time the delicate chiming of a bell heralded the arrival or departure of customers to the general store. It was a peaceful, almost soporific atmosphere, which made it all the more difficult to believe that a secret society could exist in so tranquil a setting.

But that's exactly why it would, Scott reasoned. He gazed sleepily at the rigid shape of the building on the far side of the square, offering Bed and Breakfast. Even that looked deserted, guests expected to leave in the morning and not return till after five. A second-hand bookshop had been sandwiched between it and the coffee shop where they had breakfasted, its window as dusty as the books it sold. Further on, a sign, partially obscured by the building on the corner, read: *Faro Island Self-Help Pure wool hand* – Intrigued, Scott stood up and took a pace forward – *knitted sweaters*.

Disappointed, he sat down again and stretched out his legs, casting an envious eye at the dog taking advantage of the sun's warmth. His eyelids began to droop. Pulling himself back upright, he pressed his back into the bars of the seat and focussed his gaze once more on the general store, its window a junkyard of advertising leaflets. The window blurred and he blinked rapidly to focus his eyes again. 'I need a sleep,' he said.

'What about lunch?'

He yawned widely. 'It's a bit late now, it's gone four. Anyhow sleep's more important. Then we'll have dinner. We can start again in the morning.'

Hilary groaned loudly. 'Scott, I don't mean this unkindly but we're wasting time searching like this without more to go on. It's a total washout. All that's happening is we're getting more and more miserable. Admit it; we've come to the wrong place.' She lent forward, tossing her ice-cream wrapper into the bin.

Since early morning the sun had been making its way round the square. Now it ducked behind the tall roof of the building opposite, throwing the general store into shade. The bell above the shop doorway chimed and a man appeared carrying a long pole, a gleaming brass hook projecting from one end. He hooked the pole into the frame of the awning and pushed vigorously upwards, the muscles in his arms protesting at the force needed to move the rusty iron bars. With a loud clattering sound, the awning shot up and disappeared into the wooden fascia. Unhooking the pole, the man disappeared back into the shop.

Scott stared, his body rigid like a man poleaxed. He touched Hilary on the arm and pointed at the shop window, his hand trembling. 'Want to bet,' he said.

A polished brass strip ran across the lintel above the shop doorway. On it the words: *James Nicely licensed to sell wine and spirits ...*

SEVENTEEN

Scott leapt to his feet brushing off Hilary's hand trying to pull him back. Next second, he was pushing open the shop door.

The bell chimed. The woman behind the post office counter, a fine metal grille separating her from customers, automatically looked up, as if the bell cord had been attached to one of the vertebrae in her neck, a smile of welcome on her face.

'Can I help?' The man called from the back of the shop; his voice mechanical, repeating the same words every time the bell jangled.

With a feeling of immense gratitude for his stowing the blind away at the appropriate moment, Scott smiled warmly at him. 'I hope so,' he said, 'I'm looking for James Nicely.'

'Sorry,' the man replied, his manner abrupt. 'Can't help you there.'

'But his name, it's over the door,' Scott protested.

'That's right, laddie.' The friendly voice of the woman behind the post office counter broke in, the criss-cross lines of the grille bars breaking up the contours of her face. 'Mr Nicely, he was the boss until … ooh … ten years ago … about that. Right up till one of the chain stores came along. They bought up most of the village shops in this area. And Mr Nicely, bless him, well he retired. I didn't know the sign was still there.' She laughed self-consciously. 'I unlock the door every morning. I suppose I'm so used to seeing it, I never notice.'

Scott gazed at the woman in dismay. 'You mean he's not here?'

'No, laddie, that what I've been saying. I don't even know if he's still alive, is he, Sandy?'

The man glanced up from sorting left-over newspapers. In his early-twenties, the colour of his hair seemed a reasonable explanation for his name. He finished tying a knot in the piece of string holding the bundle together. 'People haven't seen him for years,' he said.

The bell jangled again as Hilary followed Scott into the shop. One look at his face told her the news.

'Is it him in particular? Maybe I can help, I'm the post mistress,' the older woman said.

'I wanted to ask him about someone called Sky Masterson. Do you have an address? Could I write to him?'

'Masterson?' The woman shook her head, her manner kindly but not overly concerned. 'No one of that name round here.'

'I know that, but I hoped Mr Nicely would know him,' Scott persisted. 'Are you positive you don't have an address?'

'We might find one, laddie, but I can't promise he's still living. Call in tomorrow.'

'Okay! In the morning?' Scott caught his tone of voice, it sounded desperate.

The woman studied him closely. Scott flinched, wondering if she'd noticed how upset he was. She nodded. 'I'll check through the files tonight, if that will suit.'

'Thanks. Come on,' he said to Hilary. 'Let's get back to the hostel.' He hesitated. 'Where can we get a decent meal – not expensive?'

Sandy walked round the counter accompanying them to the door. He stood in the doorway and pointed. 'Go left out of the square and then first left – there's a decent fish and chip shop. It's in the backstreets – if you see what I mean – but you can eat there.'

'Och! They won't be wanting fish and chips, Sandy. They can get those in England. There's three good restaurants in the village – all on the main street where the hostel is. You can't miss them.'

'Fish and chips will be just fine – our budget can stretch to that. Thanks, Sandy.' Hilary said politely, pushing Scott out of the door. 'Bye.'

'Good luck, I hope you find your friend.'

Bleary-eyed, Scott gazed round the emptiness of the little fish and chip café, steam and hot fat sizzling away in the steel fryers spiralling up into the air. A desultory queue of two small boys waited patiently by the counter for their pieces of cod to be cooked, a pile of chips already in the warmer. Scott gazed at the boys indignantly, as if they were personally responsible for the rubbish quality of the chips. He glared down at his plate with dislike and added some more ketchup to disguise their sogginess.

He still felt tired even after sleeping for two hours. And he would happily have slept longer, if Hilary hadn't nagged at one of the guests to go up and wake him. All he wanted was for morning to come. He checked his watch impatiently. It had been half-eight before they had set out to eat.

'We go to bed early round here,' the manager at the hostel had informed them, handing across a key. 'Visitors are usually up and about by six, so I lock the main door at half-nine. In any case you won't find much open at this time of the year. A couple of pubs, except you're too young for pubs. There's a good television in the lounge.'

Scott pulled back the half-curtains screening the café window. The windows were steamed up. He rubbed at them to clear the glass and peered out into the street. It was deserted, dark without street lamps, and empty except for a couple of cars and a van, neatly parked against the kerb. 'We'd have been better off spending more money and eating in that restaurant we passed,' he grumbled. 'I've got Dad's card, we could have used that.'

'Why don't you hire a plane and drag a banner behind it, announcing to the world that Scott Anderson is at Loch Lomond.'

'*Okay! Okay*! So how much money *have* we got left?' He scowled at Hilary as if it were her fault they were short of money.

'Not a lot, not after buying clean T-shirts and underwear, but enough for another night here, if we have to. Then we must trek south again. Can't risk using the machine here.'

'Do you think she'll find the address?'

'*Oh, for crying out loud*, Scott, give it a rest.' Impatiently, Hilary pushed her plate away. 'You've asked that at least a trillion times,' she snapped. '*I don't know*. She'd better. I can't stand much more of you in this mood.'

'Then leave. I'll do it on my own.'

Hilary got to her feet, grasping the back of her chair. 'Do you know, Scott Anderson, I might just do that.'

'Where're you going?' Scott gasped, watching her walk away.

'Back to the hostel,' she opened the door. It was pitch black outside, the street-lamps dim. 'But I warn you if you aren't in a better mood in the morning I *will* go.'

'That's fine with me,' he retorted.

He glared down at the table determined not to look up again until he heard the door slam. He'd wanted to be shot of her ever since Birmingham. Now, with a bit of luck, she'd clear off altogether. He chased a chip gloomily round his plate, angry now at his own boorish behaviour. He frowned remembering one of his dad's favourite lectures: *never let a row go overnight*. He and Jay were always rowing but they always made up straight after and had stayed best friends. Feeling guilty, he stared at the door, wishing Hilary would come back in so he could apologise. She might be a right pain but she had saved his life. He jumped up, pushing aside his half-eaten meal.

'Thanks,' he called to the girl behind the counter. *But no thanks*, he added to himself.

Pulling the door to behind him, he broke into a run, crossing the narrow street, concentrating on catching up with Hilary.

Hands grabbed him and a voice whispered, 'Sorry, lad.' A hood was flung over his head and his arms pulled roughly back and tied at the elbow. He kicked out knowing it was two against one. He heard a sharp intake of breath as his foot landed on someone's shin. But it wasn't enough. He found himself being dragged along the roadway and he yelled out, his voice muffled by the hood. He kicked out again, wriggling like an eel, knowing his attacker would have some serious bruises and glad of it. Next second, he was being manhandled into a vehicle. He fell forward, landing heavily, banging his knees and elbows against its metallic surface, and cried out.

A hand touched his shoulder. 'That you, Scott?'

'Hilary! You tied up like me?' he whispered.

'Yeah, never saw them. I could kick myself but I was so furious with you.'

'Me too,' said Scott. 'I was horrid.'

'And I'm a know-it-all.'

Scott shuffled round a bit and stretched out his hand. Hilary's fingers met his and he clutched them, instantly feeling happy again, his anger gone – which was downright stupid because now they were in one hell of a mess.

EIGHTEEN

Their journey was long and bumpy. Scott, bruised and shaken, began to wonder if the driver was deliberately aiming his van at every pothole, in revenge for being kicked. Only once had they passed another vehicle, a sudden increase of pressure from Hilary's hand, telling him she had noted it, too.

Inside his hood he found nothing except a place in which to learn about fear. Yet Scott had no interest in that particular lesson – surprised by his anger, which kept him focussed and listening out for sounds and clues. At least the voices of their captors were not those of the men in his motel room. Their accents had been the ugly nasal twang of the midlands, rough sounding, ideally suited to their calling with its callous and violent actions. These voices echoed with the soft burr that surrounded you wherever you walked in the small town.

He felt the van stop. Next second the door opened and a keen moorland wind, its edges tipped with ice, flooded in. Someone helped him sit up. Then he was on his feet and outside in the fresh air. He felt hands patting him down.

He heard the sound of heels scuffing against a metal floor. Automatically, he turned towards it, forgetting he could see nothing. 'Hilary? You okay?'

'Yeah, course.'

He heard her yell. 'Hey – that's mine.'

Then a second voice, its Scottish burr very evident. 'My, what have we got here?'

'I haven't seen one of those for ages,' the man holding Scott's elbow said.

'What is it, Hilary?' Scott shouted. He struggled trying to rid himself of his hood, frustrated that he couldn't see. '*What's going on?*'

'Calm down, lad, no one's going to hurt you. But we had to remove your girlfriend's weapon. American Secret Service issue, if I'm not mistaken. You going to tell us where you got it, lassie?'

'Go stuff yourself.'

The man holding Scott laughed. 'Suit yourself. There's some steps and we have to go down them. If you're sensible and give me your word you won't remove your hood, I'll release your arms – okay, lad?'

Scott nodded. Instantly, the strap pinning his arms was loosened and his hand placed on a sloping handrail. He felt for the edge of the step fumbling his way down. At the bottom he sensed warmth and light.

'Hoods off, we're there.'

The door closed. Scott tore his hood off, squinting painfully at the empty room, his body shuddering violently in reaction to the cold and hurt.

Hilary rubbed her eyes, blinking like an owl. 'At least it's not the same people,' she said, massaging her arms to restore their circulation.

'As Birmingham, I agree.' Scott took a wary step into the room. '*And* I don't think they're going to hurt us. But where are we?'

The room was bare and there were no windows, but you really wouldn't expect that, not if they were underground. White plaster dust had trickled down the wall, leaving soft mounds like ants' nests on the floor, where it had flaked away beneath the screws fixing the electric cables into the stonework. A couple of chairs nestled against a plain pine table, above them a single light bulb. Along one wall, a stone flight of steps, covered by a ramp, rose up towards a heavy door with iron hinges.

'I think we're in a castle,' he said, answering his own question.

They heard the click of a latch and the door at the top of the stairs opened. A wheel-chair appeared. Its occupant was an old man, his face a series of tram-lines radiating outwards, like the flight-path over Europe, with sparse white hair clinging to the back of his head. A bright plaid rug was draped over him from the waist down, concealing his legs.

'I apologise for your somewhat melodramatic invitation, I hope you have not taken hurt?' The voice was not Scottish, rather the plummy accent of a movie star straight out of a black and white film, so popular in the previous century.

'I could have done without the bruises,' Scott said, rubbing his arm where the strap had cut in.

Hilary pulled out a chair and sat down, carefully retying her pony tail. 'You could have simply asked us to visit you, like normal people,' she said, her voice quite calm.

'Indeed we could, except that I remain to be convinced that you are normal people. In Scotland, we are somewhat chary about handing our address to strangers; you never know who might come calling.'

The electric motor purred as the wheelchair negotiated the ramp. It stopped part way down, remaining slightly above the two teenagers and forcing them to look up at their captor. 'Your name, young lady?'

'My name's Hilary Stone and I work for the American Secret Service.'

'Is it my extreme antiquity or is authority becoming younger every day? What are you doing in England, never mind Scotland?'

'Trying to keep Scott safe, sir.'

'Scott, I presume, is the young man you are travelling with?'

'Hang on, Hilary!' Scott rounded angrily on the old man. 'Why should we answer your questions? How do we know you're not one of them?'

'My dear boy, my accent alone would fail me at the first interview,' the old man responded merrily. 'Something your partner in crime has doubtless recognised, which is why she is sensibly sharing information.'

'That true?'

'What do you think? We go into a shop and ask for James Nicely. Next thing we're being bundled into a van.' Hilary shrugged. 'I recognised the man from the shop – Sandy. I thought it odd at the time,' she continued eagerly, 'why he recommended that horrid fish and chip place, when there were three restaurants on the high street. In any case the van spent most of its time going round in circles.'

The old man laughed delightedly. 'And how did you reach such a fascinating conclusion?'

Hilary smiled at him. 'There was a waterfall. I heard it a second time and memorised that stretch of road. When I heard it a third time and felt the bumps,' she rubbed her haunches, 'I knew I was right. Except, right at the end, the van headed out on to the moor.'

The old man applauded the sound echoing round the empty room. 'Did you hear that, Sandy?' he called.

A head appeared at the top of the stairs. Scott recognised the man from the post office. 'I heard.'

'Your elaborate plan failed miserably and, to top it all, the young people had a most disgraceful dinner.'

The head nodded. 'I'll get tea,' it said and disappeared.

'Are you James Nicely?'

'And you are Sky Masterson.' The man smiled and, swivelling his chair in a tight circle, directed it back up the ramp.

'H … h …how do you know that?' Scott stuttered.

'You are so very like your mother. I think it might be appropriate, since we have now come to the conclusion we are on the same side, to relocate to somewhat more congenial surroundings. *Ah!* But I forgot.' The chair stopped. The old man directed his piercing glance at Hilary. 'There appears to be a problem with our friends in the American Secret Service. They have developed a nasty little habit of whispering secrets to the enemy, which might, in the present circumstances, be construed as somewhat dangerous.'

Hilary flushed. 'I know,' she said. 'Scott's not convinced, either.'

'Yes, I am,' he protested loyally.

'No, you're not. Whenever anything happens, the first thing you wonder, is it me?'

Scott stayed silent.

'And is it?' James Nicely's voice was stern.

'No!' Hilary shook her head, her pony tail flipping from side to side. 'Only problem is I could be the bad guy saying this. *Except I'm not*! But it's got me so freaked I daren't even contact my boss, in case it's him. *And we need him!* Scott and me, we're on our own and somewhere out there is a highly organised team of men, who are somehow connected to government. They've got Scott's dad – now they want him. And you've got my gun.'

'Your gun will be restored to you when you leave, since I have no doubt you are most capable of handling it.' The chair headed out through the door at the top of the stairs.

'*He believed you!*'

Hilary laughed at the expression of bewilderment on Scott's face. 'It would be nice if you did,' she said. 'Let's go and find out how he knew your mother.'

The fire gleamed: glowing wells of heat burst into flame, pushing out clouds of peat-scented smoke. Tapestries of long-forgotten battles hung from the heavy stone walls, their muted colours a testament to youth and movement; while thick brocade curtains, suspended from black iron rods, had been strung across the top of the windows to keep out the bitter night air. A semicircle of deep armchairs and sofas snuggled round the fire, creating a sheltered, almost cosy atmosphere; a pathway left clear for the wheelchair to make its way unhindered to its accustomed place on the left side of the fireplace – a pair of spectacles, lodged in an open book, on a small table nearby.

The stories had been thrashed out, the elegant tones of James Nicely's voice belying an eager and warm nature that invited confidences. Here Scott felt comfortable – secure – the anxieties of the past few days wiped out.

Sandy came in with a fresh pot of tea and scones still warm

from the oven. Scott felt reluctant to move, as if movement itself would create new problems. Idly, he glanced down at his watch. It was after twelve. Who on earth baked scones that late? Whoever it was they were extremely welcome, since he felt both hungry and thirsty after talking non-stop for twenty minutes. He'd gone over everything that had happened up to that point, confident enough, in this nucleus of safety, to allow frightening incidents to take on the hue of a tale related simply for entertainment; everything, that is, except for the earthquake and how his mother had been caught up in it. That remained the stuff of nightmares.

'She was my brightest pupil.'

The old man had ignored the offer of tea, raising his eyebrows at Sandy and nodding as he was shown a whisky bottle.

'I was lecturing at Cambridge when your mother arrived to take her doctorate,' he said. 'That's where she became interested in viruses. The British refused funding so the Americans switched the entire operation to California. I went too. She met your father there.' James Nicely beamed at Scott.

'The project was named Styrus. There were nine of us plus ancillary staff, for inputting data. We had almost cracked it. Naively the Americans, instead of keeping it under wraps, began boasting of its power and erroneously it assumed the mantle of a threat to global stability. Have you heard of Star Wars?'

Hilary said, 'I have.'

'Then you will have read how foolishly the Americans acted, putting their own interests before their allies, provoking the Russians into resuming the Cold War.'

'I'm an American,' she protested.

Scott listened intently, understanding the words but somehow unable to relate them either to him or his father, as if the old man was reading a story from a book.

'So you are, Hilary, but I trust you belong to the fifty percent that make up the enlightened section.' James Nicely tilted his glass to the light, its contents the colour of amber, and took a sip.

'They appreciate that foreign policy will forever be the undoing of their country.'

'And then?'

'The World Symposium appeared. It was heralded as the greatest event of the millennium, a unique opportunity to promote world-understanding. Naturally scientists flocked to be part of it. At the very last second two members of our team were called away.' He tilted his glass towards Scott. 'Your father and David Runyon.' He smiled cheerfully, as though he was recounting an amusing anecdote, not a story of murder, told in the middle of the night to a captive audience. '*Tragic*, we branded their absence at the time, to miss an event of such magnitude taking place on our doorstep.

'Prime speeches always took place after dinner – and it was a little after nine when more than a thousand of us eagerly filed into the auditorium. The second night in, men with machine guns appeared.'

The old man glanced at Hilary. 'You will doubtless ask why a thousand people could not rush the gunmen. It is quite simple, if you are seated in rows one person can move at a time. It was tried. The men died instantly.

'Names were called, serious names, leading experts in fields relating to both software and hardware development. We were led out of the auditorium towards parkland, where helicopters were waiting.'

The old man paused, sipping at the amber liquid in his glass. 'I think it strange, even today, but it was as if some supernatural force intervened. I simply cannot explain it any other way. It was as if the realisation that they weren't planning to kill us struck everyone at the same time and the entire group stopped and ran back into the building.'

James Nicely closed his eyes picturing the event. 'At that precise second …' Putting down his glass, he raised both hands, the first finger and thumb circling one another, as if to emphasise the point. 'At that moment,' he repeated, 'we heard a vast explosion and the buildings began to rock.'

As if it had been waiting, holding back until the exact second, the clock in the corner had chimed midnight; the sound lifting Scott and Hilary out of their seats in fright, flinching round to see what had caused it, only the old man remaining unmoved.

He laughed. 'I apologise for the melodrama, it was unintentional I assure you.'

Right after that Scott began to shiver uncontrollably, his imagination filling in the gaps that James Nicely had left out. A vast explosion destroying the lives of a thousand human beings; chaos with people fighting to get back to the auditorium to see what had happened to their friends; others fleeing, trying to escape, his mother among them. The sound of a machine gun reverberated through his head. He clenched his jaw, his teeth chattering as he watched the bodies tumbling through the air to lie still on the ground.

'It was chaos. Unintended, but chaos nevertheless. Looking back, dinner had taken longer than anticipated and we were fifteen minutes late going into the auditorium. Perhaps that was all it took. The men, instructed to take us to safety, lost control and opened fire; hoping, without doubt, to restore their authority. Charlie died instantly and I was left for dead. Your mother ...'

James Nicely gave the faintest of shrugs; Scott's imagination accompanying the fleeing figure of his mother seeking a way out where none existed, experiencing the panic of the noise and vibration, the dust clouds and the screaming.

From a distance he heard the calm tones of the old man bringing his story to an end. 'Fortunately for me, I was found before the tsunami and airlifted to hospital. First the earthquake concealed; then the water washed away all evidence of a crime. But I believe, and have always believed, that the earthquake was triggered to cover up the massacre of the scientists,' he finished sadly.

'But the Americans didn't do it,' Hilary burst out.

James Nicely smiled: 'No one in their right mind believes they did.'

That was when Sandy had come in with fresh tea and scones. 'So how did my father find you?'

'It was almost four years later. David Runyon advertised through the Internet. Years before, when we first met up, the nine of us, somewhat frivolously, had assumed pseudonyms from the musical *Guys and Dolls*. If I remember correctly, it was your father's idea. He had an excellent voice and, with a name like Masterson and your mother called Sarah – and, of course, David Runyon – it was the obvious choice. We were young and there was much fun to be had. We worked hard and we played hard.

'My name was originally Neuburg. My family came from Germany, and I sang baritone. The character, Nicely Nicely, appeared a most natural one considering my shape.' The old man smiled. 'I had a tendency towards corpulence in middle age,' he explained. 'I changed my name for real after I came to Scotland. We survivors followed the clues – rather as you appear to have done, young man. David, knowing the dangers we might still face, insisted we no longer worked together but separately, connected only by mobile phones.' He paused, shaking his head sadly. 'So many precautions – none of which we ever thought we'd need. Your father devised a piece of computer software, as an alarm system – and, thank God, he did. David's best friend, who lived in the flat below, worked for Reuters. He promised to print an obituary, if anything happened to David.'

'And you never met?' Hilary said.

'Once, not long after we linked up. A celebration of life, for those of us still living. To decide what had to be done, obviously. Who wanted out? Finance?'

The man in the wheelchair waved an arm nonchalantly around the walls. 'Finance was no problem. I had money. Who was to continue?' He looked over at Scott. 'Your father was determined the project should be completed as a fitting memorial to those who had died. Although from time to time it was a sombre meeting, it was also a noisy one. Disguised as fishermen, rather raucous fishermen, if I remember correctly, I am certain our late-night merrymaking was remembered long after we left.

'I may have given you the impression, Hilary, that no one believed the US behind the disaster. That is not quite correct. At that point we had no idea what to believe. The entire world was busily denying they had anything to do with it, whilst accusing the US – in reality the most likely culprit. But, as in all good detective fiction, rarely do the most obvious suspects commit the dastardly deed.'

James Nicely broke the tension with a small laugh.

'And so it was here,' he continued. 'As the dust began to settle, we pooled knowledge of the sequence of events of that night. It became apparent that the US, however naïve, had to be innocent. Syd, who had the dubious honour of being nick-named Nathan Detroit, got away, as did David Hart – who we called Dave the Dude. Harry Bentley, alias Harry the Horse because he mirrored the character from the play, a gambler who'd bet on anything with four legs – no trace of him was ever found. Big Jule and Good time Charley were also killed trying to escape – and now your father has been captured,' he ended sadly.

'Can you help me find him?'

'I can do better than that, young man. He's in Lisse – in Holland. And already friends are heading for the town.'

'But who's behind it?' Hilary asked.

James Nicely gazed at the boy slumped on the sofa, obviously exhausted.

'That must wait for another day, young lady. I will get Chris to drive you back to the hostel. In the morning, I suggest you collect your things and come back here. You will be safe and there is still much to talk about. If we say eleven o'clock? Make your way to Balloch; I'll have Chris pick you up in the van. Meanwhile, you have a key for your lodgings?'

'Yes, but I need to contact my people in America and tell them what's happened.'

'Perhaps we can discuss that tomorrow. There's someone I'd

like Scott to meet first.' He spoke directly to Hilary, guessing that Scott could no longer absorb information let alone process it. 'I know Scott is determined to rescue his father but you have to convince him to leave that to us.'

'Why?' said Scott, unexpectedly tuning in to the conversation.

'If they get you, Scott, the entire project is put in danger and all those deaths will have been in vain.'

'I don't care about the project.'

'Scott, what Mr Nicely means, if you get captured your father will have to work for them to keep you alive,' Hilary said, her face screwed up as if she was saying sorry.

Scott was finding it difficult to think – everything so jumbled up. 'But I have to get him out. He'd do that for me,' he managed. 'Did you say that you had people already searching for him?'

'Private people – monarchists. You won't have heard of them.'

'Yes, I have. Dad told me about the rallies happening across Europe he said it was … it was …' He felt the words slip away and he shook his head to clear it. 'Growing.' It wasn't exactly the word his dad had used but it would have to do.

'Go and sleep. Tomorrow you can meet this person. After that, if you are still determined to seek your father, I will take you to the monarchists.'

'Okay,' Scott said. 'I'm dead beat and I know Hilary is. One night won't make any difference.'

NINETEEN

Scott felt something tugging at his arm, making him run, except his feet felt heavy like lead. He woke up with a start to find Hilary shaking him. 'What?'

'There's a man downstairs asking questions.'

Scott leapt out of bed, the words: *what are you doing in the boys' dormitory* frozen on his lips. He thrust his legs into his jeans. He didn't ask *good or bad!* Hilary wouldn't have come bursting in for the postman. 'How do you know?'

'I'd gone down to breakfast. He was asking the manager about accommodation,' the girl gasped, her breath coming in fits and starts from her manic dash up two flights of stairs. 'And did he get many guests? Said they were looking for a boy on a bike. Missing from home, he said. Hurry up!'

'I'm hurrying,' Scott pulled on his T-shirt and made a dive for the bathroom. 'I need the loo – man or no man. Don't go away.' Carelessly, he sloshed water over his face to wake him up and, grabbing his toothbrush, stuffed it in his pocket. 'Which way?'

'Fire Escape. Don't forget your helmet!'

The sash window slid silently open. They climbed out, their trainers making no noise on the metal treads.

'Will he tell, do you think?'

'You'd better hope not.' Hilary darted a quick glance over her shoulder. 'People round here don't like strangers asking questions, Mr Nicely made that quite clear. Said it had taken him ten years to fit in – but our hostel receptionist? I'm sure he wasn't police though. Shush!'

Hilary stepped carefully round the flowerpots decorating the bottom steps of the fire escape and padded softly along the terrace. She viewed the area in front of them with its paths circling round a neatly tended vegetable garden, its rows of seedlings standing out against the dark earth like a regiment of soldiers. Beyond it, nestling crookedly in the wall, was the door to the garage, fifty metres away.

'Not that way,' said Scott, reading her thoughts. 'You can see the door through the windows in Reception. If we can reach the lane without being seen, we can use that entrance.'

'But, we'll be spotted on the front drive,' Hilary argued, her face white and worried-looking.

Behind them a terraced area fell away, to be replaced by square beds full of roses that had recently been pruned, their red buds beginning to burst into tightly-curled leaves. Beyond that, a wide expanse of lawn dissolved into a thickly-wooded coppice of pine trees.

Through their lower branches Scott caught a glimpse of water. 'Come on.'

Grabbing Hilary's hand he ran hard across the lawn, willing himself not to glance round to see if they'd been spotted. The conifers swallowed them up. Scott dropped to the ground, pulling Hilary down with him. Crawling on his hands and knees, he worked his way back to the edge of the trees, a deep carpet of soft pine needles clinging to his jeans. The tall granite building appeared deserted.

'What now?' Hilary swallowed hard, still puffing from their mad dash across the lawn.

'We can get to the loch through these trees and then straight back up the lane. Come on.'

Hilary pulled at Scott's jacket and grabbed his hand, holding it tightly. *So how did they find us this time?* Her voice sounded frightened, its confident tone missing.

Scott bit his lip. They were tired, both of them. Besides it wasn't fair on Hilary. At the beginning she had played it like a game, to get the better of her boss and one up on the bad guys.

Now, she was exhausted and the chase had begun to resemble a long journey into hopelessness. Tiredness did that to you. His dad had told him that. 'When you're tired, Scott, a big, black boulder, almost too heavy to bear, appears on your back. Get some sleep; it's surprising how light that boulder becomes after a good night's rest.' Scott checked his watch. They'd only had four hours. No wonder Hilary was upset.

'I don't know how they got here,' he re-assured her, 'but it wasn't ...'

'I checked the bike,' Hilary broke in, 'when I removed my bug. It was clean, I promise you, so how did they find us so quickly? There are no towers and your specs are miles away. So that leaves ...'

'James Nicely.' Scott finished for her. 'But it wasn't him and it wasn't *you*,' he insisted, looking her full in the face. 'I don't know who it was, but somehow we are going to get out of here.'

'And go where?'

The second-floor window opened and a man's head appeared.

'Anywhere but here!' he shouted. 'Run!'

The carpet of pine needles absorbed the sound of their racing feet, their jackets unfastened and flying open. Their helmets, clutched in their hands, swung wildly as they wove through the pole-like trunks of the pine trees, the glimmer of water expanding as they ran towards it. They jumped the ditch on to the lane and stopped.

It was peaceful, no different from the day before. Scott glanced at Hilary knowing she felt like him, an overwhelming desire to keep on going, yet keenly aware that flying feet on a country lane, more used to the strolling feet of tourists, would invite comment.

Slowing their pace, they set off up the lane with Hilary heroically playing the part of an eager tourist, gazing in rapture at polished windows and neatly-dug gardens. But Scott knew she wasn't seeing them.

He studied her face, noticing the tension in it, aware of the effort she was putting into keeping her steps slow and leisurely. *Hilary was really scared*. The thought shocked him. For the first time her air of confidence had deserted her and she was looking to him for answers. And, right now, he knew exactly what she was seeing – the same as him – the man at the window, gun in hand, tearing down the fire escape to pursue them through the wood.

They rounded the bend. On the far side of the tall wall was the garden through which, moments before, they had fled for their lives and, beyond that, not fifty metres away, the hostel with its intruder asking questions and demanding answers. Just visible, behind the broken brickwork of the wall and half that distance again – sanctuary – the heavy wooden doors of the garage, its sun-blasted green paint peeling off in long wispy curls.

Scott hesitated, his foot poised to take the next step. He put out his hand to stop Hilary going further and touched the snub nose of the Colt in her hand.

'I'll check,' she said grimly.

'No!' Unexpectedly, a feeling of light-heartedness overtook him and he broke into a jog. 'Same format as before. You shoot – I'll steer.' He pulled open the garage door, confidence powering through him at the sight of the Suzuki. It felt like coming home. He was already wearing his leather jacket, reluctant to be parted from it in the keen Scottish air. Quickly strapping on his helmet, he pulled the keys from his pocket, feeling safe again. 'We have to see Mr Nicely. He's the key to all this I know. Besides we'll be safe there.' He shifted sideways on, speaking confidently. 'If we couldn't find his house without a guide, *neither can anyone else*; so we make our way to Balloch as planned.'

'No! We need the police,' Hilary said, climbing up behind him.

'And say what? And what happens if they're in on it?'

'I don't think they are, Scott. At least you'd be safe.'

'You've changed your tune,' he shouted angrily, his feeling of euphoria vanished. 'In any case, I doubt if they'd listen, even to me our story sounds crazy.' He waited a moment for Hilary to come up with some argument but she remained silent. 'Nothing's changed, unless you know something I don't.'

He felt Hilary flinch as if he'd hit her. 'Oh for pity's sake, Scott,' she snapped. 'And I still think you should go to the police.'

'No, I'm going to keep that appointment.' The Suzuki roared into life. 'You don't have to come, Hilary. The offer still stands. I'll drop you at the bus stop.'

'Yes, I do.' she growled sullenly. 'It's my job, remember.'

Two seconds later the narrow alleys of Arden had been left behind. In a blur of speed, the bike headed south, a streak of red surrounded on both sides by the menacing darkness of the hills overlooking the loch.

TWENTY

How the hell did they find us this time? The thought pursued Scott relentlessly, his mind replaying the events of the past two days over and over, hardly noticing his surroundings except as a check they were heading in the right direction.

He braked sharply, almost cannoning into a sheep nibbling the grass at the side of the road, a gap in the dry-stone walling creating an avenue of escape from the arid moorland. Up ahead, half a dozen animals milled about, searching for fresh green stems.

Hilary didn't speak, not even bothering to reprimand him for riding so fast, her face buried between his shoulder-blades; the wind piercing even with a helmet. Scott set the bike in motion again, slowly manoeuvring round the four-legged obstacles, before opening the throttle.

Eventually the wall, that had run beside them all the way from the village of Arden, fizzled out and was replaced by tiers of terraced cottages; lines of washing flapping in their windswept gardens. Scott slowed to thirty as he spotted the fuel station, the sole tenant of a patch of scrubby wasteland, exactly as Chris had described it.

'Can't miss it,' he smiled cheerfully at Hilary. 'And it's part way.'

In his late forties, almost bald with thick lenses, there was nothing memorable about him except his continued cheerfulness, despite a series of vivid-looking bruises on his shins, and his genuine astonishment that a young person, *"and a lassie at that"*, had worked out they were driving round in circles.

The fuel station was busy, but they saw no sign of Chris or his van among the patrons using the pumps.

'We're way too early,' Scott said, the dial of his watch pointing just past ten. He shook it, hoping it had stopped. 'What time do you make it?' He removed his helmet.

'Ten-fifteen. We'd better wait.'

'Not here, it's too visible. Anyone could see us.'

'But they couldn't get at us,' Hilary insisted, staring round at a dozen people busily filling up their vehicles. As she spoke, a police car drove on to the forecourt and parked by the flower stall, its driver putting on his cap before heading purposefully into the mini-mart.

Scott eyed him nervously, aware he couldn't afford an inspection of his driving licence. 'I'd rather wait somewhere else, if you don't mind. Besides I need something to eat, I can't think straight till I've had breakfast.' He tried to make his voice sound upbeat, hoping for Hilary's flashing smile to come back at him.

'I'm staying here,' she said, not meeting his eyes, her voice monotone. 'You can go if you want.'

'That's okay. We'll stay together. I'll eat later. But I'd better get the bike out of sight.'

Hilary shrugged and climbed off. Huddled in her padded jacket, she walked across the forecourt and sat down on the low wall next to the road, as if she had withdrawn from knowing him. Scott couldn't blame her. From the moment they had met in the motel in Birmingham they'd been running. Then, all of sudden, a lifeline had been thrown. Mr Nicely with his tea and scones, firelight glinting on his glass of whisky, had made the nightmare recede. That is, until the face had appeared at the hostel window.

Scott flicked a glance at the scudding grey clouds. A cup of tea would really have hit the spot right now, particularly after being hauled out of bed and chased halfway round Scotland. He shivered, feeling the cold even through his leathers. Pushing the bike out of sight behind the car wash, he crossed the road heading for an outlet selling second-hand cars, leaving Hilary to wait alone.

'I told you he wouldn't come.'

Scott jumped. For the past half-hour he'd been trying not to watch the road and hadn't noticed Hilary leave her post. He ran his fingers lightly over the gleaming chrome on the vehicle next to him; strings of brightly coloured streamers, designed to focus the attention of passing traffic on the elegant models for sale, fluttering in the breeze above his head.

'You okay?' he said, his insides churning miserably with hunger and disappointment.

'No, I'm not,' the girl snapped, glaring at Scott as if he was a piece of dirt that had stuck to her shoe. 'I told you to go to the police. I just knew they wouldn't come. And there's nowhere to go from here. It's a dead end.'

Scott flushed red at the put down; overcome by a feeling of abandonment, like a speck of flotsam trying to link up with another speck and being repulsed at every turn. He knew nothing about girls and their moods. How could he having never had a sister? All of a sudden Hilary had changed and he didn't have a clue why. He'd done something to upset her – that much was obvious – but what? He felt furiously angry with himself, tears of frustration not far from the surface. He had become used to her cheerfulness and, stupidly, even begun to like her bossy attitude. If only girls were like boys, and could come out with what was bothering them, life would be that much simpler. Of course she felt tired and defeated – he did, too. But she could have said, not leave him to think she hated him.

'I'm going to phone the post office.' He pointed to the garage. 'They'll have a directory.'

'It won't do any good; *they're not coming*, I tell you.'

Ignoring her, he ran back across the road and into the shop, where the shop assistant obligingly scribbled the number on a piece of paper for him.

The connection clicked in and Scott heard the brisk voice of the post mistress.

'Arden Post Office, may I help?'

'Can I talk to Sandy? I'm a friend. We spent the evening together.'

'In Balloch was it, then you'll won't be knowing what's happened?'

'Er … yes. Balloch, that's right. Um … what do you mean?' He screwed up his face at Hilary, who was standing two paces away, her expression impatient. 'Has something happened to him?'

'Aye, in a manner of speaking. He was asleep in his bed when burglars broke in. I don't know the details but he was shot!'

'*Shot!* No, I don't believe it!'

Hilary grabbed the handset. Angrily, he wrestled it out of her grasp. '*Wait!*' he hissed, covering the mouthpiece with his hand.

'*Who's been shot?*' she demanded, trying to listen.

He waved his free hand to stop her talking. '*Shush!*'

'As well you might sound surprised,' came the lilting voice over the wire. 'I certainly was; I found the police waiting on my doorstep when I arrived for work. They said they couldn't believe it either; a remote farmhouse on the moor – robbed.' Scott heard her sniff. 'They airlifted him to Glasgow,' the postmistress said, her voice unsteady.

'But he *is* going to be all right, isn't he?'

'They don't know yet. The bullet entered a lung. They said they'd phone when they had some news.'

'What about the others?' Scott said, 'the other people in the house?'

'What other people? He lives alone with his mother. She phoned the police … would you hold a moment?' The voice at the other end of the line abruptly changed tone. 'Good morning, sir. What can I do for you?'

Scott heard muttering in the background and pressed his ear into the handset, hoping to eavesdrop on the conversation. The post mistress's voice sounded loud in his ear.

'Mr Nicely? How strange! You're the second set of people that have asked for him in two days. As I told the other people – he died, you know.'

Scott listened, riveted to the phone.

He heard more muttering, then, 'No, sir, I'd forgotten that notice was even there. He died years ago – ask anyone in town. Nice old gentleman, he was too. Ran this shop ... ooohf ... nigh on twenty years. A chain store bought it. I work for them now. Sorry I can't help. Good day to you.'

Silence fell. Scott closed his eyes imagining feet crossing the floor towards the door. He heard the door close, its movement stirring the bell into life, and let go the breath he'd been holding.

The voice sounded again in his ear. 'Is there anything else, sir?' The postmistress said. 'Can I take a message?'

'No, no message. Just tell him to get better quick.' He clicked the end switch on his mobile. 'They've got Mr Nicely,' he said, his face grey.

'You can't know that!' Hilary yelled and punched him hard in the chest.

Scott's mouth dropped open in surprise. He rubbed the spot where she'd hit him, adding lamely, 'But Sandy was shot; and Sandy was guarding him.'

'When – *when* was he shot?' she demanded.

'Does it matter?'

Hilary glared. 'Of course it matters; *when* was he shot?'

'She didn't say, sometime in the night after we left,' he said in a sulky voice.

'Scott, *tell* me exactly.'

Impatiently, Scott repeated the words parrot-fashion. 'Sandy was shot and his mother phoned for the police. Then, while I was talking to the post lady, some men came into the shop. I couldn't hear what they were saying but they asked for Mr Nicely. She said he was dead.'

Hilary grabbed his arm and bounced it up and down. 'That's okay then!'

Her eyes blazed at him, her expression fierce. 'Don't you get it? They haven't got Mr Nicely because they were *asking* for him!'

Scott stared at the face full of energy, unable to believe what he was seeing. This was Hilary at her best. *But what had happened to carry her off like that and what had brought her back?* He could feel the confusion in his head, like a hive of angry wasps, questions buzzing round and round without means of escape.

'And she said he'd been dead for years,' Scott said hope lighting up his eyes. 'Right! Let's get going.'

'But where?' Hilary said.

'I don't know yet. But as far away from here as possible,' Scott repeated.

Hope was brief, despair taking over as the full understanding of the situation struck Scott. The Suzuki growled contentedly, eating up the miles, the bike once again heading towards Glasgow; except this time it was powering south towards the borders with England – not travelling north. Scott wondered how long it would be before Hilary also realised that *they* had led the men to Mr Nicely's door. *But how?* As Hilary had said before – no towers and no glasses.

Abruptly, he pulled the Suzuki to a halt. Behind them stretched miles of road like a long piece of string, the high, barren moorland melting into the horizon; its windswept outcrops of spiky heather home to birds and sheep. Anyone pursuing them would be visible from miles away. He studied the car cruising towards him. But how would they know who that was? And would there be one man or several? The car swept past full of eager tourists, presumably gossiping about the wonders of Loch Lomond. He looked round as another car approached, travelling north, its occupants eagerly anticipating those same wonders. Impatiently, he pulled off his gloves, tugging at his helmet.

'Why have we stopped?' Hilary called over his shoulder.

'Because!'

Puzzled, Hilary climbed down. She wrapped her arms round her, shivering. 'Because what?'

Ignoring her, Scott pulled the bike back on to its stand and climbed off. 'It's not the bike,' he muttered and, pulling off his jacket, undid the button on his jeans. Remembering the cuffs were too tight to go over his trainers he yanked them off, not bothering to untie the laces first.

Hilary gazed at him, stunned into silence. 'What are you doing?' she squeaked, as his second shoe hit the ground.

'Stripping, what does it look like?'

'*But we're on a main road*!'

A car passed them. Its horn blared appreciatively and heads leered out of the window.

'I don't care if we're on the blasted motorway,' Scott swore, pulling the legs of his jeans inside out. 'There's a bug somewhere on me and I'm going to find it.' He laughed as the absurdity of the situation struck him. Another car passed to the accompaniment of wolf whistles.

'Don't worry,' he grinned at Hilary. 'It's not in my underwear. They're new, remember, so's my T-shirt. You've got Dad's jacket. Start with that. I'll do my sweater and jeans.'

'I checked the jacket before, Scott, there was nothing, but I'll do it again, if you want.'

A stream of interested motorists passed; most of the cars slowing right down to gawp more closely at the youth wearing only his shirt, briefs and socks, while his companion, although fully dressed, was also coatless. This was eccentricity carried way too far, a keen wind off the moors keeping their car heaters at full blast.

'There's got to be something,' Scott insisted. 'Here, check my jeans.' He tossed them across. 'I can't find anything but you have to know what we're looking for better than me. *There's got to be something*,' he repeated. 'We got rid of Dad's specs – so how do they keep finding us?'

He got to his feet staring at his clothes on the ground; his legs naturally tanned rapidly taking on a bluish tinge. 'It's not my leathers, we've checked my jeans, nothing in my sweater,' he said. He picked up each item of clothing, examining it closely before dropping it back down on the ground.

They heard a sudden squeal of brakes and a horn blasted out. Hilary swung round to see what was happening. 'You'd better get your clothes back on fast before we cause an accident,' she giggled. 'That car almost tailgated the one in front, they were that interested.'

Scott grabbed his jeans, thrusting one leg into them. 'Check my trainers will you?'

Hilary picked up the left shoe. *'Oh no!'* she gasped.

'What?' Scott impatiently zipped up his jeans.

'I feel sick!' Hilary pointed to a piece of gravel buried between the ridges in the sole of the trainer.

'Hilary, *it's a piece of gravel*, okay. They get stuck between the ridges.'

The girl shook her head slowly. 'No, it's a bug.' Her voice sounded flat and, to Scott's amazement, she burst into tears.

Scott squatted down and awkwardly put his arm round her. 'But why are you crying? If it really is a bug, that's good, isn't it? At least we know how they found us – it wasn't the towers – it wasn't the government – it …'

Hilary knocked his arm away. *'Good!* How wrong can you get, Scott! This bug is designed to come on line with movement – you know walking and such – which explains why we managed to keep ahead of them.' Hilary gazed wildly down the road as if expecting their enemy to appear round the bend at any second. 'But it doesn't change anything. Number plate recognition still located us and that means either the government is involved, or there's someone in their computer centre passing on information.' She shrugged. 'Take your pick.'

She took a hairclip trying to hook out the small plastic-pebble. It didn't move. 'That's confirms it's a bug,' she said. 'This has been stuck in, anything else would fly out.' She searched for a piece of stick, viciously digging into the rubber tread. The grey circular object shot into the air and disappeared among the shards of glass and fine stone at the side of the road.

Scott peered at the mound of dust. 'Well, we'll never find that again.' He sat down, carefully inspecting his trainers before putting them on again. 'We'd better get going before they do get here. Oh come on, Hilary, look on the bright side,' he tried to quip. 'We can actually get lost now and no one will ever find us.'

Hilary wiped her wet cheeks with the palm of her hand and picking up her jacket, cuddled herself into it. 'Thanks.' She smiled briefly.

'For what?' Scott asked.

'For not getting on your bike and leaving me here.' Hilary's blue eyes gazed directly into his. 'Sorry about before, we're in enough of a mess, without me taking it out on you.'

Scott watched the precise way she turned towards the wind, carefully smoothing her hair before retying her pony tail, and smiled happily. The cool was firmly back in place. She was in control again.

'I was so looking forward to this being over, you've no idea.'

Scott quickly put on his jacket and zipped it up. 'Yes, I have,' he admitted. 'I want it to be over just as much as you.' He took out his phone.

'Who are you calling?'

'Travers. I don't know why I never thought of him before. Great guy in an emergency.' His thoughts flew back to the cottage, where his overriding emotion had been to find his father. And he had, he thought – well almost. The engaged tone rang out. 'Look, knowing Travers he's likely to be on a while and I'm freezing after that strip search. We'll lose ourselves in Glasgow and get some lunch. Then we'll try him again.'

TWENTY-ONE

It was ridiculous how easily everything slipped into place, as if the mention of his friend's name had instantly smoothed out the many difficulties that still stood in their way.

Remembering the black towers that held the city so tightly in their grip, Scott left his bike parked at a commuter station where it would be safe, boarding a local train that would take them into the heart of Glasgow. A few minutes walk had brought them into an area thronging with art students and coffee shops, the gaunt outline of Glasgow's famous art college casting its avuncular eye over the busy scene.

Despite knowing they were safe, Scott found it impossible to relax; the question he couldn't keep away from, that clutched his head in its vice-like grip – how did that bug get on his trainers?

Travers, on the other hand, had been the personification of calm. His greeting: *having fun tiptoeing through the tulips,* flew straight over Scott's head when finally, after a series of coffees and two tortilla wraps, they managed to contact him.

'I've been trying to get you for hours,' Scott said indignantly. 'Don't you ever do anything but talk on the phone?'

Travers chuckled. 'Mary does the talking, I add an occasional, *yes, no or that's exciting.* So what's up?'

'What did you mean – *tulips?*' Scott said, picking up on his friend's opening gambit.

'Aren't you at the Keukenhof with your dad? You said you were going.'

'You must be psychic,' Scott muttered. 'That's why I'm calling. I need to get to Holland. Hilary's with me.'

'*Well, I never!*' Travers let out a whistle of astonishment. 'Thought you and she hated one another.'

'We do – well, we don't. *Well, not any more,*' Scott's voice sounded exasperated.

'What's he saying?' Hilary whispered.

'Wait!' he hissed. 'Attend, Travers, this is serious. I'm in real trouble. I have to get to Holland and I've never been there. How do I do that?'

'You catch a ferry from Harwich.'

'I don't even know where that is.'

'On the east coast somewhere. Look, where are you calling from?'

'Glasgow. I've got Dad's bike.'

'*Wow!* Scotland's obviously the *in* place right now. Dad flew up there last night for an urgent meeting. Mum's that mad about it. They've got a party today and he's left her to deal with it on her own. Hang on a minute, I've got a brainwave. Beau's down.'

'Down?'

'From Oxford, you wally, got in half an hour ago. I'd lay you any odds he's off to the mainland for the weekend and has stopped in here en route.'

Covering the mouthpiece, Scott whispered to Hilary, 'Travers's brother, Beau, he flies everywhere. He might take us. You think he'll give us a lift?' he asked his friend.

'Don't see why not. You know Beau, anything for a lark. It'll probably cost me lunch in Paris though and it'll send Mum spare with Dad away. Still Beau won't care. I'll ring you back when I've asked him.'

Scott said into the handset. 'Can you bring me some money, too?' His words were greeted by silence at the other end of the phone. 'Travers? You there?'

Travers's voice sounded again. 'Look here, Scott, I know I'm pretty thick but you have to be in some real-serious bother if you are *a*: six hundred miles from home; *b*: have your dad's bike, which is illegal if you're not sixteen, like you; *c*: have no money and *d*: have a girl with you and *e*: sound devilish worried.'

Scott laughed. 'I am, but I promise you it's not what you're thinking. I haven't run off to Gretna Green with Hilary. But if I tell you, you've got to swear not to tell a soul – not your parents – Beau – nobody.'

Travers grunted.

'My dad's been kidnapped. I think he's in Lisse in Holland. Hilary's helping – actually she saved my life – but that's another story.'

A long whistle sounded. '*Brilliant*! Now pull the other one.'

Hilary grabbed the phone, her tone fierce. 'Travers? Look, Scott is telling you the sanitised version. I work for the American Secret Service and Scott's in real danger. *Now* will you help?'

'*What did you do that for*?' Scott yelled. 'It's so far-fetched he'll never believe a story like that in a million years.' He took the phone back. 'Travers, you still there?'

Travers lazy tones for once sounded serious, as they did when his side was behind on points in a rugby match. 'Scott, I don't know what's going on but something must be. Stay right there. I'll track Beau down and ring you back.'

Scott snatched up the phone as it rang out, anxious not to disturb Hilary who, exhausted, was using the table for a pillow, her head resting on her arms.

'Beau says he can pick you up at Prestwick about ten in the morning,'

'Not to-day?' said Scott, his voice cracking with tiredness.

'No can do,' Travers chuckled, the deep sound resonating through the mobile. 'Mum would excommunicate us but she agreed on tomorrow. Beau will drop you off on his way to Belgium.'

There'd been more but Scott had blanked that out – a day's delay – would his dad even be alive by then? 'Where's Prestwick?' he said, interrupting the chatty monologue.

'I asked Beau that. He says from our house it's straight up and on the left.'

'Thanks, Travers.'

'Haven't done anything yet. But your story had better be a real blockbuster.'

More like the stuff of nightmares, Scott thought as he clicked the phone off.

Hilary blinked and sat up. 'I was asleep,' she admitted.

'Doesn't matter, it's all sorted,' Scott smiled at her. 'Now all we need do is sleep – if that's okay with you.'

Hilary shook her head at him. 'First, I've got to find out about Sandy.'

That had started another argument though one Scott was happy to lose; insisting that trying to locate a patient in hospital, without knowing their surname, was impossible: 'like looking for a needle in a haystack,' he argued.

Ignoring his objections, Hilary continued to phone round the hospitals. Ten minutes later, beaming with triumph, she informed Scott that there had actually only been one gun-shot patient admitted the night before. *And yes, his name was Sandy.* The starchy nurse at the other end of the phone, on learning they weren't relatives only concerned friends, had relented long enough to admit that her patient was out of danger and well on the road to recovery.

It was a small success, but it brought with it the feeling that perhaps the tide had turned and, at long last, things might go their way.

Beau, as his brother had predicted, had not been the slightest bit put out by being asked to fly four-hundred miles north, before changing direction and flying south-east across the North Sea. Nor had he turned a hair when Travers and Mary elected to go with him, and the twin-engined Cessna, a present from his parents on his eighteenth birthday, had been early.

Out of breath, after a frustrating chase round and round the airport trying to locate the right building, Scott and Hilary fell through the terminal doors in time to see their friends push open the swing doors at the far end, having left the aircraft in its parking bay twenty metres or so from the building.

'We got lost,' Scott exclaimed.

Hilary rushed over to give Mary a hug.

'I've raided both our wardrobes,' Mary called out. 'Bless Travers, love him to bits and all that, but I knew he'd never think of clothes.'

Beau, the middle one of the three Randals, their elder sister at modelling school in London, had always been Scott's absolute hero, ever since his first day at secondary school, when his friend's brother had been chosen to speak in assembly, to welcome the new intake from the local primary. Now, piloting his own plane made him even more awesome.

Scott smiled shyly at him, venturing, 'We nearly ended up in Ireland,' to excuse their precipitate arrival.

'You'd be amazed at the places I've ended up,' Beau said, the sarcastic ring to his voice at odds with his casual air. It reminded Scott of the day he'd been hauled up in front of him, knees quivering, for dropping an easy catch. Tall like his father, Beau possessed the fine bones of his mother, his face attractively ugly where a broken nose and jaw had destroyed its symmetry; Travers openly boasting that his brother had been earmarked for fly-half in the England squad, before a skiing accident had scuppered his chances. 'And he'd have been pretty magical too,' he told his friends.

'One time I was listening so hard to an England-France game I ended up back where I started,' Beau elaborated, keenly aware that to an impressionable teenager he resembled some species of superhero. 'So how did you get yourself in this mess? Travers said you were due to meet up with your father at the Keukenhof *yesterday* and you'll never hear the last of it, if you don't hightail it p-d-q.' He nodded at Scott in a friendly fashion. 'Knowing you youngsters, I don't believe a word.' He raised a shoulder in the direction of his brother. 'But they did, and kindly came along to ride shotgun.'

Scott flashed Travers a grateful glance, receiving a grin in return.

'Right! They're your problem now, at least for the weekend. I'll pick them up on the way back on Sunday. I've a girl waiting in Brussels and a younger brother will cramp my style,' Beau continued. 'Go grab some coffee and a sandwich while I file my flight plan, then we'll be off.'

'What's been happening?' Mary hissed, as soon as Beau was out of earshot.

'I'll tell you when we're aboard, but honestly, Mary, do you think you should have come? It might be dangerous.'

'You think I should stay home while Travers swans off to the mainland – I should say so. In any case I can chaperone Hilary, sounds like she needs it. Travers said you'd been visiting Gretna Green.'

Scott blushed while Hilary laughed.

'Travers, you wait till I get you on your own,' Scott growled.

Travers's dark eyes glinted mischievously. He held up one hand in surrender. 'Don't blame me, your tale was that garbled, you could well be Mr and Mrs Anderson for all I know.'

'Except my name's not Anderson,' said Scott.

'NOT ...'

'*Shush*, Mary! Forget I said that. I'll tell you when we're airborne.'

Scott stared at the back of Beau's head. 'You sure Beau can't hear?'

Head phones on, blocking out sound from the cabin behind, Travers's brother seemed in a world of his own, dominated by the sky ahead. Every so often he spoke a few words into the mouthpiece of his radio or tapped the glass on one of several-dozen circular dials that formed the control panel of the modern aircraft. Despite state-of-the-art technology, the engine noise on either side of the narrow fuselage remained considerable, drowning out anything other than particularly clear and precise enunciation.

'*No way!* I can only just hear you and I'm sitting right next to you. In any case, this bit of the North Sea's so congested Beau says it's like Piccadilly Circus in the rush hour. He'll be up to his neck till we land in Holland. But I wish you'd include him, he's the best if you're in a jam.'

Scott voice was determined. 'No! The fewer people that know, the better.'

'That's rot. It's the opposite. The more people that know, the less the danger – if there is danger. Were you pulling my leg about being Secret Service?'

'No! I really am.' Hilary gave a wry smile.

'Wow! *Hilary!* But that's so exciting,' Mary burst out. 'Ever since Travers told me … well, he didn't exactly tell me. To be fair, I sort'a dug it out of him. Anyway I've been dying to see you. This has to be the most exciting thing to happen in Cornwall for ever. My life's deadly dull by comparison.'

Scott hid a grin, knowing full well that Travers could never keep a secret where Mary was concerned. Even birthday gifts had to be a last-minute purchase otherwise Mary's digging for clues spoiled the surprise.

'So how did it happen, you know becoming a spy?'

'Shut up, Mary.' Her boyfriend groaned. 'Our flight plan gives us less than three hours and I refuse to spend it listening to girls' gossiping, when I could be plunged into an exciting whodunit that will keep me on the edge of my seat. Go on, Scott. But first of all put us out of our misery, *you definitely aren't married?*'

It was out in the open at last. Travers and Mary had listened, their faces expressing a series of tumultuous emotions. But telling the story a second time, and being able to explain some of its mysteries, had made it sound more credible. Even so Mary had grabbed Hilary's hand holding it tightly, concerned that her friend had been so bullied by such powerful forces.

Scott began to feel optimistic, especially after Travers announced it was a good job Mary had brought along their clothes, since wild horses wouldn't send him back to England before the mystery had been solved. Of course, that didn't mean they would be able to solve the mystery but four heads were definitely better than two.

Travers acting as unofficial steward got to his feet, handing out Cokes. He tapped Beau on the back to attract his attention. Beau held up an opened water bottle.

'How long?' Travers mouthed.

'Twenty minutes or so, but don't make anything hot, have a gander at that lot.' He pointed downwards to where densely packed layers of swirling brown cut off their view of land.

'They look solid,' Travers said staring at the clouds.

'They feel it sometimes. Get strapped in I would, and warn the others it'll be a bit rocky. Tell them not to worry though, Isadora is more than capable.'

'Beau says it's going to be a bit bumpy,' Travers said, relaying his brother's message.

Mary hastily strapped herself in, looking nervous. 'How bumpy?' she squeaked.

Travers held his Coke bottle high in the air, waves of liquid fizzing against its side, as the small jet dived into a venomous-looking cloud, buffeting the fuselage and swinging its tail from side to side. 'That bumpy!' He showed her the bottle, dribbles of liquid overflowing down the sides. 'So to while away the last few moments, how about a tale of espionage, Hilary? How did you get into it?'

'You mean I'm now licensed to thrill,' she joked. 'It's pretty dull, after what we've gone through the last few days. My mum brought me up. My dad was in the service. He was killed when I was ten.'

'And there's your application to the school saying both your parents are alive,' Mary interrupted, her voice tight. She peered anxiously through the porthole, swirling fingers of cloud clinging to the fuselage like the tendrils of a giant octopus.

'How did *you* see my application form?' Hilary glared at her friend. She shrugged. 'I guess it doesn't matter now. Whatever happens I won't be going back. That was my cover story, two parents, ordinary family; Dad's work brings him to Cornwall.' She took a deep breath. 'No, Dad died and a few years later Mum and me – we stopped getting on and I ran away. Anyway, to cut a long story short …'

Hilary's head jerked up nervously as the light aircraft dropped into a hole in the clouds. The plane lurched sideways before steadying again. 'Hate this stuff,' she said, swallowing hard. 'Flying over the Atlantic was really rough, clear air turbulence is the worst.'

'Beau said ignore it,' Travers said calmly, undisturbed by the bumps. 'Go on.'

'Um ... well ... to cut a long story short,' Hilary repeated, 'Mum got in touch with Sean Terry ...' Her voice faded away again as the plane danced a tango, lasting several long minutes. She swallowed and kneaded her ears. 'He knew Dad well and tracked me down.'

'Where were you?' Mary said, clutching Travers's hand. 'How long's this going on for?' she gasped wildly. 'I'll need a sick bag if there's much more, my stomach's already heaving.'

'It's not going to hurt you,' Travers pointed out, 'as long as you can hear the engines.' He grinned over at Scott and winked. Mary groaned holding her head in her hands. 'Keep talking, Hilary,' he said.

'I was living in Washington.' Hilary started again her manner half-hearted, obviously more concerned with what was happening outside the plane, than her story. 'Are you sure Mary's okay, Travers? She's gone awfully white.'

Mary shut her eyes. 'Ignore me, Travers is. But when we get on terra firma he's for it,' she threatened. 'I wouldn't have come if I'd known it was going to be this rough.'

'Don't blame me,' Travers said indignantly. 'I'm not responsible for the weather.'

'What were you doing in Washington?' Scott said, hoping that talking would keep Hilary's mind off the turbulence.

'Living rough. But I wasn't into drugs or anything like that,' she protested. 'There's always work if you want it. No one bothers about age in the US. All the kids work – waiting tables, washing-up, factory work – that sort of thing. Sean told me that kids from age fourteen were being recruited to report on classroom activity, because terrorism has to start somewhere. I got the training and found myself back in school. Two months after that I got a crash course in English and sent to London. You know the rest.'

'So where you used to live, there wasn't a river?'

Hilary's laugh sounded false and she wrapped her arms round her middle, as if she was hanging on to her insides, holding them steady against the relentless pounding.

'And how I hated you, Scott, keeping on about it,' she said trying hard to create the impression of being relaxed. 'If you really want to know I'd never even seen a river till I was ten and I watched a video about London on the flight to Dublin.'

Travers roared with laughter. 'I'm not surprised she got mad, Scott, asking all those questions.'

'But you still think there's a mole in your outfit,' Mary said. She swallowed and swung round in her seat to stare at Beau's back, as if wanting to check for herself that he remained unconcerned about the plane's acrobatics. The drone of the engines sounded solid and re-assuring, not varying at all despite the wind's furious pummelling. She looked round again, appearing a shade calmer as the plane steadied.

'Definitely! You can't explain any of this without.'

'I've gone over and over it. It has to be Sean Terry,' Scott insisted. 'You've avoided his name, Hilary, skirting round and round it, saying *headquarters*. You know that's no longer possible,' he accused.

Hilary said miserably. 'But I still don't think …'

'Because he brought you into the service?' Travers helped out.

'I guess that and because he knew my dad.'

'I agree,' said Mary. 'So it has to be somebody else.'

'But until we know who,' Scott added, 'we're on our own, which might sound great, except we're four kids in a strange country.'

Travers grinned at him. 'Look at it this way. If you're the underdog, you've nothing to lose.' He peered out of the window. 'We're down – never felt a thing. Told you Beau was good.'

Beau declined the offer of food, maintaining that lunch in an airport terminal was something he preferred to skip.

'Well, a sandwich then,' suggested Mary.

'No, thanks. I'll head straight off. Compared to oysters in Bruges, a sandwich just doesn't grab you.' Beau grinned and ruffled Travers's hair, much to his brother's annoyance. 'Enjoy yourselves, kiddles. Give me a ring if you are still there after the weekend and need a lift back. But don't ring before, okay.'

He watched the little group walk across the tarmac towards the terminal buildings. As the brown cloud base had promised, rain fell in stair rods, puddles already gathering on the runway surface. He hesitated a moment, waiting for the doors to close behind the four teenagers, then dialled a number on his mobile. There was no reply, except for the recorded voice of the answer machine suggesting he left a message.

'Dad? Pity you're not there. You know that boy you were looking for? Well, I've just deposited him at Lisse airport. Seems like he's on his way to meet his father. Thought you'd like to know.'

TWENTY-TWO

The four friends watched the Cessna taxi towards the runway, holding for a passenger jet. The huge aircraft surged forward hurtling along the runway, its ungainly lift-off reminding Scott of a swan attempting to become airborne; its wheels dangling awkwardly before snapping up into the fuselage. It disappeared skywards in a roar of noise and kerosene fumes. A few minutes later the small jet began to roll forward, quickly accelerating and reaching lift-off in a quarter of the time it had taken the heavily-laden charter plane. They watched it climb steeply, banking sharply westwards before vanishing into the low cloud base.

There was an awkward pause, the words: *so where do we go from here* on everyone's lips. Scott was uncomfortably aware that his friends expected him to come up with some answers, especially after hearing about the heart-stopping escapades of the previous few days. He had promised them he was going to find his father. Now Beau had delivered them to Holland, they were waiting for him to make his promise good – except he hadn't a clue how to do that.

'Don't all look at me,' he said backing away slightly. 'I don't know where we go from here either.'

Hilary checked her watch. 'We could start by finding somewhere to stay,' she suggested.

'And now I've recovered from that ghastly plane ride,' added Mary, 'I could do with something to eat.' She glared at her boyfriend who had drifted away from the small group towards the glass counter of the airport snack bar, and was eyeing up their stock of tired-looking baguettes; wisps of salami and finely shredded cheese escaping from their edges. 'I don't fancy that cafeteria either, Travers.'

'I was only looking,' Travers protested. 'Besides food helps me think. Let's find out if there's a bus.'

A long queue of people were already waiting for the bus into Lisse and, by the time they had paid their fare, it was standing room only.

The bus pulled out negotiating its way past a line of illegally-parked cars, their passengers hoping to avoid notice long enough to manhandle several pieces of large and cumbersome luggage onto a trolley. Designed by some malevolent genie, they appeared to have wheels that pursued several directions at once, constantly drifting into the path of oncoming vehicles. The bus driver, well used to the lunch-time crush, drew up, waiting patiently for a woman to rescue her trolley from his front bumper, before setting off again.

Scott ducked his head to look out of the window, the excitement of actually being on the mainland momentarily overriding his concern about finding his father.

The fine rain had transformed the jumble of buildings into featureless concrete, while the people and cars looked no different from those at home. The bus slowed and, after a brief pause, pulled out onto a main highway, the ground on either side drab and uninviting. Surprisingly there were few cars. Instead bicycles dominated the dual-carriageway; stolid-looking machines, with wide handlebars and baskets perched on the front, quite unlike Scott's own with its twelve gears and thin tyres. The driver gave the huddled groups a wide berth, easing the heavily-laden bus past on the far side.

From time to time bright green road signs urged them on towards Lisse, where the coach was scheduled to make a brief stop before heading out again to the Keukenhof, the world-famous park of flowers and its final destination. The other occupants of the bus appeared to be mostly retired people on holiday and, with the exception of their little group, it was likely the entire bus load of passengers was planning to visit the park. Scott listened eagerly, hearing a dozen different conversations in as many languages. Constant expressions of surprised delight flowed into the air, as the bus drove between fields of tulips, their glittering array of colours escorting the vehicle towards the small town.

Scott dug his elbow into Travers's ribs. 'Look, a windmill, they still exist,' he breathed, now entirely convinced he was in a different country. Bending low, he screwed his head round to catch sight of its sails revolving, their gossamer fabric dramatically outlined against a backdrop of dark-grey clouds, its gleaming white-board body planted among a carpet of scarlet tulips.

'You remember those school trips to museums to look at art?'

'Never managed to go on one yet,' Travers stifled a yawn, 'too busy playing rugby, why?'

'I was just thinking; if you lived here you could understand all those famous men wanting to paint. I mean, *look at that.*'

He pointed to where a group of brightly clad children on bikes were leaning up against the heavy black timbers of a loch, watching a painted barge disappear from sight into the bowels of the canal. Enviously, Scott wished there was a bus stop handy, so he could stay and see it emerge on the lower level.

'Can't appreciate anything on an empty stomach, Scott, you know that. Now if you were showing me a restaurant full of flame-grilled burgers, I might show some interest, but a canal – I'll give it a miss, thanks.'

Soon after, an outcrop of modern brick and glass factories heralded the outskirts of Lisse. The bus slowed, passing streets of houses that might have a purpose in the economy of the region but, architecturally, were no different from any other town in northern Europe; the town's historical gems restricted to several streets near its centre. It slowed some more and its tyres bumped over cobblestones fronting a row of curiously narrow, yet elegantly tall, townhouses. Hilary and Mary craned over the seats to watch a sofa being off-loaded from a large furniture van.

A length of rope came snaking down the wall of the house. Next minute the sofa was swinging in the air. It headed up the face of a building before entering the house through its upper windows.

The centre of town, its streets still wet from the downpour, which had now moved on towards the North Sea, was quite ordinary except for one thing – the fragrance of spring flowers. For residents, for whom the delicate scent had long worn off, the sight of passengers descending from the airport bus, only to become rooted to the spot wearing an expression of stupefied delight, was a constant source of entertainment.

Flowers were obviously big business and a row of market stalls clung to the pavement edges, their green and white striped awnings protecting the delicate buds and stems from the weather. And, in case anyone managed to avoid these, large wicker baskets – overflowing with a dozen different varieties of narcissi and tulips – were positioned on every street corner to give the air a perfume boost; their owners cheerfully chatting while they waited for any one, remotely resembling a tourist, to pass by.

Hilary and Mary gazed entranced and darted towards the nearest stall; its owner, a white-haired matron wearing the traditional black dress, with its gaily-embroidered apron and a bonnet with curls. She greeted the two girls cheerfully, her English hardly accented at all, not the slightest bit offended by the two girls examining her outfit inch by inch.

'It was my grandmother's,' she explained, pointing to her apron. She pulled up the skirt on her long black dress, to show them her clogs, the pattern on the wood matching the one on her bonnet. 'Everything is, except for the long wool socks.'

Hilary shivered in the cold wind. 'You need them too,' she agreed. 'Doesn't the sun ever shine here?'

The woman beamed. 'We have our carnival on Sunday; there will be sunshine for that, I promise you. You will be staying?'

'Hope so,' Mary smiled eagerly as Hilary, unable to resist the temptation, picked up a bunch of hyacinths, burying her nose in them.

'What happens then?' she said, lifting her head.

'There is a parade of carts, many different themes but all of them made of flowers. That is why the town is so busy.' The elderly matron sketched a hand over the crowds of people thronging the streets, the majority laden with armfuls of flowers.

'Can I buy these?' Hilary asked, separating a half-dozen bunches from the rest.

The woman laughed. 'My dear, that is what you do when you come to Holland, buy flowers. And you, my dear?'

'I'd love some.' Mary hesitated, staring covetously round the stall. 'But it's impossible to choose.'

'You said, there's lots of people in town?' Hilary handed over some euros.

The old woman wrapped the wet stems in a triangle of paper. 'Yes, it is always busy for the flower parade.'

The two girls stared at one another with dismay.

'We need somewhere to stay,' explained Mary.

'You may have to go to Amsterdam or The Hague; the hotels here are always full. Wait a minute.' She rummaged under the counter. Hilary and Mary exchanged glances, both girls wondering if they would find themselves sleeping in a bus shelter for the night. 'Here!' She waved a white card triumphantly. 'Try number seven Kanaalstraat, a friend of mine owns it. When I saw her this morning she still had rooms.'

'Oh that's wonderful. Thank you! *Thank you!* Mary, *do* make up your mind, we can't stay here for ever.'

Travers lent his chin on Mary's shoulder. 'I haven't got enough money to buy the entire stall,' he said, with a cheerful smile at the stall holder.

Mary glared. 'If you want to know,' she said, her tone haughty, 'Hilary and I are seeking accommodation, which we have discovered will not be easy since the town is overflowing with tourists.' She pointed to a bucket filled with narcissi, the clusters of miniature flowers pumping their fragrance into the air. 'Oh, I just love those.'

'Ah, so that's what you're doing.' Travers smiled lazily. 'We might have believed you except for the flowers.'

'You can't come to Holland and not buy flowers,' Mary insisted stubbornly.

Scott stood on one side, his expression bleak, the euphoria of being on the mainland wiped out the moment his foot had touched the pavement. That was where it had hit him – it should have been his dad standing there. Making a real effort, he joined the gathering round the stall. Then he noticed the tulips leaning against the side of a bucket. Brilliantly purple, they were tall and elegant, identical in every way to those in the picture he carried of his mother. He patted his pocket feeling the hard rim of its frame. A storm of emotion rampaged through him, aware, for the first time, how much he missed her. It was the strangest of sensations; a great bleeding void he never knew existed till now. He pushed it away and smiled, trying hard to join in the fun.

The woman finished wrapping the white blossoms, handing them to Mary with her change. 'Canal Street, don't forget.'

'We won't,' Mary promised, tucking her arm into Travers's. 'Thanks.' She waved goodbye.

'I suppose you have understood that flowers need water to survive,' Travers said as they strolled off down the street. He stopped to sniff the large bunch. 'They do smell.'

'Oh Travers, *you really are a pain*, they're supposed to smell,' Mary groaned. 'I guess you need food. Come on, let's feed the beast, then we'll find the hotel.'

Travers stared down at his large plate, only a piece of it still covered by a delicious-looking veal escalope and chips. 'That's better. I feel halfway human now and my brains are back in order.' He took another mouthful. 'So there's something I need clearing up. How did they – whoever they are – keep on tracking you down?'

'We told you that,' Scott said, smiling gratefully at his friend. Travers made it all sound so easy.

'I must have missed that bit, so tell me again.'

'I expect the plane jumped sideways at that point,' Mary took a bite of her ham omelette. 'This is good. And, to be honest, I didn't follow that bit either, I was more concerned about my insides, which were threatening to become my outsides,' she joked. 'I mean, if those motorway barriers are only there for terrorists, why did they pick you up, Scott?'

'I'd never heard of them till Hilary put me straight. Did you know about them, Travers?'

'Beau got caught once,' his friend said, studying the remaining pile of chips on his plate with interest. 'He'd borrowed a mate's car without telling him. It was reported stolen, and the next thing Dad knew about it was a summons. He was slightly peeved, made Beau work off the fine.'

'Anyway that's when he told us,' he continued after a pause for laughter, his eyes sparkling with mischief. 'Said it was against government policy to warn people of their existence. Do you think your dad's fallen foul of the government and they're after him?'

'Scott and I've had this out a dozen times. My boss said ...'

'Stop quoting Sean Terry, you know I hate it,' Scott snapped, frowning at Hilary across the table.

She flushed. 'Okay,' she said, her voice sharp. 'Anyway, after talking about it, *we* came to the conclusion that someone, with access to the central computer system, was instructed to keep an eye out for Scott, who just happened to be riding his dad's bike. And the only people that knew Scott had taken the bike were ...'

'The American Secret Service,' Travers finished triumphantly. 'Okay, got it!'

'And someone Scott came into contact with bugged him,' Mary added.

Travers chewed thoughtfully. 'Yeah, I forgot that bit. So now what? It's almost four.'

'We find our hotel then explore the town,' Hilary said.

'Looking for what?' Scott said. He glanced down at his plate, thankful he had only a couple of chips left because the thought of pounding the streets had taken away his appetite.

'Anything that doesn't fit.' Hilary put her hand on Scott's

arm. 'No one but you would have come up with those clues about Scotland. I honestly thought you were mad ...'

Scot nodded, resisting the temptation to agree with her. All through lunch he'd been going over and over the clues. It had been sheer luck; nothing clever about it at all. Mr Nicely had found them, not the other way round – *luck*! And someone else had traced his father to Lisse – not them – *luck again*! If it had been left to them... Scott didn't pursue that thought, only to aware that he would be travelling back to Cornwall no wiser than when he set out.

'... but because of that we're here,' Hilary said, her voice firm and confident. 'Anything might happen, Scott, we just have to keep looking,' she ended. 'So let's get ourselves booked in, the flowers in water, then we'll scour the town. Finished, Travers?'

'For now.' He rose to his feet. 'But I'll probably need another layer before bedtime. Come on.'

The small restaurant situated on the main square had looked rather dingy from the outside, with a yellowing lace curtain tacked across the lower half of its window. Both girls had objected vociferously when Travers, ignoring the brightly lit and busy establishments on the far side of the square, had opened the door to look inside, announcing this was the one.

'But it looks ghastly,' Mary wailed.

'Not on the inside and that's where it counts. Anyway this is where the local people eat.'

'How do you know that?' Scott said.

'Because,' Travers retorted.

'Because what?' Hilary said standing her ground. 'The place over there ...' She pointed to the far side of the square, where elegant patio heaters extended the restaurant's seating to include a dozen tables and chairs under an awning, 'looks far more comfy.'

'Trust me on this. That restaurant,' he said, scornfully, 'is filled with tourists. Local people are the ones *not* carrying maps and rucksacks, and they've chosen to eat here.'

With a flourish he ushered his friends into the small room,

boldly sitting at one of the rickety wooden tables curiously covered by a small carpet; although the instant the waiter had appeared to take their order, this had been swathed in a fresh white tablecloth.

Now, having been proved right, Travers felt honour bound to pay. He and Scott wandered over to the pay-desk, a brass metal cage near the door, tended by an old woman garmented in black from head to toe. At least ten years past retiring age, she was perched on a high stool carefully counting the lunch-time takings, her spine bent from long years of tending the caisse. Her equally-ancient spouse was serving behind the bar; a number of men, huddled in heavy navy jackets and caps, still drinking their schnapps and coffee.

Scott picked up his coat waiting for Travers to finish his conversation with the old woman. Hilary and Mary were excitedly swopping girl talk and ignoring him completely. He listened half-heartedly to their banter. Thanks to them his feelings of being pursued had vanished; but the constant diversions to buy flowers, dawdling through the streets, drooling over the sights and smells, had reduced him to a churning impatience – as if every second counted, which was ridiculous because they didn't even know where to begin.

Anxious to get going, he picked up Mary's suitcase and opened the door, flinching slightly as the cold wind struck. Hilary followed him out, leaving Mary to wait for Travers who was still chatting. Scott cast an eye over the busy thoroughfare. He was not really thinking about anything in particular, rather satisfying some subconscious whim; refreshing his gaze with the scene he'd last looked on before entering the restaurant. He stopped dead quivering, exactly like a pointer dog when it locates its quarry. Grabbing Hilary, he backed into the restaurant and swung the door shut behind them.

Travers collecting his change looked up. 'Scott?'

'I don't believe it! *It can't be!*'

Mary peered over his shoulder into the square. 'Who can't it be, Scott?'

Ignoring her, he grabbed the flowers out of Hilary's arm and held them across her face. 'For God's sake don't look up,' he hissed. Pulling open the door, he pushed the two girls out of the doorway and into the nearest alleyway.

Startled, Travers grabbed his change and raced after them.

'Keep walking,' Scott insisted, digging his fingers into the small of Hilary's back. 'And pray he didn't see us.'

'Who?' Hilary yelled, dragging her feet.

'Sean *bloody* Terry, *that's who!* He's only sitting in that restaurant across the square. Thank God for Travers, otherwise we'd have been sat there, too.'

Travers grabbed his arm and pinned him against the wall. '*Calm down!* No one can see us from here.' He pushed Scott and Hilary into a shop doorway. 'Stay there. Mary and I'll go and see. He doesn't know us. What does he look like?'

'Tall and thin, dark hair with designer stubble,' Hilary said, from behind her flowers.

Scott crouched down against the wall, his head in his hands. The nightmare had resurfaced; he could sense it crowding in on him, making him want to run, to get away. He hated feeling like that. His dad had always encouraged him to face what frightened him. But this? There was nothing rational about this fear. It was like a black mass hovering just out of sight with Sean Terry at its core, leaving him shaking and sick at the sight of him.

Hilary opened her mouth to speak. She hesitated, a curious expression on her face. 'It's okay, Scott, we've had worse.' She bent down and put her arm round his shoulder.

'Not right on our heels,' he muttered.

Travers and Mary reappeared.

'He's still there,' Travers called. 'Talking to someone. Can't see who – a load of tourists in the way.'

'That really puts paid to wandering round the town,' Scott's voice took on a bleak, empty tone. 'I wish I was brave enough to go right up to him and demand to see Dad. You can bet your life if I did confront Terry, he'd deny everything – say he was looking for Dad too. Next minute some big black car would appear and bundle me into it.'

'You don't know that,' Hilary argued.

'*You willing to* give me *guarantee?*' Scott hurled at her. 'If you're that convinced – *you walk up to him* 'cos I'm not risking it. The only way I know to save Dad is by staying alive and free.'

Mary, seeing that Scott was close to losing it, slipped her arm through his. 'She didn't mean it like that, Scott.' She screwed up her face at Hilary. 'What she really meant was ... er ... that we don't know anything for certain. But we have to hang together – don't fall out now.'

TWENTY-THREE

A motley collection of bars and coffee houses had replaced the pertly smiling shops of the main street projecting a seedy image, with fresh paint and clean windows left at the top of the alley. The dingy buildings huddled together, destroying what little light the rain-filled clouds had allowed through. No one was about, the bars tightly shuttered till night; only a beggar sheltering from the drizzle under a wall, a tarpaulin draped over his head to keep him dry. He called out, holding his hand in the air and Mary, grateful for anything that relieved the tension between Scott and Hilary, dropped some coins into it.

'I agree.' Travers put an arm round Scott's shoulders. 'No good falling out.' He stopped, glancing casually at the shop windows, selling liquor and tobacco and cheap souvenirs. Some appeared deserted, the shop windows empty except for a string of light bulbs round the edges of the window pane and a chair; a backdrop of material obscuring the shop floor itself. 'Strange-looking shops,' he said and burst into laughter.

'What's up?' Scott said.

'Nothing at all,' he said, smiling broadly. 'You're not going to find anything much down here though, unless you want to get laid.'

'*Travers!* Honestly!' Mary broke into a relieved giggle.

'What! But the shops are empty,' Scott said, gazing round.

'They could be busy,' Travers smirked.

'Will somebody tell me what you're all talking about?' Hilary demanded, her tone indignant.

'Only that Scott has led us straight into the red-light district.'

'Prostitutes, you mean,' Hilary said, her voice disapproving, as if it was a word she found difficult to say. She glared and grabbed Mary's arm. 'In which case, if you don't mind, I'd quite like to get away from here.' She peered up and down the small alleyway, as if undecided which way to go.' You may find it funny, Travers, but I know Mary doesn't and I'm damn sure I don't,' she said pompously.

Mary laughed. 'I'm just cross Travers knew about it.'

'You do, too.' Her boyfriend grinned at her.

'That's different,' Mary said. 'They're women and I should know what happens to women, but I don't think you should.'

'That's cock-eyed logic if ever I heard it,' Travers protested, forcing a reluctant laugh from Scott.

'I can see why you two are so devoted, you never stop quarrelling. Hang on, Hilary,' Scott grabbed her by the sleeve. 'I know that man.'

The door to one of the shops had opened and a man appeared, lighting a cigarette. Of medium height, his brown hair was thinning and receding from the temples and although his raincoat was smart, and obviously expensive, it fitted rather too snugly, as if its wearer was carrying a few unwanted pounds. He buttoned his coat; the air still filled with a fine drizzle left from the earlier rain storm, his cigarette hanging loosely from his mouth.

Hilary peered over Scott's shoulder. 'I've never seen him before.'

As if he had sensed their interest, the man glanced over his shoulder, giving the alley a cursory inspection. Scott quickly buried his face in the flowers pretending to smell them.

'Hey, watch my flowers will you!' Hilary yelped.

'I'll buy you some more. He didn't see me, though, did he?' Scott said, dropping his voice to a whisper. 'I could swear he was the man checking George's sheep. *Holy crap!* This is getting weird.'

'Sheep!' Mary exclaimed.

Scott spoke into the air, keeping his back firmly turned. 'Yes, Mary. Sheep! The day before Dad disappeared there were these ministry men checking the farmer's sheep for radiation. I spoke to them. What's he doing now?'

'He's gone,' Travers reported. 'You're safe.'

Scott looked after him eagerly, his face vividly alive. 'It's him all right, I'd know him anywhere. Come on, let's follow him.'

'But ...' began Hilary.

'It's the clue we've been waiting for, Hilary, and for that I'd risk meeting your boss any day of the week. *Come on*. But keep back, he mustn't spot us.'

Scott studied the broad back, now more than fifty metres away, memorising his shape, what he was wearing, the way his feet clipped neatly on to the pavement, even though he was walking quite leisurely. Flimsy trails of smoke rose into the air from his cigarette, each step the man took leaving Scott more and more convinced that this was the man that had taken his father.

Hilary grabbed his arm, pulling him back. 'You sure, Scott?' she murmured staring intently at him.

He watched the strolling figure and pictured him wearing the navy overalls, a gold crest over the pocket, absolutely positive he was right.

'One hundred percent! There were three men.' He paused remembering the incident of the alarm. *If only he'd spoken out*! 'That man – he had an accent. George Beale called him a foreigner.'

The man appeared to know exactly where he was heading – zigzagging through the narrowing streets; his head constantly half-turned to check for oncoming cyclists and cars, making him difficult to follow. They emerged onto a highway, a sudden break in traffic allowing their quarry to cross unhindered. Scott swore loudly, teetering on the edge of the pavement and stepped carelessly into the road. A car swerved, banging its horn as Hilary hauled him back out of danger.

'Don't be stupid,' she shouted.

'But he's getting away.'

He pointed despairingly towards the figure, now vanishing into an underpass, and yanked his arm free.

On the far side, the outline of a typical inner-city estate could be seen, a series of apartment blocks huddled together, their tall silhouettes angled into the sky like upended dominoes. At intervals along the kerbside, ugly steel barriers had been erected to prevent small children wandering into the busy thoroughfare.

Throwing himself almost under the wheels of some approaching cyclists, Scott dived across the road. Travers, grabbing Mary's arm, followed leaving Hilary to bring up the rear, shouting an apologetic, 'sorry,' to the leading group – their brakes screeching in protest. A lorry coming in fast on the far side slowed, its driver impatiently waving the hurrying figures across in front of him.

Scott tore through the underpass, closely followed by Travers, loudly protesting that bunches of flowers and a heavy bag weren't exactly the right gear for a cross-country run.

He slowed down, allowing his friends to catch up with him.

'Sorry, but he mustn't escape.'

'We know,' said Mary, 'but if he disappears again, you and ...'

'*Hang on*!' Scott hastily dragged his friends behind the rust-spotted remains of a white van that had been dumped on the grass verge, its wheels no longer in existence.

Their quarry had stopped by a group of small children, who were squatting on the kerbside playing some game; the girls, with black headscarves covering their hair, adding to sombreness of the atmosphere. As the man passed they had called out, holding up their palms beseechingly. He laughed tossing coins down into their eager hands and casually glanced back over his shoulder.

'Oh hell! Now he's seen us!' Scott said, ducking down.

Never at a loss, Travers wrapped his free arm around Mary's shoulders and, hugging her towards him, walked slowly out from behind the body of the van, the man still gazing curiously towards them. Travers bent his head and planted a lingering kiss on his girlfriend's cheek.

'What?' she exclaimed, startled.

'Acting,' he whispered. 'Keep walking,' he added, his voice stern. 'He doesn't know us and, if you're a good girl, you can have a real one later.'

'Ugh!' She smiled coyly, nestling her head into his shoulder. 'Acting,' she repeated, 'and don't you dare think I'm doing this all the time.'

The man gave a brief smile and, waving to the children, took off across the deserted play area; its scrubby blades of grass battling with winter mud and broken bottles for survival. Against the dark brown of the sky, its metal and wood shapes looked strangely alien. Idly, he tugged at the chains of the solitary swing, setting it in motion.

Scott waited, his thoughts nagging impatiently, convinced he was the only one totally aware of the magnitude of the clue.

'They won't let him disappear,' said Hilary, reading his mind. She peeped round the edge of the van. 'Okay, we can go now but stick to the paths.' She tugged on Scott's arm pointing towards the last of the apartment blocks, their quarry still visible on the far side.

Sounds of traffic, with bicycle bells ringing out, alerted Scott to a busy main street ahead. He broke into a run, keenly aware that in a street full of people wearing raincoats, their quarry could easily vanish without trace. They arrived in time to see the man enter a coffee house, a plate-glass window giving them a clear view of its interior.

A waiter had looked up as the door opened, his gesture clearly inviting their quarry to sit down and take the weight off. The two men exchanged words; then the waiter disappeared from view only to reappear a moment later with, what looked like, coffee and a beer on a tray.

The square was awash with light and movement, its bistros and bustling shops busy; bicycles and cars constantly manoeuvring in and out of parking bays – a far cry from the air of poverty that had hung over the housing estate.

Travers beckoned. He and Mary were already seated on one

of the benches in the busy square, hidden from the coffee shop by several dozen bicycles piled higgledy-piggledy in a bike rack.

Scott smiled, a sense of excitement lifting his spirits. Once again luck had been on their side and now he felt almost grateful to Sean Terry. If they hadn't seen him and dived down that alley, they'd still have been looking.

After ten minutes or so their quarry stood up. Dropping a coin on the table, he strolled out of the café and, casually mounting one of the bicycles parked against a lamppost, rode off down the street.

Startled, Scott jumped to his feet; the moving silhouette quickly diminishing in the gloom. Then, he was across the square and, grabbing the first bike, set off after him.

'What do think you're doing?' Hilary yelled.

Travers broke into a run. 'Come on.'

'But the flowers and the bag,' wailed Mary.

Travers grabbed one of the machines from the bike stand. 'I'm borrowing it,' he called, 'in case someone asks. I'll put it back. I'll follow Scott. You stay here.'

He pushed down on the pedals and, waving to the two figures staring forlornly after him, sped off. Quickly accelerating, he closed the gap on Scott.

'Well, I like that, leaving us here,' Mary protested. She swung round in a circle taking in the square. 'In the middle of nowhere, too.'

Hilary glared resentfully. 'I was all set to follow,' she said, 'but Travers beat me to it. It infuriates me that boys automatically think girls are useless at anything that requires a bit of action.'

'I don't expect Travers actually thought,' Mary defended her boyfriend. 'It's the same in a match. His auto-pilot clicks in. And since he looks on us as a team – if someone's in trouble, the one nearest to him goes to help, which usually means Travers. In any case you had your arms full of flowers.'

'You really like him, don't you?'

Mary blushed. 'They're a nice family,' she said not committing herself. 'I adore his mum. His dad's strange though.'

'Why strange?' Hilary said, beginning to calm down. 'He looked fine on the boat – really nice. So funny.'

'He's that all right. Travers says he's always flying off to meetings – most of them in Europe. Travers says they're nothing to do with television either. He gets a phone call and off he goes.'

Hilary glanced down at her watch. 'Oh help! It's gone five. We'd better find a taxi. I don't feel like finding my way back to the town – not carrying this lot. Only hope the rooms are still there. You got your phone?'

'Yes, Travers will get in touch. Oh!' Mary groaned. 'I hope they're safe.'

'They'd better be,' Hilary said. 'I can't believe Scott left me behind. He, of all people, should have remembered how useful my gun has been.'

'*Gun! You've got a gun!*' Mary's eyebrows disappeared into her hair.

Hilary laughed. 'How do you think we escaped from the motel?'

'You told us they were shooting at you,' she said, 'but you never said you shot back.'

'We must have forgotten to tell you that bit!'

'It seems you and Scott only told us half what's going on. While we're waiting, I'm going to hear the rest.'

Scott wasn't thinking; his gazed fixed on the dark shape ahead. If he had been he'd never have stolen the bike, particularly not in a foreign country, without a clue as to its laws or what might happen to someone caught breaking them. Holland and England might both belong to the Federation and share the same laws, but Holland was dramatically different from anything Scott had ever experienced; its flatness, its flowers and windmills, driving on the wrong side, carpets on tables in the restaurant – those things alone were enough to convince him – he didn't need to hear the language, with its guttural-sounding vowels or view the general use of pedal power instead of cars.

'Do you think we can find our way back?'

Scott swerved, startled to hear Travers's voice. 'Where's Mary and Hilary?'

'Back at the square. I don't suppose it occurred to you to look at its name?'

'Why?'

'We've got to put the bikes back.'

Scott gazed down at his bike, as if seeing it for the first time and his anxious expression faded into a grin. 'Dad's always telling me I'm too law abiding, that I need to take an occasional risk. Except that's generally when we off camping, or something to do with school. He might even approve of this. Does it bother you?'

'Not much,' Travers said. 'Dad'll bail me out if we get arrested. I'll get a lecture but … no.'

On either side of the road streams of cyclists, their work over for the day, queued at the factory gates, waiting for a break in the traffic to feed into the circulation. Cars added to the congestion, forced to crawl behind the dozens of bicycles spread across the entire width of the carriageway. Fortunately, the road was straight and the figure riding ahead of them seemingly content to stay on it, which suited Scott fine; knowing their chances of finding the small square again lessened with every turn he took.

A few minutes later, the wrought-iron railings that marked the boundary of the industrial park disappeared, allowing a main road to cut in from the left. The by-now familiar shape turned across the traffic island and vanished into a small lane bordered by a lone factory building, its sculptured shrubberies investing the site with an air of extreme affluence.

Scott, checking the name on the building so they could find it again, swerved violently.

'Look out,' Travers shouted in alarm, steering his bike into the kerb to avoid him.

Scott stopped and took off his glasses, peering at them. He swore and put them back on.

'What's going on?' Travers sounded concerned.

'I'll explain in a minute. Lend me your specs first.'

'What's the matter with yours?'

'Not regulation.' Scott held up his hand. 'Forgot to tell you that bit.'

'Strikes me you only told us half a story,' Travers handed across his glasses. 'So what?'

'Fredericé et cie. That's the place that makes our glasses.' Scott pointed to the building, its elegant façade of glass and white panelling interrupted by swirling pillars of dark-grey granite, like the curve of a wave. 'How weird!'

'What?'

Scott heaved a sigh. 'Don't know. Strange coincidence, that's all. Come on.'

The road dwindled into a muddy track. Scott, furious with himself for losing precious minutes, pushed his bike hard until the figure came into view again; although, in the bad light, it was no longer possible to tell if it was even the same person. On either side open fields bordered the lane, with rows of dreary-looking stalks reduced to shades of brown and grey in the half-light. Scott wondered if they could be tulips, although there were no flowers only stalks and leaves.

'Where's he going?'

'That house?' Travers pointed towards the distant silhouette.

The bicycle stopped. Casually dropping it to the ground, the man strode out into the field.

'Where's he going now?' Travers said, repeating Scott's question.

A lack of cover kept them well back, the figure in front simply a distant blur, bobbing up and down as he stepped over the greenish-grey ridges. He came to a halt, carefully checking all about him. Scott and Travers ducked, hugging the ground. They waited a few seconds before cautiously raising their heads. The field was empty.

Behind them, lights burned on every floor in the factory but too far away to pose any threat. Dumping their bikes, they traced the muddy footprints, deep impressions in the wet earth taking them towards the centre of the field.

'Nothing!' exclaimed Scott. He peered at the ground, which

was heavily scored as if an animal had been scratching about. 'But there has to be something; people don't vanish into thin air.'

Taking care not to slip in the mud, Travers inspected the ridges on either side of them, scrabbling about in the earth.

'*Got it!*' he exclaimed triumphantly and pulled at a ring. A circular manhole cover swung upwards, exposing a short ladder.

'*Dad!*' Scott made to climb down.

Travers grabbed him round the waist and hauled him back, lowering the cover back into place. Once down it was impossible to distinguish it from the earth, unless you knew it was there.

'No, you're flaming-well not,' he grunted keeping tight hold, as Scott struggled to free himself. They struggled and Scott toppled to the ground, dragging Travers with him.

'*Have you gone mad?*' Travers yelled.

Scott flushed. 'Dad's down there. I know it.'

'Even if he is ….' Travers climbed back onto his feet, standing astride the manhole cover. 'You can't just barge in. I've seen far too many movies where the hero walks into a strange place and, next second, he's wishing he hadn't.'

'You mean you're just going to stand there and do nothing?' Scott wanted to scream aloud his frustration. 'Why the hell did I ask you, if this is all the help you're going to be.'

'Nice try!' Travers grinned, his even temper not the slightest bit dented. 'That was so crazy! Arm wrestling in a mud pool! We need the police.'

'How can we go to the police? We've no evidence, nothing to go on. Where *is* Hilary? Now, when she could really be useful, she's nowhere about.' Angrily, Scott got to his feet, brushing the wet earth from his jacket.

'*Hilary?* How can she help?'

'She's carries a gun and …'

Travers tugged at his ear-lobe. 'I know I get kicked about a bit in rugby, but did you say *gun?*'

Scott grinned, his anger gone and, despite the uncertainty, grateful that Travers was there – so totally unfazed by anything.

'Did we forget to tell you that bit?' Travers nodded. 'That's how we got away. She's a good shot, too.'

'Sorry! No Hilary. But the next best thing – man's best friend.'

'A dog?'

'*No!* A mobile, you wally,' Travers glowered.

'Not here! The sound'll carry.' Scott glanced nervously towards the factory.

'Okay, we call them from the lane. Tell them where we are. Then we go back and collect reinforcements.'

'No, I'm staying.' Scott indicated the mess of muddy footprints crowded round the manhole. 'If there's rain in the night we'll never find it again.'

'It's twenty-six rows from the lane.'

'That doesn't help much, the rows are miles long.'

'*Oh, for crying-out-loud!*' Travers pointed towards the wrought-iron railings separating the house from the field. 'From here to there is about eighty yards. And we're exactly in line with that corner rail. Don't bother to argue. I've kicked enough drop goals to know what I'm talking about.'

Scott nodded his thanks. 'But it still doesn't make it any easier to leave.'

'Well, I'm not camping out here all night.'

'If it was your dad …'

'I'd probably go charging in – like you want to – and end up a prisoner like him. But since you're not thinking straight, you'd better leave that to me.'

Scott turned away reluctantly, unable to bear the thought of chucking in the towel. Innocent people didn't duck into holes in the ground. He stopped, staring back at the manhole. 'Okay, so it's stupid, it makes no sense, it's dangerous, it's crazy – I agree with all that,' he said, his voice trembling. 'But, *we've got to take a look*. Unless we have evidence, no one's going to believe us. You stay. If I don't reappear…'

'Honestly, Scott, I've known you dozens of years and never …'

'Come off it!'

'Well, eight anyway! Never once, in all that time, have you ever been anything but cautious. You never speak without thinking first and then you don't say much. So why now?' Travers saw Scott hesitate and glance over his shoulder, as if the words he was going to say were so special he didn't want anyone overhearing them.

''Cos there's only Dad and me.'

Travers sighed. 'I never thought of it like that. Okay then. But we go down, check round and leave. No risks! Promise?'

'Okay, thanks!'

Leaving the cover open, the two boys slid silently down the steps. Their trainers were muddy, leaving pats of impacted soil on the rungs but the man they'd been following would have left a trail too. Six steps took them to the bottom; a narrow box, its walls solid to the touch.

'Feels like a cupboard,' Travers whispered, scrunching his shoulders to make way for Scott. He swiped his hand over the wall in front. Silently it swung back; red-glowing safety lights allowing them to identify stacks of linen piled on shelves. 'I'll go and check,' he pointed to the door. 'You stay here.'

'No, I'm going,' Scott insisted. 'It's my dad, no contest.'

Tiptoeing over to the door, he edged it open.

At first it was difficult to decide what he was seeing. On the face of it, it could have been a hotel – a long carpeted corridor with dozens of doors on both sides – although it was highly unlikely that anyone would build a hotel under a field. Scott took another step, craning his neck. The corridor emptied into a brightly-lit concourse, with trees and shrubs. There were glass-fronted offices, furnished with computers, and a cafeteria where people were eating. Others wearing casual dress were hanging round the lounge area, chatting. It looked relaxed and friendly.

Scott stared down at his leather jacket. Without that on he could easily pass as one of them. Rubbing his trainers on the carpet to clean them, he slipped it off. Immediately, he felt

Travers breathing down his neck.

'I was only going to look,' he protested, standing back behind the half-closed door.

'I don't care what you were just going to do,' Travers said. 'We *agreed*. If necessary I'll drag you out by force. So what is it?'

'It's like an underground city. Let me, please. Just a couple of minutes more,' Scott pleaded. '*I promise.*'

'No way! Now we go and get help.'

TWENTY-FOUR

Scott crept out of the bedroom clutching his muddy trainers. From all five floors of the tall house silence reigned; the rest of the guests still fast asleep.

The four friends hadn't come across any of the people staying there. The owner had explained, in her faultless English, that she had room for ten people, most of whom returned every spring to see the flowers. And when Mary feeling curious asked, the owner laughed, not at all put out.

'My dear, Dutch is such a beast of a language. Whatever else we are, as a nation we are exceedingly practical. We have never expected foreigners to learn our language. I speak German, of course, and a little French.'

The decision to contact Doug Randal had been a majority one; Hilary declaring that she might take on the man they'd followed if forced to, but not stick her head into a hornets' nest without help.

'It's not a hornets' nest,' Travers grinned at her. 'A den of thieves perhaps.'

'*Whatever*! I'm not that stupid.'

Travers's quip had been almost the only instance of light-heartedness that had appeared in their sometimes heated discussion. If there had been joshing about, Scott would have found himself resenting it; his nerves jagged like broken glass, eating only because it helped pass the time, wincing at the slightest thing, not understanding that his friends were doing their best to help.

Mary had grabbed at the lifeline of calling Doug Randal, her face pale and worried at the thought of Travers even contemplating anything more dangerous than an exploratory cycle ride. It was Scott who resisted the plan – because of the time it would all take. No one had been at home when Travers had phoned and his dad's mobile had been on answer-phone. Even if they found him, Scott argued, it would be at least lunchtime before Mr Randal could possibly reach Lisse. By the time a rescue had been organised, yet another day would have passed.

Scott hadn't slept much, the night black and airless and the narrow bedroom he shared with Travers chock-a-block with dark-brown mahogany; its small windows camouflaged with thick lace, over which heavy velvet curtains had been draped.

He'd got up once or twice in the night for a drink of water, the effort of trying to relax and sleep leaving him hot and restless. Eventually he had fallen into an uneasy doze, waking again as light crept into the sky, knowing exactly what he was going to do.

They had replaced the bikes in the square, relieved to find no police or angry owners waiting for them. It was left to Travers to suggest that perhaps the town possessed a pool of bikes that anyone could ride, as their gesture towards global warning. Unwilling to test this hypothesis, in case they found themselves spending the night in a police station, they had taken a taxi to the house where Hilary and Mary were anxiously waiting for news.

The small landing was gloomy, the lights on a timer from eleven. Any later than that, and guests were forced to fumble around for a switch that gave just enough time to complete a single flight of stairs, before plunging the stairwell into darkness again. Hilary, tucked into the shadows on the staircase above, her mobile buried in the folds of her borrowed dressing gown, recoiled in horror at seeing the silent figure. She drew back, scarcely breathing, and shut her eyes.

Scott didn't look up. Ignoring the light switches – which puffed loudly as they blinked out – he used what little natural light was creeping up the stairwell to make his way down the precipitously-narrow stairs. He glanced at his watch, as he gently closed the door behind him. It said six fifty-nine.

'That was close,' Hilary whispered into the handset. 'I'll get dressed and follow. You can guess where's he's gone. *You* have to pick him up now. You can't put it off any longer.'

Scott shivered as the wind struck him, the air tipped with ice blowing in from the North Sea. It had rained in the night, the pavements wet, and the canal looked forlorn and unappetising, with an oily film streaking the surface of the dark-grey water.

As far as he was concerned, almost the only positive to come out of their endless discussions of the previous night, had been the realisation that several miles could be cut from the journey back to the lane. The street map, thoughtfully purchased by Mary, showed the main road to The Hague as a straight red line. Bypassing the industrial centre, it connected with the road at the traffic island. Even on a bicycle, it would take only about twenty minutes.

Crossing the cobbled roadway over the canal, Scott followed the bus route. He wished now they'd had time to travel over by ferry so he could have brought the motorbike. The act of walking, even with no one around, left him feeling exposed and vulnerable, whereas riding the Suzuki empowered him with enormous confidence. At that moment a couple of workman passed him, doing what he desperately wanted to do – cycle. He had already passed several dozen bikes, decorating the railings and kerbs, without a single chain in sight. The temptation was there. It would have been so easy to lift one. But Travers's theory about a pool of courtesy bikes, remained exactly that – a theory. They should have asked their landlady but it had been forgotten in the furore of deciding on a plan of action.

His route to the main square would have been dull, even on a sunny day but under the early morning drizzle, every attempt at colour on the facade of houses and offices was reduced to monotones of beige. Gradually the street opened out into the wide pavements of the centre.

Scott still felt cold, the walk failing to warm him up. In the square the cafés remained tightly closed-up, their patio heaters locked away in some back room, the awnings and tables as cold and forlorn as Scott felt. He needed something hot. Tea was out; the stuff he'd tried last night, when they went out for something to eat, quite disgusting.

A solitary truck crawled into the square, stopping at its far edge. Workmen jumped down and began unloading lengths of green and white canvas which would, in a matter of minutes, be transformed into gaily-striped market stalls.

He walked over to them. 'Excuse me, do you speak English?'

The men paused and pointed towards one of their workmates who was busily sorting out the metal pieces of the framework, passing them down to the men on the ground. Noticing Scott, he jumped down off the lorry and came towards him. He was tall and fair, like so many of the people Scott had seen in Holland and, although he appeared very little older than Scott, his face was already set, laughter lines permanently established at the corner of his eyes.

He smiled and nodded, taking the question seriously. '*Ja!* Always in Holland.'

'I need some coffee.'

The young man grimaced and called out to his workmates. From the sounds he made, he could have been insulting them. They laughed.

'I asked my friends if they would like a cup, too. It is cold, no?'

'Yes,' Scott agreed.

'Go down there.' The young man gestured to a street across the square. 'Good coffee. My name is Gerrard – in Dutch that is pronounced Hheracht.'

Scott started at the guttural sound. He laughed and held out his hand. 'I'm Scott! Now I can see why you don't expect us to learn your language. You sure I can't get you anything?'

'*Ja*, sure, I was joking. We had breakfast and we are finished by three in time to watch the football.'

Scott waved goodbye. Crossing the forlorn stretch of pavement that centred the square, he headed down the narrow street, a lighted shop already in view. Its windows were steamed up, reminding Scott of the all-night café they had used north of Birmingham and he hoped this would be cleaner.

It was. Sparkling blue Delft tiles formed a frieze round the walls and lined the table tops, the fogging of the windows due only to the bitterly cold wind outside. A middle-aged woman, plain but cheerful looking, stood behind the glass-topped counter; she smiled a welcome.

'Coffee, please.' Scott rubbed his hands, trying to restore their circulation.

'Well, look what the wind's blown in.' The voice was American.

Scott spun on his heel, feeling the blood drain from his face.

'Hey, kid.' It was Pete. Sunglasses still firmly in place, he looked as if he belonged there; comfortably relaxed, with a cup of coffee in front of him.

'Is Sean Terry, with you?' Scott gasped, wondering if he could reach the door before Pete reached him, praying for Gerrard's friendly face to appear.

'Kid, for crying-out-loud, you look like a startled rabbit. Sit down and take the weight off.' Pete moved one eyebrow. 'It's good to see you. We've missed you.'

'*Is Sean Terry with you?*' Scott repeated, rolling on the balls of his feet.

'Don't see him anywhere, do you?' Pete swung round deliberately to take in the whole café. 'Your coffee's ready.' He flipped the index finger of his right hand, as if firing a gun at the counter. 'Hey, why not sit down, you're quite safe, it's a public place.'

Scott quickly counted the number of people in the café – at least a dozen, most of them heavy-set, burly working men.

Quickly shoving some coins across the counter, he sat down in the seat opposite Pete, his mind still playing leapfrog. *How? Why? When?*

'So what's your problem with my boss? I know he's a shit, but I don't normally get this reaction when his name comes up.'

Scott leaned forward. '*I don't know* and that's the truth.'

Pete sighed. 'Okay, so tell me what you do know. The last time I saw you, you were tearing out of the drive at ninety miles an hour. Great escape! I figured you out all wrong. And it isn't often I do that. You struck me as the silent, no action type. But that took real guts. The boss was furious.'

Scott laughed and took a sip of his coffee. 'I know, Hilary said.'

'So she and you palled up, did you? And you've been having adventures. So how did you get here?'

'How did *you* get here?'

'Kid, we've had people at headquarters searching for your dad for fifteen years. They followed the trail to Lisse. Got here yesterday. The boss, Pearson, and me – all looking like tourists.'

Scott felt as if bands of steel were encasing his chest. 'Who's Pearson?'

A puzzled frown crossed Pete's face. 'He's from headquarters, why?'

'Where's that?'

'A haulage firm in Exeter – only a couple of guys left there now. The boss sent Tulsa and Arizona back to the States. He only brought Pearson along because he happens to know what a flower looks like.' Pete grinned, his smile self-mocking. 'So how did you get here?'

Scott ignored the question. He burst out, 'I know where Dad's being held, but you can't tell Mr Terry.'

Pete's glance was gimlet and searching. Without his sunspecs it would have drilled right through you, Scott decided, flinching away.

'He's my boss – so explain.' The tone matched the look, no longer casual, leaving Scott in no doubt that the hundreds of muscles in Pete's body had woken up ready for action.

Scott hesitated, watching the door open and shut, with one labourer being exchanged for two shop assistants; both girls ordering lattes and croissant, before taking up the free table in the window. They immediately wiped the window clear so they could have something to look at while they chatted.

'You found Dad the sensible way, I took the long way round,' he admitted and blinked, remembering the hundreds of miles he had ridden pursuing fragile clues. 'But always the bad guys found us. Do you know who they are?'

'Nope!' Pete cradled his coffee cup in his hands. 'Never had the pleasure.'

Although Pete gave the appearance of being relaxed, only interested in the bottom of his cup, Scott was only too aware the agent wasn't missing a trick.

'We discovered I'd been bugged and although Hilary keeps trying to be loyal, even she was finally forced to admit only Sean Terry could have done it.'

'No way!' Pete shook his head. 'Sean's one of the good guys.'

'How do I prove it to you?' Scott argued.

'*You can't.*' Pete got to his feet. 'I need more coffee. You?'

Scott drained his cup. 'Wish it was tea but yes, thanks.' What should he do now? What if Pete refused to believe him and contacted Sean Terry.

He gazed bleakly at the row of blue tiles on the wall, the stylized scenes of milkmaids carrying wooden churns staring back at him, horribly aware that he should have left while he still had a chance. He fixed his eyes on Pete's back, daring his hand to reach for his mobile and alert his boss.

A second later Scott's heart skipped a beat, his feet ready to break into movement as the agent's hand reached down into his pocket. It reappeared clutching a fistful of change.

Pete angled his body into a V-shape slithering past the table edge, a couple of croissant on a plate clutched in one hand. 'Food'll help,' he said, pushing the plate across the table. 'So how *did* you get here?'

'Travers, a friend from school, his brother owns a plane.'

'Nice! *And?*'

'Well, yesterday afternoon we saw this man. I recognised him as one of the men checking the sheep.'

'Sure?'

'Positive. Remember, I spoke to them. He told me they'd found radiation in one of the fields. But they couldn't have, because that's where the sheep were all winter. I even asked the farmer. And, if the sheep were clear, it wasn't possible for the field to be contaminated. I guess they were keeping an eye on Dad.'

'So why didn't you tell us any of this?'

'I didn't trust you,' Scott said frankly.

'Okay!'

'We followed him. He left his bike at a factory in the outskirts and went into this field. He disappeared but we found this manhole with a ladder. At the bottom was an underground city. Trees and stuff. People ...' Scott gazed round the busy space, conversations with occasional bursts of laughter floating into the air, despite the early hour. 'There was even a coffee shop, like this one. I was going to explore further but Travers dragged me back. Still I'm positive that's where Dad's being kept. I saw this room. It had computers in it.'

'And you were going to rescue him, with what?' Pete's tone was relaxed.

Scott held up his half-eaten croissant.

Pete laughed. 'Unusual weapon, I'd prefer a Colt or a sub-machine gun.'

'The people I saw, they were wearing jeans and T-shirts – you know ordinary stuff. I thought I could mingle and have a look round, without being noticed. I mean the way I got in ...' Scott frowned. 'It was more like an emergency exit. I bet no one knew it existed.'

'So why not get help?' Pete's tone was mildly curious.

'We have.'

Pete sat up straight. 'Much more sensible than going it alone. Who've you called, the police?'

'No, Travers contacted his dad. Travers said, knowing his dad, he'll bring the cavalry.' Scott broke off a piece of his croissant, crumbling it between his fingers. 'Only problem is, it'll take them a few hours to get here; and I can't wait that long.'

Pete pulled out his mobile.

'No! Pete! Not Sean Terry, you can't!'

Scott's voice was loud enough to stop all conversation in the café. Pete held up his hand nodding amiably at the occupants of the other tables.

'Relax, kid! It's not Sean, though it would be better for you if it was.'

'Please, not till Dad's safe.' Scott begged.

Pete shrugged. 'Have it your own way. But you can't go alone. I was ordering us a taxi, that's all. But I'm not promising anything. At best we might have a look round, okay?'

Scott nodded, his fingers pushing the crumbs round his plate.

Pete dialled, speaking casually into the handset. 'Travelight? A taxi to one-two-seven Centrestraat. Okay. Five minutes, two passengers. Thanks.' He snapped the mobile shut. 'What the hell we did before we had these, I don't know.'

'Pay phones, I think,' Scott said.

Pete's slid along the seat and got to his feet. 'Okay, kid, if we're going to do a spot of rescuing, we'd better go. Finished?'

Scott's middle griped nervously at him, the croissant in his mouth like a block of concrete. He hastily took a sip of coffee, almost choking in his efforts to swallow it.

Pete waited by the door, eyeing up the shop assistants. Something about his casual manner made Scott think of Hilary. She'd been excited, hyped up with adrenaline when they'd been escaping the bullets at the motel. But not Pete. This visit could end in bloodshed or with his dad safe. Whatever was going to happen appeared of no consequence, the agent more interested in the two girls. Would Hilary change? Would she become so used to danger that she became blasé about carrying a gun? Or using it?

In the time it had taken Scott to drink two coffees, a line of market stalls had sprung up, their green and white shells waiting for the flower sellers to arrive and festoon the air with perfume. Nearby, talking to the workmen, was a young woman.

A taxi – its engine still running – was waiting for them a little way down the street. Pete spoke to the driver and was about to open the back door when Scott grabbed his arm.

'There's Hilary!' he exclaimed, pointing towards the square. 'She must have followed me.' The American brushed Scott's hand from his jacket, swivelling on the balls of his feet to see where Scott was pointing. 'I'm still not sure about her. Mostly I believe she's okay but if she came with us, you could keep an eye on her.' Scott smiled apologetically. 'And if she is okay a second gun would be ...'

'*Sorry, kid, not today.*'

A heavy blow in the centre of his back knocked Scott onto the floor of the cab, the driver speeding into gear long before Pete had closed the door.

Scott looked up, winded and unable to speak, seeing the muzzle of the Colt not a foot from his chest.

'Sorry for the dramatics,' Pete indicated the gun. Dropping his arm, he rested the black steel on his knee. 'You can get up now. *Hell*! Of all the bad luck, seeing Stone.'

Scott hid in the corner of the cab. 'I don't understand,' he gasped, trying to drag air into lungs that were still hurting.

'Look, Scott, I like you. Full of spunk! I don't know many kids your age that would have gone on and on till they found their dad; most would have given up ages ago. So this is nothing personal. I have a job to do. Deliver you.'

'Deliver me ... to who?'

'My boss. He already has your dad.'

'But ...'

'You thought it was Sean Terry.' Pete shrugged. 'You've only got yourself to blame. I kept telling you, he's one of the good guys.'

'But ...'

'We've been trying to get your dad for fifteen years, Davois and me,' he added. 'He's the bloke you followed – stupid bastard,' he swore, his tone savage. 'We traced him to Sacramento, but no sign.'

'Why me?' Scott managed to spit out.

'Because your dad will never work for us without. But I can promise you, no one means you any harm. Once your dad sorts out their little computer problem, you and he will be living the life of millionaires. Nothing will be too good for you.'

The taxi had slowed, now travelling the empty streets at a speed unlikely to attract attention. Scott wondered if he could reach the door handle and leap out before a shot could be fired.

'Don't try it, kid.' Pete warned, his glance homing in on Scott, his pistol moving at the same time.

'Okay!' Scott sighed painfully. He'd got it wrong, so bloody wrong. Sean Terry was okay and Hilary had been telling the truth. He should have believed her right from the start.

He stared helplessly out of the window. The taxi was now travelling in a straight line, mimicking the red line on the map that ended at the traffic island. He felt like an animal in a trap, terrified, despite the assurance that no harm would come to him. But it could to his dad – and he was responsible – *responsible because he'd got it wrong*.

'Why didn't you kidnap me at the cottage?' he said.

'Thought about it, but Stone was there. Only a kid herself. I would have had to kill her. I hadn't a problem with that ...'

Scott shivered.

'But most likely, I'd have blown my cover. Terry's no fool. He'd have guessed if I survived an attack it was because I was part of it. This is different.'

'You must have thought me a real patsy, I even liked you; it's laughable.' Scott said, the bitterness in his tone carrying across the partition to the driver. He tilted his head back listening.

'This doesn't change anything. It's not personal. I told you, I think you're a swell kid. This is politics. I happen to work for someone who dislikes the way the world is going. And in politics there has to be casualties.' Pete ended the sentence on a shrug.

'*You* killed that man?'

Pete nodded. Dropping his pistol into his lap he removed his sunspecs, wiping them on a tissue; his eyes the ice blue of an artic sky, his tone of voice once again as casual as it had been when sipping at his coffee. 'Couldn't take a chance on his talking. You can't spill the beans if you're dead.'

Scott's mind stopped working; his eyes automatically absorbing the images of places as they passed by, his subconscious unscrambling them into recognisable objects – fields dotted with an occasional tree, a traffic island ahead; on its far side ornamental gardens belonging to a factory.

The taxi slowed and drove in through its gates, the elegant white shape of the building looming over the black vehicle, like a preying mantis devouring its prey. A line of young people hurried out of the building towards them.

Scott blinked and a thought leaped through the frozen conduits. Ordinary people finishing their shift. Help! They could help.

He felt Pete's eyes move and focus on the line. 'You said an underground city with kids in T-shirts and jeans.'

It wasn't a question.

Scott shut his eyes hoping that Travers would wake early, see he was missing and follow. Except they weren't going to the field. Why not? He opened them again and pushed the thought into speech. 'Why here? If you're taking me to my dad, the place is further on. So why are we stopping here?'

TWENTY-FIVE

For Bill the four days of captivity seemed endless. Not being able to stretch his legs in the open air a worse punishment than he realised, leading to sleepless nights from lack of exercise; while the knowledge of being trapped underground was something he found impossible to shake from his thoughts. It wasn't fear for himself; it never had been. His nightmares about the tsunami had never involved him. After all, he hadn't been there. But his friends and colleagues had, and it was these faces that wakened him sweating in the night.

Surprisingly, no one bothered him. No heavy mob, with baseball bats, threatening him to hurry up and unlock the secrets of his computer. This lack of urgency was in itself a clue; an acknowledgement that the people he was dealing with had aeons of time.

It was ironic that despite losing all their data and half his colleagues, it had only taken seven more years to recreate the project and bring it to fruition. Styrus did work, although now Bill wished they had destroyed it. But a desire for the world to acknowledge their efforts had overridden common sense. In the right hands, like the Internet, it would have been of immense value, particularly for the United Nations committed to fighting terrorism wherever it reared its head. In the wrong hands, Styrus could destroy the world as they knew it. And if Scott were found, he, Bill, would be forced into wielding this weapon of destruction.

Now it was Saturday, and a repeat of the previous four days.

More coffee than was good for him, fretting about Scott, living in dread of the announcement that he'd been found; exhausted from lack of sleep and the constant search for a way out – all of it useless. Mr Smith had been right. There wasn't one – if there was, he hadn't found it yet. In the daytime too many people about; at night, his bedroom door locked from the outside to stop him finding a way into the conduits, the heavy galvanised tubes that carried the air-conditioning.

'Bill. We're leaving. Come on.'

The crossword, Bill's only means of whiling away the endless hours of the morning, slipped from his fingers. Aquilla was standing in front of him, as fastidiously dressed as always. He was carrying a small briefcase.

'Luggage!' he nodded towards it. 'But you won't be needing any.'

Bill suddenly became aware of activity; a hurried criss-crossing of the lounge area by numbers of young people. Most appeared to be making for the boardroom; uniformed firemen heading the opposite way, trailing wire behind them.

'Fire?' he said hopefully.

'There will be if we don't leave now. By the way, we have your son. He'll be with us shortly.'

Bill felt sick, his face stiff with shock; the frank and open demeanour that he'd worked so hard to maintain, wiped off.

'He didn't do badly though, did he?' he managed. 'A kid, not yet sixteen, on his own out there. Led your lot a merry dance.'

Aquilla smiled. Not his usual tight-lipped Teutonic offering that never reached his eyes; this was a genuine gold-plated smile which, if repeated daily, would lead to laughter lines round the eyes and deep groves permanently etched on either side of his mouth.

'If I had a son, I'd be proud to have yours,' he said.

Bill started.

Aquilla waved an arm nonchalantly, embracing the activity. 'He's responsible for this little lot.'

'How …?'

'Only found out where you were and brought a rescue party. Picking him up now is rather like locking the stable door after the horse has bolted, wouldn't you say?' The smile disappeared. 'Unfortunately, his success necessitates a change in our direction. We have a helicopter waiting, after which this place will disappear under several-hundred tons of water. Anything caught in it will disappear, too. But don't be fooled, Bill. In the big scheme of things, this doesn't even register. Let's get moving.' A gun appeared in his hand. 'This way.'

At the far end of the boardroom, tucked away behind the video screen, appeared a corridor. Brightly lit along its entire length, it sloped steadily uphill, a number of figures already hurrying along its walkway towards safety; aware that the trailing lengths of wire meant an imminent explosion.

All at once Bill felt like bursting into song and risking the shocked expressions of the youngsters walking alongside, their eyes flicking curiously from the gun barrel to his face. He stopped himself in the nick of time. Superfluous gestures would take energy and, before long, he was going to need every scrap he could summon up. If Scott could wreck their operation, *he* could find a way out. This sudden exodus was something the enemy hadn't planned for. There would be mistakes. Adrenalin surged through his body wiping away the inertia and fatigue of the past few days, stretching his muscles ready for action at an instant's notice.

At the end of the corridor, double doors opened into a concrete-clad lobby housing a lift and emergency stairs, a young man politely holding them back for the two men to pass through. At the far side of the lobby, heavy glass doors led out onto a driveway, with shrubs and grass.

'Up!' Aquilla indicated the open doors of the lift with his gun.

Bill eyed the weapon cautiously. When purchasing it, Aquilla's primary purpose may well have been to buy something small enough not to damage the elegant cut of his suit. Despite that, it was still likely to be deadly at close range.

Aquilla followed the direction of his glance and gave an abrupt laugh. 'Don't think for one second you're going to make it through those doors to freedom.' He inclined his head towards the glass doors. 'You may be invaluable but that wouldn't stop me killing you. And I'm a good shot.'

'I thought you probably were,' Bill said agreeably. 'But what about those poor beggars?' He pointed to the youngsters, a continuous line passing through the glass doors. 'Unless you've got a coach waiting outside for them.'

Aquilla punched the button for the roof. 'They simply walk out into the sunset. Regroup in another country and start again, working for the cause.' Behind him the doors swung silently into place, a low whining noise accompanying the lift on its ascent.

Bill felt the gears slowing the heavy machinery to a stop, then the doors opened and a blustery wind blew in. With every sense on high alert, he stepped out. He glanced down at the emergency stairwell – listening intently for the telltale sound of footsteps echoing against the concrete – but heard nothing. Then, leisurely, as if making an entrance to some party on the cocktail circuit, he slowly ascended the four steps to the roof, stopping on the last one to take a deep, lung-filling breath – the swirling expanse of oxygen-laden air tugging at his jacket. He moved out on to the exposed deck and was instantly blasted backwards by the fierce wind. Aquilla, leaning into it, indicated for Bill to keep tight-hold of the safety rail, securing the perimeter of the bitumen-covered platform.

Keeping his face blank, and his body like that of someone having a spot of bother staying upright, Bill flicked a glance down over the safety rail. Immediately beneath his feet, a heavy granite slab folded itself into the edge of the roof space. The inspection lasted no more than a second or so, but it was enough. It had to be. When you climbed mountains, you became used to entrusting your life to the accuracy of your eyesight. Six granite pillars swooped down the side of the building. Mimicking the fold of a wave, they generously formed a ninety-degree angle with the white-panelled fascia.

He looked up, his eyes watering in the biting wind.

Two people were already seated in the helicopter; its engines revving, its rotor blades swaying awkwardly under the torrent of air, as if unsure which way they should go. The German bodyguard, Arnulf, was positioned by the door, his right arm held up across the front of his jacket, a pistol in his hand.

Waiting to escort me in, Bill thought ruefully. He turned, hearing the whine of the lift.

'*Scott!*'

The barrel of the small pistol lodged in his ribs, stopping him in his tracks.

Scott, ignoring the gun in his escort's hand, a tall, rangy fellow wearing green reflective shades, flung himself into his dad's arms; the man making no attempt to stop him.

'They're coming, Dad, we've got to hang on.' Scott whispered, his face buried in Bill's jacket.

Letting go of his son's arm, Bill stood aside to force Aquilla to pass in front of him. The man hesitated then took a step towards the helicopter, gesturing with his gun for Bill to follow.

Bill glanced pointedly at the guns fixed on him, then at their owners, and gave a wry smile. Backing-up towards Aquilla, he raised his hands.

'Look,' he said, keeping his expression carefully neutral. 'We're on a roof. We're not going anywhere except in this helicopter. Come on, chaps, put away the fire power.' He made his voice as persuasive as the buffeting wind permitted.

There was a lessening of tension. That was all. But it had to be enough. In a blur of speed Bill brought down his elbows, knocking Aquilla to the ground.

'*This way, Scott!*'

Grabbing his son's hand, they fled towards the lift. Pete raised his arm, squinting along the barrel already aimed at the centre of Bill's back. As his trigger finger moved, Arnulf sprang forward, fast for such a large man, his weapon raised. He cannoned heavily into Pete, and the shot spun harmlessly off into the air.

'*NO!*' Aquilla yelled at the same time. '*We need him!*'

'Get him,' Seagar instructed from the helicopter. 'Wound him with pleasure, but take him alive. *Hurry!*'

'Dad?' Scott yelled as they reached the shelter of the lift housing, only to hear footsteps clattering below them on the staircase.

Bill shouted back, the wind whipping away his words. Ducking the open entrance, he ran on. 'We'll have to climb,' he repeated. 'The staircase is out. And we'd never make the lift before they reached us.' His words sounded staccato in the swirling wind.

'*But we're on the top of a building, Dad!*'

'I know. It'll be a great climb. Checked it out. It's easy. Slopes like mad and the windows all have great ledges.'

Scott looked down over the edge, hesitating. No way was it easy. On the ground, foreshortened by the drop and looking no bigger than ants, dozens of people appeared to be milling about.

'No time to think, Scott.'

Scott risked a glance over his shoulder at the two men chasing after them. A shot whistled by, so close he jumped with fright.

'That was a warning shot,' Bill called out. 'That lot, if they want to kill, don't miss. Come on.' His head vanished below the fascia, his hand reaching upwards to help Scott.

At that moment, the air blew apart with an explosion, the violence and force of it stopping their pursuers. They ducked as shards of glass were blown upwards, like a shower of rose petals, landing on the roof.

That decided it. Lowering himself on his arms, Scott concentrated all his thoughts into his feet, feeling his toes scrape against the smooth surface of the top-floor window.

'To your left, Scott.'

He felt Bill's hand steering his foot. It touched the rough surface and held on, his brain informing his foot muscles to remain in place. He swung his second foot to join the first. A shot flashed past his hand. Automatically he flinched and his hand sprang away from its grip so, momentarily, only his feet were keeping him anchored; his left arm still moving, in the process of searching for a handhold.

Bill was talking, his voice steady.

'Ten floors, Scott. Identical, except there's a gradient. Not much but it's still a bonus – and the pillar is rough granite which is great for climbing, no different from climbing on Snowdon.'

Except it was. Scott moved his hand, not saying a word. They had climbed so many times together his dad knew he listened, their lives depended on it.

'Two floors behind us now. Take the next the same way. Hang from the ledge at the corner of the window, while your feet gain a purchase.'

Scott simplified his thoughts. Nothing of importance now, not even counting the number of the floors as he passed them; letting his dad do that. All that was important was steady, safe movement; repeating the same action, not allowing his brain to become over-confident simply because he had safely manoeuvred his way past two floors.

'Eight floors left, that's all. Feel the slope yet? Lean into the rock, it'll hold you.'

Out of the corner of his eye, Scott spotted movement. A window in the white wall had opened and a figure leaned out. He daren't look to see, the figure remaining a blur, only the rock face in front of him in focus.

'*Dad*!' he shouted, hesitating in his next step.

'I've seen him. Take no notice.'

He heard the sound of a shot and a blast of wind whipped past his cheek.

'*Damn*!' Bill yelled out.

There was a scraping sound; the noise a body makes when it grinds over a rough surface. At the same time a roar of noise rose up from the ground and a shower of bullets patterned against the windows, rupturing the reinforced glass. Scott became aware that the head had vanished, the window slammed shut.

'*Dad*! You okay?' he shouted, his voice panicky.

223

He let go his breath when he heard the words come back to him. 'Lucky shot, hit me in the shoulder. Bleeding like a pig.'

'Stay there. I'll get you!'

He heard Bill chuckle, wiped out by a grimace of pain. 'Can't go anywhere – hanging on, though.'

Closing his ears to the sound of his father's breathing, Scott tried to visualise the face of the building, aware he had to detour round his body, which was blocking his path down. He dropped his hand, his fingertips gluing themselves to the window ledge, his second hand joining them. Leaning his weight into the windowpane, he stretched out his foot, his toe brushing the surface of the ledge below. He pulled it back up – resting. He had to drop onto that ledge. To skirt round his father's body tucked into the corner of the granite, he had to sidestep down that panel, trusting his entire weight to a single hand. Not daring to think he wouldn't do it right, his toes reached down for the sill; then his left hand stretched towards the roughness of the granite, fastening on to it, the fingers of his right hand slowly following.

'Great manoeuvre, Scott. Proud of you.'

Bill's face, now on a level with his own, shone with sweat, his colour already patchy.

'I've got you, Dad,' Scott said and, using his body as a counter weight, shielded Bill's crumpled form from the pull of gravity. 'I won't let you drop.'

'How long till help gets here?' Bill gasped, leaving Scott to imagine the warmth of the blood soaking his dad's back.

'If that was an automatic I heard firing from the ground, Dad, any second now. So hang on. Take some deep breaths.'

TWENTY-SIX

Scott waited, not daring to talk, in case the energy needed proved too much for his father's body, teetering between hanging on and plunging to the ground. Unable to see anything, he concentrated on holding his dad steady.

He heard the sound of a helicopter overhead, seeing the machine gain height before it accelerated forwards, the sound of its engines masking any noises from above. There were shouts from the ground too but he ignored them, knowing that to keep his dad safe meant he couldn't afford to let his attention waver for a second.

After a minute or two, Scott heard scratching noises coming from the roof and the sound of people talking. He no longer cared if it was Pete or one of the other men; merely relieved that someone – anyone – was coming to help. He could feel the weight of his father's body, increasingly unable to hold itself upright, pushing him out from the safety of the rock face. He heard feet against the glass of the window and Sean Terry came into view.

Scott held his breath, not knowing what to think or believe.

Above him, he heard the whine of a rope being paid out and a second set of feet jumping their way down the side of the building.

Then a cheerful voice said, 'Cavalry's here, Scott.'

Attached to a heavy climbing belt and several ropes, Beau's head, with its dark hair and crooked jaw, appeared. Momentarily Scott closed his eyes to stop the moisture leaking from them.

'I thought you were in Belgium?' he gasped.

'I was! But Dad thought this little party much more interesting. He was right, too. Wouldn't have missed it for the world. You okay, Mr Anderson?'

Bill raised his head, his face grey with pain and fatigue.

'If you really are the cavalry, I'm fine.'

'That's brilliant! Now we're going to pass a belt round you. Hold on a couple more seconds, Scott, okay.' Beau sounded as cheerful as if he was demonstrating a move in the gym, with mats below to catch you if you fell.

'Can you move your arm at all, Bill?' the grating tones of Sean Terry's voice cut across the air.

'Who are you?'

'Name's Terry.'

'The reporter?' The voice sounded exhausted, the two words using up vital strength.

'Don't worry about it. We can work on that once we've got a few pints of blood into you. All you need to know right now is — I climb.' The abrupt tone flew back at Bill, the stick-like figure on the end of the rope walking across the face of the building. Nonchalantly, he passed a heavy belt round Bill Anderson's waist and clipped it to his own.

'Let go now, youngster.'

Scott let out a strangled cry as he felt his father drop, before understanding it was simply his father's body relaxing into the belt, experienced enough to know it would hold.

'I thought you were one of them,' he admitted, glancing timidly at the steel-blue eyes, watching his father like a hawk.

'And very proper, too,' Beau broke in; the tones of his voice absurdly cheerful for someone marooned eighty feet in the air. 'I would have felt exactly the same had I not seen him abseiling down the face of this building.'

Scott felt a belt pass round his own body and heard a clunk as the clip snapped shut.

'Any man who climbs like he does, you can definitely trust with your life. Okay, Scott, relax. I've got you and there's a number of very-chunky, ex-rugby players who've got me.'

Scott felt an insane desire to giggle, wondering if he dare ask who had got them.

'What's happening on the ground, Terry?' Bill said his voice faint.

'The Dutch police are up to their eyeballs in water and they're not best pleased. Where did they get you?'

'Shoulder, splintered the bone, I think.'

'Careless, for someone they wanted alive.'

'They're the sort to reason you can always operate a computer with one hand.'

Now he could move his head, Scott saw his father not making any attempt to keep a hold, his feet simply resting on the rough granite surface. He's hurt bad, but I've got him back, he thought, delight momentarily overpowering his anxiety.

Sean Terry's voice cut across the air like a knife. 'I'll have to strap it tight. This may hurt but you've lost a lot of blood. I need to get you down without delay. There's an ambulance standing by, it'll get you to hospital.'

'But the men?' Scott interrupted.

'They've gone. And if that blast was anything to do with them, blew the place apart, too.'

'So it's not ended,' Bill whispered.

Scott saw Sean Terry studying his father closely. 'No! Not for me. But it is for you, pal.'

Bill lifted his head painfully. 'Got a lot to say. I'll be fine by tomorrow.'

Scott watched anxiously, gasping with sympathy as he saw his father flinch and turn very white, a second strap fixing his arm into place across his chest.

Sean Terry tugged on the rope. Slowly the two figures began their descent, the reporter cradling Bill's body with his own.

Beau waited a moment. 'Let them get clear,' he confided. 'Don't want a traffic jam on the ground. Right, off we go.'

It was the strangest of sensations and one Scott wasn't quite sure if he liked. It was different abseiling yourself. Here, he had no control; the only thing needed was total belief in the person you were strapped to. Seconds later, his toes bounced on the ground. Simultaneous bear hugs almost knocked him to the floor, despite Beau's remonstrations, as Travers, Mary and Hilary, seeing Scott safe and sound, rushed up to greet him.

'You lot go with Scott to the hospital. And get him something to drink. We'll clear up this mess here.'

Scott stared round at the number of vehicles homing-in on the factory forecourt; a half-a-dozen people closeted against the side of an official-looking car, deep into some serious conversation. An army truck appeared, soldiers adding to the general confusion.

TWENTY-SEVEN

Scott listened to the questions; most of them he never heard, a thick blanket of exhaustion like a rain cloud in front of his eyes. Those he did hear, most he was unable to answer. He concentrated on the things he did know and could remember – like being in a hospital; although the language spoken by its staff left him with a feeling of immense bewilderment, despite the sparkling-white surfaces and an appearance of efficiency. The doctors, switching from English to Dutch, only added to the confusion; as did his friends. While one stayed the others ate, bringing him food that wouldn't go down. Yet, when he opened his eyes, to take in something other than the still figure lying in the hospital bed, someone different was always sitting there, keeping him company.

Doug Randal had appeared, his larger than life persona bulldozing his way through the fog that surrounded Scott.

'I'll be back tomorrow,' he had said. 'Beau's about if you need him. If you will trust me with your dad's bike, I'll get it shipped back from Glasgow. It'll be waiting for you although I don't think Bill will be riding it for a while, Scott.'

Scott remembered that bit, handing over the keys; grateful to think he didn't have to leave his dad's bedside in order to ride the bike back to Cornwall.

'It'll take more than a bullet to stop me, Scott, don't worry,' had been his dad's final words, as they wheeled him into the operating theatre. Since then he hadn't uttered a word; a red streak of blood, coursing through the drip hanging from the top of his bed, the only indication he was alive; except, of course, he had to be alive otherwise he wouldn't be all bandaged up.

A nurse bustled in. Scott tried to count how many times she had come in since the operation. And was that a good sign or a bad? She bent over the bed.

'Your fader, he is waking.'

Scott stared out through the fog. How could his dad be waking? He'd only looked at him a second ago and he was still unconscious then.

'Here! Look!' She handed him a stick of iced water. 'He is thirsty. You give it.'

Scott bent over the bed. 'Dad?' He moistened the cracked lips.

'Told you!' Bill mouthed the words.

Scott grinned. 'Yeah, you told me. Here, have this. A couple of these and you'll be giving me a lecture, a mile long.'

'Get some sleep,' the voice a little stronger. 'Leave the talking till morning.'

'Okay, Dad. Dad?'

The figure stirred, the blue eyes drooping with pain and fatigue. 'Mmm?'

'It's great,' Scott said and was answered by the ghost of a smile.

The mist suddenly cleared. For the first time, he noticed the room in which he had spent the last fourteen hours, its large windows overlooking the street; Travers sitting silently in a chair.

'*Travers*! You here? Whatever time is it?' he said, forgetting he was wearing a watch.

'Gone twelve.'

'At night?'

Travers nodded.

'And you've been here all this time?'

'No, Mary and Hilary were here too. We were worried about you.'

'I'm okay, now. So where are they?'

'Sleeping, I hope.' Travers yawned. 'Bad day all round. What the devil were you doing, going off like that?' he accused Scott angrily. 'And after all I said, too. Frightened us half to death. If you'd been a member of my squad, I'd have given you the boot.'

'You were right,' Scott apologised. 'I wasn't thinking straight.'

'Damn good job Hilary couldn't sleep either. She saw you leave. We came after you in time to see you being bundled into a black car. I hailed a taxi and followed.'

'But how did Mr Randal get here? It was him I saw a little while back, wasn't it?'

'Dad? He was already here.'

'*How?*'

'Don't ask me. Gosh, I'm tired. Ask Beau. He's around somewhere. He's organised storm troopers at the entrance. Went off for a long chat with that American guy. Ever since they shinned down that factory wall they've been joined at the hip. Wouldn't be at all surprised to hear they'd got hitched.'

Beau's face, its broken nose and kink in the jaw noticeably evident, appeared round the door. 'You talkin' about me? Hey, youngster you look happier.' He winked at Scott. 'For a moment back there, I began to wonder whether the hospital had got the right patient. So now your dad's off the danger list, I don't suppose I could tempt you into swopping an uncomfortable armchair, with wipe-down vinyl seat covers, for a spot of horizontal in a nice comfy bed with breakfast at the end of it?'

Scott stared blankly. Then, figuring out what Beau meant, laughed out loud. 'No, I'll sleep here, thanks.'

'Okay, then, so here's the drill. In a moment, a devilishly attractive nurse, who doesn't speak one word of English so don't bother trying, is going to come in and hook your dad up to a morphine pump. That's because, until the anaesthetic wears off he won't feel any pain. Once it has, he will. There's a bell …' Beau crossed to the bed and picked it up. 'Press it and people will appear, as if by magic.' He grinned. 'And, just in case you are concerned, the men outside belong to the Dutch police and are armed. Oh yes, if you happen to want the loo in the night, it's likely you will be followed there by a tall, blond Nazi type in a mac.'

Beau laughed at the glazed expression on Scott's face. 'Don't be alarmed, he's not a pervert. The Dutch authorities have, rightly or wrongly, found the events of the day somewhat worrying. The owner of the factory is kicking up a storm. Yelling "terrorists" and pointing his finger at you and your father as the most likely suspects. On the other hand, the authorities have a strong aversion to foreigners being abducted at gunpoint and pot-shots taken at them, and are determined to keep you safe from further harm, until they've had a chance to find out exactly what did happen. In which case, either he, or his twin brother, will be your shadow until you step onto a plane and wave goodbye.'

Scott blinked. Travers had always described his brother as *something else*. He definitely was that all right.

'But it's okay, isn't it?' he said.

'No more bad guys?' said Beau, the sarcasm quite strong.

Scott nodded.

'Depends what you're looking for. If your aim was to get your dad back ...'

'Definitely ... to get Dad back ... yes.'

'Then you have undoubtedly triumphed.' Beau's eyes twinkled. 'However, if you are talking about defeating the bad guys ...? Terry, with whom I have had a long chat, says the spoils of war are pretty much even. In other words, they might think they have the belt but we definitely have the braces.' He spotted Scott's puzzled frown. 'They have the computer files but we have your dad,' he explained. 'And since they don't have your dad, and their base has been destroyed, it will take a long while for them to re-group and, hopefully, longer still to decode the files. If we're lucky, the good guys will get there first. If we're not, then we can expect all sorts of fun and games. But I doubt Terry will say it quite like that.'

Scott gave up trying to work out whether Beau was joking or not.

Beau's smile was mocking. 'Terry will probably throw the

term, *real and present danger* half a dozen times into every conversation, to get your father back to the States.'

'But how did Mr Randal happen to get here so quickly?'

'Oh that! I rang him from Lisse airport.' Beau said calmly, perching himself on the bed.

'YOU!' Scott and Travers burst out together. 'I don't understand,' added Scott.

'Name James Nicely mean anything?'

'Yes, what about him?' Scott said excitedly.

'It seems that Dad and this Nicely character have been hatching plots. This one was to rescue your dad,' he explained. 'He happened to be wearing a trace bug in his shoes, just in case the day ever arrived when he was kidnapped. It went off the screen near Lisse.'

'But why your father?'

'Dad's an old-fashioned monarchist.' Beau's face broke into a puzzled frown. 'Guess I am, too; never thought about it before.' He held up his hands. 'Don't ask me how they met. I know they go way back. I never ask questions like that.'

'Is Mr Nicely okay?'

Beau raised one eyebrow. 'You mean the attack? I guess so. Dad flew back to see him. He wanted to check he was okay and let him know what had happened. Dad says he's the most extraordinary character. Did you ever meet him?'

'Yes, I did, I mean we did – Hilary and me. Three …' Scott rubbed his eyes, 'No … four days ago.'

'Talks with a plum in his mouth and keeps an automatic down the side of his wheel chair.'

Travers whistled with astonishment. 'Now I know what Mary meant. Nothing half this exciting ever happens in Cornwall. Did you know he was loaded, Scott?'

Scott grinned. 'We had tea and scones. So, what happened?'

'Apparently, he saw off the intruders but his nephew got hurt.'

'We knew that bit. Hilary rang round the hospitals in Glasgow but we didn't know if Mr Nicely was okay and daren't go back to check, in case we were being followed.'

'I think the old man is curious to know how they found him.'

Scott said slowly, 'My trainers were bugged.'

'Aha! That makes sense with all these wicked Secret Service agents on the loose. Sorry now I won't be taking you back to England. You could have donned earphones and recounted the amazing adventures of that intrepid duo – Scott and Hilary, super sleuths.'

Scott blushed.

Travers laughed. 'Have you worked out the mystery yet of why I'm the quiet one in the family and never say much?'

Beau's eyes twinkled. He got to his feet. 'So, brother of mine, how about I take you back to the hotel, where I will occupy the bed so kindly left empty by Scott. If you can persuade Scott to give us the pleasure of his company for breakfast, we can lay bare the remainder of these fascinating mysteries.' He put a friendly arm round his brother's shoulder. 'Come on, Travers,' he added seriously. 'You look done in. Let's get some sleep.'

Scott slept. In the night someone covered him with a blanket, sliding a pillow under his head, but even that failed to wake him.

He woke to find his dad propped up against a bank of pillows, the stubble on his chin flecked with grey, reminding Scott of Sean Terry's hangdog look. Still, he seemed a shade better, not quite so drawn.

'You look terrible, Scott,' he greeted his son. 'Go away, get showered and come back after lunch, clean and tidy, and ready to talk to the dozens of people asking questions and demanding answers.'

Scott groaned; then smiled. 'You look better, too, Dad, but still pretty grim. What about your shoulder?'

'Wonders of modern medicine. Can't feel a thing, unless I try to move it.'

'Is it broken?'

'The scapula is. It's that flat bone on the back of the shoulder,' Bill explained. 'In several pieces, so they tell me. But

234

it will heal. I just have to be patient. Perhaps, at long last, you will learn to cook something more exotic than stir-fry and pasta.'

Scott yawned and stretched. 'I doubt it but I could do with a bath,' he admitted, 'except I don't want to leave you.'

'You might as well. As soon as I've seen the doctor, this room will be full of suited officials demanding answers as to why someone should blow a big hole in their canal.'

'Is that what they did?'

'Apparently so. And I'm the only witness. Everyone else has vanished.'

Scott frowned, keeping quiet about the sliver of information Beau had let slip. 'But I want to hear your story,' he said instead. 'I don't even know what happened to you.'

Bill smiled and let out a long, painful breath. 'If I know officialdom, I'll be explaining what happened from now till Christmas and, by summer, we'll be bored to death with talking about it. So go. I'll see you after lunch.'

Scott waited on the steps of the hospital, wondering which part of the town he was in, the buildings quite unfamiliar and the street empty. Sunday, he reminded himself, no one works. He swung round to go back into Reception and ask which way to Kanaalstraat, only to find a tall blond man almost breathing down his neck. He started back, viewing the long, black leather coat with suspicion.

The man gave a slight bow and clicked his heels. 'Good morning, sir. My credentials. There is a car waiting.'

He passed across an official-looking card for inspection. Like Sean Terry's Secret Service badge, this meant nothing; a series of lines of gobbledegook. Scott froze. The last time he had entered a car there'd been a gun in his face.

The man saw his hesitation and his face broke into a smile, his blue eyes sparkling, at odds with his sombre attire.

'Is all right,' he said. 'Your brother, he explained you hate cars. You would prefer to walk, is not far.'

So Beau had even thought of that. Scott didn't bother to

explain that he didn't have a brother. 'No, it's okay,' he agreed. 'The car's fine.'

Mary, thrilled that her friend was receiving so much attention, insisted Travers bought the policeman breakfast. If she'd had her way he would have sat at their table, but Travers decided it was time he put his foot down.

'We can't gossip with the police present. I'm quite aware you think he's a hunk, but I'm not having it, Mary,' he said sounding indignant. 'I'm not taking you to Holland to fall in love with a policeman.'

'I've no intention of doing that, Travers. You're being stupid,' Mary said, her face pinking up with annoyance. 'But look at him, poor man, all on his own. And that coat! I mean, everyone's staring. I mean, who wears long black leather today?'

'The Dutch police for a start and that's why everyone's looking, they're wondering why a policeman's eating pancakes in a restaurant when he should be working,' her boyfriend grumbled.

'They're good pancakes and the police have to eat,' Scott winked at Hilary who smiled. 'Isn't Beau joining us?'

Travers shook his head, saying grumpily: 'No, the bro's gone to check out Isadora.'

'Isadora?' said Hilary. 'I thought his girlfriend was Belgian.'

'He never made it to Belgium. Isadora's the name of the Cessna.' Travers grinned suddenly, his good humour restored. He slipped his arm around Mary's shoulders. 'The sooner I get you back to Cornwall, the better,' he admitted.

'When are you going?' said Hilary.

'Beau says straight away. He says the Dutch police are the sort to arrest all the usual suspects which, he thinks, will probably includes us, so it would be sensible to leave as soon as possible.'

'Isn't your brother ever serious?' said Scott.

Travers stared, genuinely astonished. 'He's the most serious person I know and the bravest. He and that reporter guy were first up the stairs to rescue you. He just talks funny. Besides, we have to go, Mother is having kittens,' he said, his expression gloomy again. 'I thought we could have stayed till you left, Scott, but she insists I don't miss school. Says I need all the education I can get. Don't see why, I'll be playing professional rugby in a few years. You're not coming either, are you, Hilary?'

Hilary, clean and tidy in her borrowed jeans and T-shirt – both a shade too big – shook her head, her pony tail flapping sharply from side to side. 'I don't know what will happen to me. It depends on the boss.'

'Who did the shooting?' said Scott.

'That was Sean Terry. Calm as you please. He was there before us and went heavily armed. Good job, too. Whoever it was made quite a mess of your dad.'

'I liked Pete,' Scott smiled sadly. 'So weird! How can you like a killer?'

'That's just the problem,' insisted Hilary. 'You can't tell what a person's like from the outside. I have to admit though, and I'm not saying this just because we know about him now, but I was always scared of him. The way he moved – like a cat – you never heard him.'

'I noticed that – but Sean Terry ...' Scott shivered dramatically. 'He really put the frighteners on me – that is until he saved Dad.'

Hilary laughed. 'Don't worry, I hate him, too. So does half the Service. But he's a great bloke if you never expect a *well done*. I mean, I told him about you but the moment he saw me, he bawled me out – remember?'

Scott did. It felt a long time ago now. 'What did you tell him about me?'

Hilary bit her lip, looking uncomfortable. 'Um! At the river, when your dad didn't appear? I could see you were worried to death so I rang him. That's why he went to the house.'

'Oh! I thought you were gossiping about your rotten day,' Scott confessed, with a grin.

Hilary laid a friendly hand on his arm. 'But we're okay, now, aren't we?'

Travers leered and winked at Mary. He stood up, checking the time. 'Let's go see the parade. Mary'll never forgive me if she misses it, after coming all this way. Then we're off.' He took a step towards the door. 'What about him?' He nodded in the direction of the young officer, already on his feet. 'Can't we slip out the back way and leave him here?'

'You can't do that.' Mary sounded shocked.

Travers grinned. 'Watch me.'

Scott laughed. 'Don't worry about him. I'll take him back to the hospital, in a minute.' He threw his arms round his friends. 'Thanks, Travers. You too, Mary.'

Hilary gave her friend a hug. 'Can I keep the clothes till I get back?'

Mary sniffed. 'I'm about to burst into tears, Travers. Let's go and see some flowers.'

The flower parade was in full swing, the streets now alive with people; the sun shining as they had been promised. The carts were full of people dressed as cartoon characters, all of them wearing the most amazing headgear, flowing with tulips and narcissi. They made their way through the square, creating a kaleidoscope of flamboyant colour. Scott glanced up at the blue sky, drifts of cloud floating across the sun. On a day like this, with all the worries over and done with, the sky should have been deep blue and cloudless.

'I ate a little,' Bill greeted his son; Sean Terry already occupying one of two armchairs provided by the hospital, with Doug Randal in the other. Both men looked as if they'd been there a while.

'So you're Hilary.' Bill's face, its laughter lines camouflaged by pain and exhaustion, sketched a smile, as the girl appeared in the room carrying a stacker chair. 'I understand Travers and Mary have left. I was sorry to miss them. When I'm back on my feet, they'll have to come for dinner, so I can thank them properly for looking after Scott.'

'Isn't it time you went home to the US?' Sean Terry said, the tones of his voice harsh and rasping, like a cat's tongue over the palm of your hand. 'You've been away fifteen years.'

'Yeah, I guess,' Bill agreed.

'Once you've told your story to the UN in Switzerland, there's nothing stopping you.'

'Do you think they'll believe me?' Bill said. 'The Dutch police obviously didn't.' He winced with pain.

'*Dad!*'

'I'm okay. We started without you,' he explained. 'They've all left now and I'm a bit tired.'

'They want to interview you, too, Scott.' Doug Randal intervened. 'We've been talking this over. From what I can see, it's going to be a case of, "least said, soonest mended,"' he quoted. 'Someone's trying to throw the blame on terrorists. So let's go with that. Your father went missing. You confided in me and learned he was in Lisse. You came to find him and were abducted at gunpoint. That's all you know.'

A zillion questions flooded into Scott's brain. It was no good keeping them to himself – that was how the whole mess started in the first place. 'Why the United Nations?'

Sean Terry broke in. 'Your father now knows for certain it wasn't the US behind the attack on Iran. We need him to say just that. But, as he said, without something to corroborate it, it probably won't be enough.'

Scott continued looking at him, wanting more.

'We need to catch the people behind it. Thanks to Bill here, a large chunk of my puzzle is filled in.'

Scott shifted his gaze to the big man, totally relaxed in his seat, an aura of innocence and openness enveloping him. 'How did you get involved, Mr Randal?'

'I'm not.' The tone was frank, confident.

'Then how …?' Scott protested.

'James is an old friend. He couldn't chase after your father himself so he asked me. I know a lot of people – *have-a-go* people. I was on my way to Scotland to meet up with you when the sky fell in.'

Scott was silent a moment. In the past week he'd become quite adept at only telling half the truth and now he recognised the skill of a master. 'Will you tell Mr Nicely I'm sorry,' he said accepting the futility of further questions.

'I expect he knows you weren't to blame. A bit headstrong though. Good job Travers had enough sense to warn me what was likely to happen.'

Scott bit his lip. 'I know. It was stupid; I should have listened to him.'

'Fortunately, we got away with it, thanks to some pretty nifty work with an automatic from our friend here.' Doug indicated the silent figure of the reporter. 'I've persuaded the authorities to leave your interview till tomorrow when your dad is stronger, since he's determined to be there.'

'Do *they* know who's behind the kidnapping?'

'Not a clue, if you mean the Dutch authorities.' Sean Terry intervened again, the sarcasm strong and biting. 'And they'd feel more comfortable if it *was* an act of terrorism. That's why we decided to run with it. Much simpler. Your father told us what he knows, so has Hilary. Hopefully, you can add to it. Their leader goes by the name of Smith. Not particularly original. But, whoever he is, he has to be pretty powerful if he's going to make two kidnappings, several murders, and a bloody great hole in a canal disappear.'

'And your work, Dad?'

Bill sighed. 'You know about that? I guess Terry told you,' he said; adding wearily, 'I figured if you didn't know you'd stay safe. Some great idea that was!'

'I wish you'd told me. I could have been more use.'

'I think you were pretty useful as it was. But how did you find me? I couldn't believe my ears when they said you'd brought help.'

'I followed the clues, Dad. Actually, we followed the clues.' Scott indicated the silent figure on the chair. 'Hilary came after me.'

'What clues?' Bill Anderson's expression was curious.

'Well, first there was the obituary, then the posters.'

'*Posters!*' repeated his father, sounding astonished.

'Yes,' Scott insisted. 'The ones on the wall about the bike: "So take the High Road" and "That'll do nicely."' Scott's voice trailed away. 'You *did* leave clues, didn't you?'

Bill broke into a laugh. He clutched his shoulder, an agonised expression on his face. 'Remind me not to do that, it's far too painful. Scott, I promise you, I left no clues. The only thing I left was a letter with Jameson's dad, in case anything ever happened to me. It tells you everything. *But you always go there*, so what happened this time?'

Scott appeared on the brink of tears. 'Jameson met this girl and decided to stay away for the week. And when I got back to the cottage, Mr Terry's lot were waiting. You mean it was *coincidence?*'

Bill nodded painfully. 'I swear! I never knew James Nicely lived in Loch Lomond. I never asked. He never said. We communicated by phone.' Bill shook his head. 'How extraordinary!'

Hilary sighed, shutting her eyes briefly, as if to say: *I told you so.* 'Brilliant, we *were* going round in circles,' she muttered under her breath. Then more loudly, as if unable to stop herself, 'So if we'd stayed at home we'd have found out the truth anyway and I'd have not got bruises from riding that damn bike.'

'No, we wouldn't!' Scott hurled back. 'I might have known about Dad's work but he'd still be lost. And we got there, didn't we, coincidence or no coincidence. And it was a pretty *great coincidence*, that's all I can say.'

Bill watched his son and the youthful American agent glare at one another. 'You did say you were friends, didn't you,' he said mildly.

'But why the posters, Dad, if they weren't clues? I mean, our house is bare ...' Scott's voice trailed away. 'What was I to think?'

Surprisingly it was Sean Terry who replied. 'Look here, kid. You led me a right dance; I cursed you to kingdom-come. But, if you hadn't done it like that we'd still be wondering who the snake in our organisation was – and your dad would still be lost.'

Hilary smiled a little enviously, wishing her boss would praise her like that. 'He's right, Scott,' she said generously. 'I guess it doesn't matter *how* it's done, as long as it gets done. Still, you know me, prickly as anything without clean clothes.'

Scott swallowed, feeling the ready tears trying to push their way to the surface.

Sean Terry glared at Hilary for interrupting. 'There's something else you need to know, Scott. Are you going to do it, Bill, or shall I?'

Bill leaned into his pillows, pumping a shot of morphine into his vein. 'I will. I meant to, this week anyway.' He moved his head slightly. 'Those posters – stupid really. I don't think I ever looked at what was written on them. Not once. They were simply a reminder of the last day your mother and I spent together. She picked them up in a market.' He took a deep breath wincing with pain as the muscles attached to his ribs and shoulder protested. 'I don't know if you will ever forgive me for this, I hope you will. But your mother's alive. She didn't die.'

Scott heard the words but they made no sense. '*What do you mean?*'

'Can you explain, Terry, I'm shattered.'

The silence in the room was intense – everyone aware this was one of those life-changing moments, with Bill wishing he was strong enough to do the job himself. That's how it should have been. But, with all the emotional baggage the confession would engender, he knew it was beyond him.

'What your father's trying to tell you, is that your mother, like him, has been hidden all these years. She escaped the earthquake, made her way inland and then to Miami, before losing herself in the Caribbean. She joined a charter vessel as a cook, spent three years up and down the Caribbean – long enough, she thought, to be safe.' The chair creaked as Sean Terry shifted round to face Scott full on.

'What you've got to remember, Scott, before you start to judge your father, is that he genuinely thought her dead. His only aim was to stay alive himself *and keep you safe,*' he said, emphasising the final four words. 'He had no clue as to who was behind the explosion, no one to trust; not till several years later when David Runyon surfaced.'

'You definitely started without me, if you know all this, already,' Scott threw at him.

'Kid, I know all this because I know all this. I've been searching for them for almost fifteen years, *goddamn it*.'

Bill smiled and said in a tired voice, 'You don't take prisoners, do you, Terry?'

'Your son's old enough to face facts. To go on. Your father found your mother when, four years later, she responded as Sister Sarah. At first, he didn't believe it. When he did, they met up secretly. But all they had, in the last fifteen years, was a couple of lousy weekends. Not much of a life, was it? It was a joint decision …' Sean Terry glared at Scott as if he'd been going to interrupt, 'to stay apart, to stay safe. I come into it, later. I traced your mother to Wales.'

Scott looked across at the figure in bed. 'Is that why we always went there for holidays?'

'So she could see you, from a distance, yes,' Bill said. He shut his eyes, the effort of talking obviously exhausting him.

'I found her two days after your dad went missing,' the agent continued. 'Fortunately, I was on my own. I didn't take my team, left them chasing-up Bill, otherwise your mother would have been taken too.'

'Except Sarah has nothing to do with the project now. It was the only way,' Bill said, his voice faint.

'Yeah, sure,' he dismissed Bill's effort. 'But that wouldn't have stopped them.'

'But didn't you suspect Pete?' Scott said, all of a sudden glad he could ask something innocent, something that didn't leave him feeling like mashed potato, with the masher still pounding his brains.

'No! Not Pete. He'd been with me too long; we'd shared too much together.' Sean Terry's expression was bitter.

Scott suddenly remembered what Pete had told him. 'He killed that man.'

'I guessed he had, that is once we knew it *was* him.'

'How did you know?'

All of a sudden, Hilary appeared badly rattled. She put out her hand as if to stop her boss talking and shook her head in warning.

'Look, Stone, if the kid falls out with you because you put loyalty to me first, tough. You saved his hide. He wouldn't be here with his dad, if you hadn't.'

'Hilary was in touch with you all the time?'

Sean Terry nodded. 'I don't go much on women agents as a rule, but at least Stone had the good sense to tell me your dad had gone missing and you were worried.'

'At the harbour, you mean?'

'Yeah! We were planning a visit anyway. But we got there too late.' The reporter leaned forward. 'I recruited Stone for one purpose only. To help me find the rotten apple in our barrel. She was new, not contaminated, and she reported to me, no one else.'

A blaze of clarity swept through Scott's head. 'So *that's why*,' he said, his tone almost triumphant. He swivelled round in his chair to confront Hilary. 'That's why you were in such a state when they found Mr Nicely. You thought Mr Terry behind it, didn't you? Go on, admit it. I dare you.'

'So what if I did. I was wrong, it wasn't him,' she snapped back.

Scott beat his fists on his knees. 'And that's why you burst into tears when we found the bug …'

'Steady on, Scott,' murmured his father.

'No, it's okay.' He shouted the words. 'It's all quite clear now. I wondered and wondered, what was the matter with you? I thought *I'd* done something wrong. But it was nothing to do with me after all. When you saw that bug – it got Mr Terry off the hook.'

'Right on the nose, kid!' Sean Terry's smile was bleak, like his eyes, as if his job, keeping the streets safe for decent people to walk in, had obliterated the ability to create warmth. But it was a smile nonetheless, and the first Scott had seen on the man's face.

'*And* I can tell you something else. That's when you knew about Pete, because if Hilary was okay, the only other person that could possibly have bugged my trainers was him. I never thought about it before. I tossed them off in the kitchen and none of your men came into the house afterwards; only you, Pete and Hilary. But how did you keep in touch?'

Hilary held up her phone. 'Mostly, this. But for safety ...' she added, staring down at the floor. She stretched out her foot. Clinging like a leech to the sole of her shoe was a small grey pebble.

Scott stared, stunned into silence.

'You're not mad, Scott, about my lying to you?' Hilary's voice sounded nervous; her precise, confident tone missing.

Scott's head filled with words he desperately wanted to hurl at her. Words she had used to lord it over him. *How many times had she told him to trust her, when all the time .... What did she have to do, get shot! Pretending to be too scared to get in touch with her boss.* Of all the sneaky ...' He opened his mouth and spotted his father watching him closely.

He swallowed hard and sketched a smile. 'I got Dad back.' He shrugged. 'I guess nothing else really matters. And you weren't the only person telling lies.' He glanced at his dad, smiling shyly.

'Scott?'

'It's okay, Dad, at least I think it is. I'm not quite sure yet. But I'd quite like to meet her. There's a lot of catching up to do. Do you think she can cook more than stir-fry and pasta?'

Bill felt a wetness on his cheeks; instantly blaming the morphine for leaving him so vulnerable. Then he understood why he was crying, it wasn't because he felt weak, it was with pride, great pride, that he'd reared a son who was rapidly becoming a halfway-decent human being.

'She's in Holland, Scott. Doug went back last night to get her. We were going to meet up. It had already been decided, when last weekend happened. But whether we stay here or move back to the States ...'

'I don't mind living in the States, Dad,' Scott boasted, his eyes sliding towards Hilary.

Bill noted the glimmer of a smile. 'What I'm trying to say is: wherever we live, it has to be out of the way – for the time being at least – and probably with a permanent guard. At least we now know who our friends are.' He smiled gratefully at the two men occupying the armchairs; one of whose face was ravaged with exhaustion; the other, someone that believed in the stability of the monarchy and was prepared to do something about it.

Sean Terry got to his feet. 'We'll get it sorted, don't worry. But even if we fix this one, it won't be long before another maniac comes along demanding our attention. Well, I'm off to tie one on. Doug, here, will fetch the missing momma. Stone, you coming?'

Hilary seemed about to speak. Reluctantly, she stood up as if waiting for something.

'Scott?' his father said.

Scott swung round. 'See you tomorrow?' he said, smiling broadly. She smiled back and, lifting her hand in a wave, joined her boss in the corridor.

Sean Terry stuck his head back in the room, his bleak eyes erupting into a smile. 'Oh! I forgot! Just in case your dad decides to take another fifteen years to get round to telling you; you've also got a nine-year-old sister! And grandparents! I've met *them. They're nice!*' He grinned encouragingly at the exhausted figure lying in bed; his voice, with its Irish lilt, innocent sounding. 'I find sick people get better much more quickly if their conscience is clear.' He raised his hand in a salute. 'Come on, Stone, Let's find a decent bar, I need a stiff drink.'

Look out for …

Time Breaking

Barbara Spencer

"I so hate my life. Why can't I be someone else?"
But plunged into the nightmare world of the 17th century is not exactly what Molly had in mind when she said this.

While staying in an old manor house, Molly inadvertently triggers a time-chute and re-appears in 1648, towards the end of the English Civil War, to find she has taken the place of Molly Hampton, the eldest daughter of a Puritan family. With the manor house now barred to her, Molly is forced to continue with the charade, discovering in Ann Hampton and her new sisters and brother, the family she has always dreamed of. When she realises that Richard, the son of Sir Richard Blaisdale, is someone who really cares for her, gradually Molly begins to change her mind, believing that she can stay and take Molly Hampton's place – little realising that danger and disaster wait for her …

Exerpt

'You go first,' I whispered.

Janet didn't argue. In this matter of life or death she presumed that neither of us had any intention of playing the hero. Besides, she was far too anxious to get home. Pointing downwards, she stepped on to the stone.

Nothing happened!

Her face changed – utter disbelief sweeping over it. I ran across the room peering down at the circular stone. We both stood on it, turning to face the fireplace, turning to face the door, face the window. We moved the fire screen – *nothing* – *nothing* – NOTHING!

Janet giggled hysterically, her hand flying to her mouth to stem the noise. Covering her face with her hands she collapsed, her body rigid with shock. I simply felt cheated, the decision on my future once again whisked away from under my nose. Pulling wildly at my hair, I tried to focus my thoughts and recall the exact sequence of events, before I fell down the time-chute.

'For God's sake, Janet; pull yourself together, crying won't get us out of here.' I bent down and pulled her hand away from her face. 'There's something – something different. Try and remember.'

She gazed up at me, her face all screwed-up like a lost kid.

'Janet, it's the sun. Did you have sun?' I hissed urgently, suddenly remembering how warm the sun had been and my feeling cold.

She stared across at the windows reflecting only the grey of the afternoon clouds. 'Then it's no good – all this for nothing,' she said, as if the world had just ended. She stood up and began stamping her feet on the stone, trying to bulldoze a response out of it. She glared at the window; willing the clouds to move aside and let the sun through. I put my arm round her.

'No big deal,' I said lightly, as if it really didn't matter. 'We got in once; we can do it again, easy. But next time, it'll be sunny.'

Her feet were super-glued to the stone and I had to drag her away. I guess if I'd been stuck here for two years, working as a servant and terrified of my own shadow, I wouldn't have wanted to leave either. She'd got in and now wild horses weren't going to drag her out again.

We reached the wicket gate safely. Janet cast yet another lingering glance at the sky. I knew she'd have waited forever if there'd been the slightest sign of sun, but there wasn't; the sombre clouds thickening and spits of rain now beginning to fall.

I opened the gate, flinching backwards as I spotted the dour figure of the steward – Mr Perkins – his arms folded, waiting outside in the lane.

A shrill voice piped up. 'I told yer, I told yer I seed 'em.'

I know I went white. My hands fell to my sides and we stood there, for all-the-world like a couple of ten year-olds caught smoking in the school toilets.

'What are ye doin'?'

'I came to see Richard, Mr Perkins,' I said, my voice high-pitched and quivering with nerves.

'Callers don't use the wicket, they use the front gate. You an' that girl,' he pointed to Janet as if she was a bit of filth he'd just scraped off his shoe, the nails on his fingers black and pitted, 'were up to no good.'

I noticed his eyes, narrow and cunning like a weasel.

'You was in the parlour wiv her spells.'

'That's ridiculous, we were looking for Richard. You know perfectly well we're friends.' I caught Janet's sleeve, taking a step round him.

He ignored me and, swinging round, pushed his face at Janet.

Gross – his breath would have floored a skunk at twenty paces. 'I know what I saw. You may have fooled Sir Richard with ye innocent ways, but I know ye're a witch and her too,' he jerked his head at me.

Janet, looking terrified, took a step back while I took a step forward, drawing myself to my full height.

'That's nonsense,' I said, staring him straight in the eye, trying to tell myself this was simply another bully I had to face down.

Bully or not, he wasn't backing down. I watched nervously as he hitched up his trousers, hiking his belligerence up a notch at the same time.

'We'll see about this sneakin' about. My boys saw ye cavortin' together – let's see what the pastor has to say.'

He grabbed my arm and I pulled away.

'Don't be so stupid, Mr Perkins, I can't see why you're making such a fuss. You know I often meet with Richard; we've been friends since we were children.'

I might have been speaking to a brick wall for all the notice he took. He grabbed my arm again, his nails digging viciously into the flesh. I stared at his face, almost spitting into mine, lines scalding their way downwards – like deep furrows in a ploughed field – ending at the corner of his mouth, others criss-crossing his forehead. This wasn't about me seeing Richard or saving his child; this was because Janet had made him look a fool in front of his employer. He wanted revenge and he didn't care how he got it; the worst type of bully possible and I knew he'd stop at nothing to regain his pride.

Janet knew it too – her face ashen, her eyes wide and staring. With a gasp of fear, she pulled free and ran.

'Janet stop, he can't hurt you.' I shouted and then, without thinking, I yanked my arm free and ran after her.

My wooden clogs were heavy and slowed me down and I scrunched my toes to stop them falling off. I would have been better bare-footed, except my feet were already cut and bruised. I heard thuds on the ground behind me and increased my pace, trying to catch Janet. I wanted to call out – *Janet, Janet, not that way, run towards home where it's safe* – the words hammering in my chest, but I hadn't enough breath to shout them.

She reminded me of a wounded animal running haphazardly in circles, aimlessly darting from cover to cover, anything to escape its pursuers. She reached the bridge flying across it, the door of the chapel banging open. I ran in after her and stopped. She was crouched near the front of the chapel, where the pastor had stood to address the congregation, her eyes staring.

'We're safe,' she panted. 'We're safe in the chapel.'

She hadn't been running heedlessly after all, she had purposely sought sanctuary.

My chest heaved too; not with the need for air but with fury that one person – one single bullying person – could create such mindless fear in someone else. I put my arm round her. 'He can't hurt us, Janet, we've done nothing.'

'Molly, you're so stupid. Of course he can.' She screamed the words at me. 'This isn't the twenty-first century. Men rule here; you're a woman – of less worth than an animal. This may be 1648 but they're still barbarians, and if they don't understand something they're scared shitless and lash out. Can't you see that?'

Everything in me begged for her to be wrong, because if she was right we were in big trouble.

I don't know how long we sat in the chapel, watching the light change, becoming gloomy and then dim, while the sky outside grew dark. The hours ticked by and I began to feel hungry and stupid. Mr Perkins had wanted to frighten us and he'd succeeded big time. Here we were cowering in the chapel while he was at home, sitting in his armchair by the fire, a contemptuous smile on his face. And no one had come looking for me, so I hadn't been missed but if we were to escape a beating, we had to get back as quickly as possible.

I got up and stretched, tip-toeing to the door to listen. All was quiet. Janet joined me.

'Come on,' I said. 'They must have gone by now. Let's go home.'

Cautiously, I pushed open the door. It was dark and quiet – nothing moved. I stepped out, Janet following.

The door slammed shut behind us, the noise making me jump. A torch burst into flame, illuminating the faces of the men waiting patiently for the fox to crawl out of its den.